JOCK BLOCKED

PIPPA GRANT

COPYRIGHT

Mackenzie Montana, aka a woman on a mission

I NEVER MEANT to become a criminal. But in the grand scheme of life, I don't think I'm technically engaging in criminal behavior.

At least, if it is, you could call it a crime of passion.

And I am *very* passionate in my belief that while the Fireballs need to make changes to halt their record-breaking streak of being the worst losing team ever to play professional baseball, they don't need to do it with a new mascot. Which is why I decided to take two weeks off work and fly to Florida for spring training, where I'm not saying that I've snuck into my home team's ballpark after hours to steal the worst proposed mascot costume, but I'm not saying I haven't either.

Meatballs?

They actually let a *meatball* make the final cut.

I needed at least another full season to get over the fact that the new Fireballs ownership *killed the last mascot,* and here they are, letting fans vote on replacing Fiery the Dragon with *flaming meatballs.*

I snort to myself while I creep through the darkened concrete hallways with a flaming meatball swallowing half of my body.

If you're going to steal a giant meatball costume, it's best to act like you know what you're doing. And striding out of here with zero shame means two things—one, no one's going to stop me, and two, even if they do, I'm incognito.

It's the perfect crime to counter the crime of killing Fiery.

I'm one turn away from the door that I left propped open for myself after hiding out in the family bathroom after today's game when voices drift toward me.

One male.

One female.

Neither is familiar, but as I get closer to my final turn, I realize the voices are between me and my exit.

No biggie.

I got this.

I can stroll on by, flash a thumbs-up, pretend like I'm heading out to prank the Fireballs at the team compound they're all staying at, or to make a fast-food run for publicity.

Acting like I know what I'm doing inside this mascot costume is as easy as breathing. When you've seen thousands of baseball games in your lifetime, it's not hard.

So I turn the corner.

And then I suck in a surprised breath, because that's Brooks Elliott.

Oh. My. God.

Brooks Elliott.

The Fireballs' newest acquisition. Like, so new he arrived *yesterday*. A mid-spring training acquisition, which is practically unheard of.

He plays third base, and he hits the ball like it's evil incarnate and he's an avenging angel and it's his job to send that evil into another dimension.

He could be the reason we legitimately have a shot at making it to the post-season.

And I am *not* going to hyperventilate like I did the last time I was face-to-face with a baseball player.

Pretending to be a mascot?

I got this.

Talking to the players?

It's like talking to the gods.

Tall, muscled, chiseled gods who put on a show for me every day from spring to fall with their acrobatics on the field and their powerful swings at home plate.

I've had the chance to be in the same room with several of the players in the past two years, and every time, I do the same thing.

I turn mute and make an utter fool of myself, because *I cannot talk to gods.*

My breath is coming short and choppy, so I give myself a little pep talk. *You don't have to talk, Mackenzie. Just walk. Walk and do a few hand signals that they won't understand, and he'll never know it's you.*

Brooks is in jeans that fit his muscular thighs like a second skin, with his arms bulging under a tight black T-shirt featuring a bull in a leather jacket smoking a cigarette on a motorcycle. And his forearms.

Oh, god, baseball forearms.

They're lethal to women's panties everywhere, because *baseball forearms.*

He's leaning a shoulder against the cinderblock wall, aiming smoky hazel eyes and an orgasm-inducing smile at one of the janitor ladies in a blue smock, who's giggling, because *of course she is.*

That smile is so potent, I can feel it through this costume. I want to be that smock just to be closer to the smolder.

Alas, even if my tongue worked when I'm around baseball players, Brooks Elliott is off-limits.

He's a virgin.

Intentionally.

According to my very reliable sources, when he tries to score with the ladies, he doesn't score on the field. And I very much need him to score on the field for my team this year.

Work, I silently order my legs, and look at that.

They're moving. With a bounce, even, because that's how a meatball mascot in a Fireballs jersey would move.

Huh. If my nine-to-five trash engineer job thing ever fails, maybe I can get a job as a baseball mascot.

But not the meatball mascot.

If I had to pick a new mascot—which I'm not, because I'm running the *Bring Back Fiery* campaign—I'd angle for the firefly, because at least it has fire in it naturally. I get why the duck is in the running after that thing with the ducks at Duggan Field—the Fireballs' regular season stadium back in my home city of

Copper Valley, Virginia—but the echidna is strange and not at all related to baseball, or fire, and even if his spiky hands are sort of threatening and cool, no one even knows what an echidna is.

Not in this hemisphere, anyway.

Plus you don't want to know what the internet is saying about echidna penis. You really don't.

In short, the Fireballs need to bring back Fiery the Dragon, which is my number one mission this year.

"So, you wanna go get a room?" Brooks says to his companion. His eyes dart to me, then back to the janitor lady.

She reaches out and strokes his chest. "Oh, yes."

Wait.

What's this?

And I'm not talking about the fact that she's twice his age, which I didn't notice until I was nearly right on top of them.

I'm talking about how she's angling in like she's going to kiss him, murmuring things in Spanish that I can't understand because I'm only fluent in English, baseball, and drag queen, and how he's tucking his arm around her waist like he's going to press her against him.

Did I say bringing back Fiery was my number one mission?

Not anymore.

"Oh my god, *stop!*" I shriek.

They both jump.

Naturally, because a talking meatball isn't normal. First rule of being a mascot is that you *stay silent.*

"Uh, are you okay?" Brooks's hazel eyes scan me—or rather, the meatball—and even though my vision is a little dark from peering through the costume, I'm still getting a hot flash from him looking at me.

Which isn't relevant, because *he just invited this woman old enough to be his mother to GO GET A ROOM.*

"No!" I shriek. "You're hitting on her!"

His face goes adorably pink. His thick brown hair's standing up like he ran his fingers through it after a shower, and *gah*, it is *so* working for me.

He murmurs something to the janitor and turns to fully face me. "Who are you, and what are you doing?" he hisses.

I point at him. At the growing bulge in his pants that has me getting warm, and not from being half-encased in a flaming

4

meatball. "What am *I* doing? How about what are *you* doing? Because it looks like you're going to try to have sex with her!"

She stutters something and backs farther away from him.

"That's none of your damn business," he growls.

"But if you lose your virginity, you'll never be able to hit a ball again."

The janitor lady gasps and crosses herself, then scurries down the hall.

And Brooks goes from cute and pissed-off pink to redder than a flaming meatball in the cheeks. After a split second of freezing so hard I swear he creates his own gravitational pull, he looks back at the janitor, who's slipping out my escape route, then turns to prowl toward me like a leopard barely containing its fury. "Who the hell are you?"

"I'm Meaty the Meatball."

"Take your head off."

"No."

"Take. Your fucking. Head. Off."

This is where I should really run. Or call my best friend. Or the Fireballs' owner, who happens to be a good friend of mine, and who didn't listen to reason when I told him the meatball was a bad idea, which is why I have to do this even if it means I'll lose a friend.

But I'm *talking to a baseball player*.

For the first time in my life, I'm talking to a baseball player without hyperventilating.

I back down the hall. "You're trying to sabotage the Fireballs."

"They're the worst team in baseball. There's nothing left to sabotage."

"*Last* year's team was the worst team in baseball. Which is why *you're* here now. To make them better. And you can't do that if you have sex."

"Who told you that?"

I try to clamp a hand over my mouth and end up knocking myself in the meatball instead. I can't tell him where I heard about his virginity.

That really wouldn't be nice.

"I have my sources." I'm backpedaling hard now, but I don't have eyes in the back of my head—even though the damn meatball does—and I stumble over a water fountain sticking out of the wall. "And aren't you supposed to be at the compound with the rest of the team? Why aren't you getting your rest? Don't you have catching up to do with arriving so late? When's the last time you ate?"

It's not often I need to shut up around a baseball player, but I really need to shut up now. And run. Not that I have any faith at all that I can outrun him, because *hello*, baseball gods can run fast, but I can make enough racket that possibly some security would hear me.

"Who are you?" he repeats.

"You're not denying the virgin thing. Also, if you're going to lose your virginity, *please* at least do it with someone you like, and not for the first woman willing to jump in the sack with you. Trust me. Your memories are better if you—wait. Never mind. *Don't sleep with anyone.*"

His jaw clenches. So do his fists.

And this is it.

He's going to kill me. I'm going to die in a meatball costume, at the hands of the man who's supposed to turn around my favorite baseball team and he'll be in prison, and the Fireballs will never win a championship. Ever.

"Don't you want to win?" I say as he gets right up in my face. Or, rather, as close as he can get.

This has to look weird from his perspective.

"I'd like to fucking *live*," he snarls.

"You can't do that from prison if you murder me."

He shoves back and thrusts his hands through his hair again, this time gripping those thick brown locks, and I assume that's so he doesn't have his hands free to strangle me. "I'm not going to murder you. I'm going to citizen's arrest you, because I don't know who you are, but I know for damn sure you're not supposed to be in that meatball costume."

Oh, nuggets.

Now he's reaching for his phone.

He's going to turn me in.

Adrenaline surges in my veins, and before I can think better of it, I knock his phone away, kick it down the hall, shove him, and yell, "Fiery forever!"

And then I take off at a dead run.

_____

Brooks Elliott, aka a man who's clearly down on his luck, in so many ways

WHEN I GOT up this morning, I didn't expect I'd end the day getting cock-blocked by a flaming meatball.

A meatball who knows my biggest secret.

And a meatball who's stupidly fast in that costume.

After a split second of hesitation while I regain my balance, I leave my phone and dart after the damn mascot.

I'm about to grab her when the door swings open and Cooper Rock steps in, then leaps out of the way of the running meatball, but unfortunately, right into *my* way.

He jumps out of my way too, still staring at the mascot. "Whoa, Meaty, where's the fire?"

Once again, I'm scrambling for balance. "Stop that meatball!"

He snags me by the collar and yanks. I make a gurgled noise and spin, but he's got a tight hold. "Hands off the mascots, dude. You don't want beating up a meatball to be your legacy."

"She's stealing the damn costume."

"Huh."

I yank myself free, but he leaps between me and the rapidly retreating meatball.

"Get out of my way." I finish the order with a shove that doesn't budge him.

"Elliott, man, you really want the meatball to win the mascot contest? *Let it go.* Fly and be free, meatball, but don't be the Fireballs' new mascot, right? Also, you didn't hear me say that. I promised Lila I liked the meatball best. But I swear, she was going to trade me away if I didn't."

My chest is heaving while I glare at him. First, because what the *fuck* is wrong with him that he *wants* to play for this team—the guy's good enough that he could've had three championship rings for any other team at this point in his career by now—and second, because I can't tell him why we have to stop the damn meatball.

Not like I can blurt out *the fucking meatball knows my secret*, because I don't talk about the pristine condition of my V-card with anyone.

Which begs the question, how did she know?

How the *hell* did she know?

I don't have a lot of practice denying it, because I don't have a lot of practice being confronted with it. Which means she caught me off-guard, and now I've basically confirmed it for her.

Fuck.

If I have nightmares about meatballs, I'm gonna be pissed.

Cooper punches me lightly in the arm, one of those *I got you, buddy* hits. "Look, we'll put a pirate eye patch on you and say you got meatball sauce in your eye while you tried to stop it, and you'll be a hero, plus you'll only have to sit out maybe two games. No publicity is bad publicity, and a kidnapped mascot? This is like *gold* for getting more people to talk about the Fireballs."

This.

This is what I've been traded into. We need a meatball-napping to get publicity, because the team's game sucks so hard.

I squeeze my eyes shut and try some of that deep breathing stuff my brother swears by since he married a nutcase, and I wish for the umpteenth time in the last seventy-two hours that this is all a bad dream.

"Huh." Cooper glances back at the door. "Knowing Lila, this could be a planned kidnapping."

Lila. The woman who inherited the Fireballs a few months back, and one of my sister's best friends. Long story.

"You think Lila set up a meatball kidnapping for publicity?"

This is the most insane conversation I've ever had, and my brother's married to a woman who knows over a thousand euphemisms for *penis* and uses them liberally, and my sister's autocorrected text messages need their own museum.

He nods. "She definitely set this up. Which means we can both put it out of our minds, and head out to the club."

At that, I perk up.

A club?

Oh, hell, yes.

The damn meatball was probably right about something else —I should at least be legit attracted to the first woman I bang, and not just getting a hard-on at the idea of the first vagina that signs up for the job.

The meatball was right?

I have issues.

"Point the way," I tell Cooper.

Out in the parking lot, I hop on my bike and follow Cooper's truck through the Palm Bay traffic to a less congested area of citrus groves. He turns down a dusty road that feels close to the compound, but I don't see a club.

All I see is a dilapidated shack with half a dozen cars and trucks parked at it.

Half a dozen sports cars and souped-up trucks that were parked at the ball field a few hours ago.

Dammit.

I'm not getting laid.

I'm getting initiated.

Initiated into the worst team in baseball.

And I'll do it, because that's what you do for your team.

It's not being on a new team that has me pissed. Not the guys. Not the management. Not even moving away from New York and family.

Wait.

Yes, I'm pissed that I'm not playing for New York anymore. It's my home team. The team I thought I'd retire from. The team so close to home that my family frequently showed up for games, and sometimes joined me for parties afterward.

But the shit icing on the sewage cake of being traded away from my home team is that they didn't trade me just anywhere.

Nope.

They had to trade me to the worst team in baseball.

Tell me all you want that the new ownership and the new management and the new coaches will make a difference for the Fireballs this year, but there are two things I know for damn certain:

One, curses are real in baseball.

And two, my game goes to shit anytime I get past second base with a woman.

If I'm going to play on a losing team, then why am I going to keep my pants zipped for another year in the name of my game?

My agent tells me I'm stuck. The Fireballs won't budge on the idea of trading me away as fast as they got me. *They want your experience,* he keeps saying. *Lila knows you'll be good for the team. She's probably good for the team too, Elliott. Get your head out of the superstitions and give them a chance.*

Says the guy who won't negotiate a deal without his mango-kale-acai power smoothie in his special smoothie cup sitting by his side, who still carries a lucky rabbit foot on his keychain, and who can't operate without his monthly psychic readings.

I'd fire him, except he keeps getting me sweet endorsement deals for everything from motorcycles to axes.

He can't break a curse though. And I'm sorry for Lila that she inherited one, but I'm getting laid.

Be a team player, show up for work, and play a damn good game? Sure. That's what I always do, because it's what the job requires. But it's not my responsibility to give up what every other guy on the team has to try to fight the impossible.

And the Fireballs winning anything?

That's fucking impossible.

"How's this go?" I ask Cooper while we walk to the shack. "Strip me naked and leave me to find my way through the trees to the compound? Or are we getting drunk?"

He barks out a laugh. "You've been playing for the wrong team."

He swings the door open, and there's half the team hunched around a table that's as rickety as this whole tinderbox.

"Welcome to a new era, gentlemen," Max Cole says while Luca Rossi—a fellow new guy on the team this year who was with New York for his rookie season a few years back—gives me a *help!* look from the corner. "We have work to do."

Work.

Not partying.

Not drinking.

Not getting laid.

"What kind of work?"

Darren Greene flashes a bright white grin, his dark eyes lighting up like he hasn't played for the worst team in baseball for the last three years. He leans back so I can see the spread on the table. There's a baseball, a voodoo doll, a pack of cards, a matchbox, and—is that a dildo with the Fireballs logo on it?

He points to a hand-knitted orange and yellow bat cover, which is as strange as you think it is. "I promised Tanesha our baby wouldn't be born to losers. We're breaking curses, because we're gonna fucking *win* this year."

Win.

Right.

Darren would have better luck keeping that promise by asking to get traded.

But I scrub a hand over my face and dig deep to find my team spirit, because this is the team we have.

Sure.

Win.

I'll humor them, even though I know that the Fireballs are where baseball players go for their careers to die.

I hope I'm wrong.

I hope the new ownership is going to make a difference.

But when a team has this much talent, and still sets records three years in a row for progressively worse seasons, without going to the play-offs in forever, it's hard to have hope.

Especially at the price of my blue balls.

3

Mackenzie

THE NEXT AFTERNOON sees me at the ballpark for another afternoon of eating popcorn—two handfuls between innings, and one
kernel at a time while the Fireballs are batting.

"Are you sure you don't want a hamburger?" Sarah Dempsey,
my best friend in the entire universe, asks me as our home team
heads into the dugout for the bottom of the eighth inning. She
flew in from Copper Valley to join me for a few games, because
we've always done games together, even if this is our first spring
training.

I shake my head. "It's time to turn over a new leaf. All of last
year's habits and superstitions didn't do squat. We finished with
a record I can't even think about without crying. So I'm turning
over a new leaf and trying some new things." I gesture to the
field. "Like attending spring training to get the team off to a good
start."

And like anonymously texting the Fireballs' owners video of
Meaty the Meatball waving goodbye from a dolphin cruise boat
this morning.

Sarah's boyfriend, Beck, is good friends with Tripp and Lila,
the team's new owners, and I've spent hours and hours having
in-depth conversations with them about everything the Fireballs

need to do to improve, which means I do feel guilty about stealing the mascot.

But it had to be done.

They weren't listening to reason, and it's completely unreasonable to replace Fiery the Dragon with a flaming meatball.

"Do I still have to go to the bathroom when we have runners in scoring position?" Sarah asks.

"It worked the last two times today, didn't it?" I sent her to the bathroom for both the second inning, when Darren Greene was on second and Cooper Rock hit him in, and then again in the seventh, when Brooks hit a home run, which means he *didn't* go out and get laid last night after I made my getaway.

Phew.

I was pretty certain Cooper would make sure he got back to the compound where the players are staying, because Cooper loves this team as much as I do, maybe more, but Cooper's also a total horndog, and to the best of my knowledge, he doesn't know Brooks needs his virginity to hit home runs, so there was that bit of doubt.

Like they might've gone out and had an orgy or something, which I really don't want to think about, since even though I can't talk to Cooper, I've started thinking about him like a brother I never had.

Sarah laughs about the bathroom superstition, and I smile at her. She's adorable, with dark hair and dark eyes and a bright smile. She glows without any makeup at all, which is basically the opposite of me. We bonded in college because we both got the socially awkward gene. I cover my awkwardness with makeup. She used to cover hers by hiding from the world, but now she owns who she is, which is what completely and totally charmed her boyfriend into bending over backwards to win her over.

Beck's an international fashion mogul and recovering underwear model who got his start in the Copper Valley-based boy band Bro Code. While Sarah and I are hanging in the bleachers, he's up in the owners' suite with Tripp—also formerly of Bro Code—and Lila.

Basically, Sarah was my in with the Fireballs higher-ups. She's also my in with the players I've met, if you can call it *meeting* when I simply sit there and gape at them, since Beck is also friends with like all of Copper Valley, which includes the pro sports athletes.

I haven't told her what I did to Meaty, because she'd probably tell on me, and I don't want to make things awkward for her.

"Look! The mascots are up. I didn't think we were going to see them this game." She points to the field, where the firefly, the duck, and the echidna are scratching their heads and looking around.

Glow the Firefly, has this huge round glowing ball behind his butt, because that's what makes him a firefly. His wings are awesome, and he'd make a great mascot.

For another team. Not for the Fireballs.

Firequacker, the duck with attitude, is here because a family of horny ducks invaded Duggan Field back home, and so when Tripp was tormenting Lila over an encounter they apparently had with the amorous creatures, Firequacker ended up on the finalist list.

I'm seriously worried the Fireballs will end up with a duck as a mascot, because the ducks back home became real celebrities over the winter.

As for Spike the Echidna, I have no idea why he's an option. I'm running a website and social media pages to bring back Fiery, and every single day, people ask what an echidna even is. Apparently it's some kind of fireproof spiny anteater from Australia, but all I know is that he's not Fiery, and that's the important part.

The three mascots stop at home plate, silently trash-talking each other before the base-running contest that the announcer is talking about, Glow shaking his big firefly butt—and yes, I know he's Sarah's choice, since he's a firefly, and that's her favorite canceled TV show—and Firequacker thrusting his hips and Spike wiggling his claws.

Then they all stop and look to an empty space beside them, because there's a mascot conspicuously missing.

My face flushes, and I have to try hard not to squirm in my seat.

Sarah frowns at home plate. "Where's the meatball?"

The video screen over center field suddenly flickers, and *oh my god.*

It's the video.

The video I sent of the meatball waving as he headed out to sea.

Sarah bursts into laughter.

So does the entire stadium.

The other mascots look at each other and start gesticulating wildly, and it's like they're saying *why didn't I think of that?*

"This fan re-engagement campaign is really working." Sarah's beaming as the mascots do their mascot thing, clearly debating if they're going to run the bases while Meaty's abandoned them. "I mean, *everything* Tripp and Lila are doing is working, but the mascot competition is really taking it up a notch."

I seal my lips together to keep from blurting out my question about why Tripp and Lila aren't concerned that their meatball was kidnapped, and how could they betray their team by turning Meaty leaving into a promo opportunity for the mascot?

Because now everyone will be talking about the mascot that ran away.

And what if someone starts a *Save Meaty* campaign?

What then?

I channel that inner peace that my dads are always talking about, breathe deeply through my diaphragm, and go back to concentrating on my popcorn while my brain spins about what the hell I'm supposed to do with the mascot costume *now*.

That's a problem for later.

After we win this baseball game. Which means I need to get back to eating one kernel of popcorn at a time, because the Fireballs are up to bat.

Sarah nudges me. "Tripp told Beck that your *bring back Fiery* campaign is driving a ton of fan mail to the home office with write-in votes."

I mean, *duh*. That's the point. But I still give her the surprised eyes. "Seriously?"

"I'm not supposed to tell you. Tripp's worried you'll do something extreme if you think your efforts are working."

Uh-oh. I dive for my water bottle to cover my reaction to how very, very close to the truth she's getting. After a big gulp, I yank my Fireballs hat lower over my eyes and stare out at the field. "Like he doesn't want Fiery to come back too."

"Like he'd tell Lila no for anything these days," she counters.

16

"By the way, were you planning on telling me about the picketers you're gathering for the home opener next month?"

"I don't want to make anything weird for you. Like, making you pick between me and your boyfriend's best friends."

"Mackenzie, there aren't sides. *All* of us want the Fireballs to win and find their fans again. Family doesn't abandon family just because we don't always see eye-to-eye about how to reach a common goal. Plus, it's fun to watch Tripp squirm when Beck points out that Lila's totally wrong about the Fireballs needing a new mascot."

"He is *not* giving Tripp trouble." Beck's the nicest man on the entire planet. He'd never intentionally make anyone uncomfortable.

But Sarah's smile is turning devious. "I wish you could've made it to lunch. He was hilarious." She drops her voice an octave to imitate her boyfriend. *"Lila, are you putting all of the mascots on a pension plan? Like, what happens if it turns out Spike develops a heart murmur caused by all the anxiety over people not knowing what an echidna is? Or if that bird protection group puts Firequacker on an endangered species list and needs to use him for genetic and fertility testing? I hear that doesn't pay well. And a baseball can do some serious damage to a real firefly. I'm talking SMUSH, you know? Can the Fireballs really afford to be the team with multiple failed mascots? Fiery can be rehabbed. He can get back to eating right and exercising and meditating, and he can come back. You have to BELIEVE."*

I tip my head back and laugh. "He is such a nut."

"We're both firmly on Team Fiery. Oh, I almost forgot. Cooper invited Beck to the compound for a little get-together tonight. You should come with us. I'll bet you can rally some of the players to give testimonials about Fiery too."

Almost forgot. No, she didn't.

I slide her a side eye while Francisco Lopez does that thing he does where he plucks his uniform at both his shoulders, then grabs his crotch before squaring up to the plate after tipping a foul ball for strike two, and I force myself to remember that she doesn't know I actually *talked* to Brooks Elliott last night. "You mean so I can go catatonic in the presence of that many gods?"

"You know how we're trying new habits and tactics for good luck for the Fireballs? Maybe they *need* you to talk to them."

I gasp.

She arches a dark brow.

"You did *not* go there," I whisper.

The crowds around us erupt in booing, and I whip my head around to see Lopez kick the grass and throw his bat as he marches back to the dugout.

"Oh, come *on*," Sarah yells as we watch the replay on the jumbotron. "That wasn't a strike!"

I dive for my popcorn and go back to eating it one piece at a time. It's a close game—we're winning by one run with our primary team playing, instead of some of the guys here at spring training on a testing rotation to see if they have what it takes—and I can't take any chances that I quit doing what's working.

But at the top of the ninth, Milwaukee's freaking *pitcher* hits a two-run homer, and we're not able to close the deal at the bottom of the inning, which means we lose.

Because the *pitcher* hit a home run.

That's about as likely as the ghosts of the bats—the animal bats, not the baseball bats—that blessed the Fireballs all those years ago, the last time they made it to the post-season, coming back and blessing the team's balls from the afterlife.

Baseball-balls, I mean.

The last thing we need is ghosts blessing Brooks Elliott's testicles and giving them a mind of their own so that he goes out and bangs anything that moves, and after last night, I'm pretty sure he's either *very* particular with his unique type, or else he's not picky at all.

"Come with me tonight." Sarah links her arm through mine while we head up to the owners' box to gather Beck and offer our condolences on the loss to Tripp and Lila. "Even if you don't talk, you know you'll love the inside look at how the players live. And I don't want to be the only woman there. Again."

"Lila's not going?"

"No, management's trying to give the players space to do their team thing without pressure. There'll be a few girlfriends or wives, but most of the guys are single."

I give her another side eye. "You don't want me to talk to the players to see if I'm good luck. You want me to talk to them because the Lady Fireballs are low on members and want honorary members for raising money for the Fireballs Foundation now that Lila's got it started again."

"I want you to get comfortable talking to the players for *all the reasons*, Mackenzie. It's been almost two years since you met Cooper for the first time. Eventually you're going to stop coming to see me at Beck's place if you think any of the Fireballs guys will be there. And then I'll be sad, because you're my bestie, and while I will absolutely always make time for you, I'd miss you terribly for having to split my time between you and Beck instead of seeing you both together."

"I'd miss you too."

"So you'll come?"

As if there was a question. Sarah's the closest thing to a sister I've ever had—I mean, in most people's traditional sense of the word—and even if she wasn't, what she's offering is basically in the team's best interest.

Because so long as I'm there, I can make sure Brooks Elliott doesn't get laid.

4

Brooks

EVEN KNOWING the odds were stacked against us by the universe, this afternoon's loss is sitting on me like a pile of moldy lucky socks that didn't do their job.

However, with the disaster of Stafford giving up the game in basically the worst way possible short of all of us lying down in the field for naps in the middle of the inning, it's clear that me having a slump wouldn't be the worst thing for the team.

We're fucking cursed.

So I'm gonna do some fucking. And the more I think about it, the more it's clear that if I'm going to induce a slump, I should do it in spring training.

Begs the question why I've never gotten laid in the off-season, doesn't it?

I'm not much of a scientist, but I remember high school science from my junior year. Hypotheses. Tests. Theories.

That was the year I almost went all the way with my girl-friend. I'd barely gotten her out of her pants when my brother Jack walked into the basement and flipped on all the lights, gave us both the *don't fuck up your lives by doing this without protection* lecture, and sent her running.

Like I hadn't caught him—and our other two older brothers—making out with their girlfriends on that very couch.

But he was right.

I couldn't hit a ball for the next four months, and it took another four months after that to get back to where I was before.

Same with my freshman year college girlfriend, though that time, we got interrupted by a contingency of my frat brothers crashing into the room, chasing a goat that had gotten into the house.

I went into a slump, and two weeks later, I broke up with her. Came back strong the next fall, but a few months later, I started dating another girl. Made out hot and heavy on the first date. She left me with the hard-on to end all hard-ons, and I couldn't connect at the plate for months.

I wanted to blame the blue balls, but I knew that wasn't the problem.

I knew.

Once I got to the minors, I wasn't really into testing the theory anymore.

Didn't want to risk it. Especially when going all the way once wouldn't be enough. Plus, there's no telling how long it would take to recover.

Now?

When I'm playing for the worst team in baseball?

When the job that I've given my all to has stabbed me in the back and told me I'll never get the one thing I've been dreaming of and hoping for since I was a kid?

Hell, I don't know if I even have dreams past winning myself a championship ring.

So yeah, now I'm definitely willing to risk a slump.

I download six different dating apps while I'm doing my fifteen minutes active recovery time on the bike after the game. I settle on inviting a woman on the fifth app to the low-key party we're having at the compound tonight.

Yes, *the compound.*

Every other year I've been at spring training, I've stayed at my own house. Bought it my third season with New York, because I knew I'd retire from my home team.

Wrong.

This year, two games into training, they shipped me to the Fireballs.

Hey, good news is, you don't have to set up housing, New York's general manager had said on my way out the door. *Not for the next month, anyway. You get bonding time with your new teammates.*

And that's exactly what the Fireballs' new management has set up. We're having a slumber party every night for six weeks while a small group of us brainstorm ways to break curses, and no, I can't tell you what we did last night. Especially with the dildo.

What happens at the club during curse-breaking stays at the club.

Thank god tonight's an actual party. With women.

Including Ainsley.

According to the app, she likes playing Pokémon, lifting weights, and binge watching *The Bachelor*.

Who puts that on a dating app unless it's real? Which leads me to believe that her picture—featuring a smiling brunette with dimples—is probably real too.

And if she's half as hot as her picture, I'm putting a sock on my door and shedding my virginity like a scaly second skin tonight.

I grab dinner from the spread in the clubhouse and head back to the compound to get prepped for the party. We're in a gated community with six houses around a central courtyard, and when the guests start arriving, there's a fire going in the outdoor fire pit, catering manning the chicken breasts and lean steaks on the grills, music coming from the speakers Rossi set up, and light beer flowing freely from a few kegs.

Plus the women.

Apparently I'm not the only single guy wanting to get laid tonight.

When Ainsley arrives, she seems as normal—and as attractive —as her dating profile said she was, and I make up my mind in an instant.

We are definitely getting it on before curfew.

"Oh my god, you're really Brooks Elliott," she says with a laugh. Her voice is a little high-pitched, but that's not going to bother me. "I thought I was being pranked."

"You really play Pokémon?" I ask as I put a hand to the small of her back and lead her through the gardens to the courtyard.

"And Dungeons and Dragons," she whispers conspiratorially.

"Stafford and Greene are D&D junkies too. I was going to

introduce them to my sister-in-law, but you're less scary than she is. They'll like you. You should hook up."

She gives me a funny look, and I realize that while I've watched dudes date for years, I've never seen another guy try to hand off his date in the first thirty seconds of meeting her.

Not when he's into her, anyway.

"Your sister-in-law is scary?" Ainsley prompts before I can stutter out something about Darren being married with a baby on the way, and figure out how to make Stafford sound like a dick without sounding like a dick.

"Terrifying. She can hack your bank accounts in her sleep." Fuck. I just said that. *Hi, I'm Brooks Elliott, and I know people who can ruin your life if this goes south.* "Not that she'll do it to you. She uses her powers for good. So as long as you don't run a sweatshop, send dick pics, or troll people online, you're safe."

"Um, okay."

Shit. *Shit.* I'm already losing her. "You hungry? We have carrots."

Her smile turns smoky. "*Carrots*, hm?"

"Yeah, and celery, and steak too. We all eat healthy during the season, but steak's steak. I love meat."

She blinks at me again, and I realize she probably meant *carrots* as a phallic reference, and hopefully I didn't just tell her we all like *meat*, like *man-meat*.

Jesus.

I need to text my sister. She told me a while back that my flirting game is weak. Maybe she has some pointers on how to recover.

"And zucchini," I blurt. "We have zucchini."

"Hey, Elliott, who's your friend?"

Saved by Cooper Rock.

Saved being a relative term, because this guy gets more action than a bobblehead in a New York taxi. So I hear.

We stop near a fountain, and I gesture to my date. "This is Ashley."

"Ainsley," she corrects dryly.

Rock visibly stifles a snort. "Go easy on him, Miss A. Took a ball to the head at practice before the game. But he still hit a home run. Not bad, eh? You guys meet my buddy Beck? This is Beck Ryder, his girlfriend, Sarah, and their friend Mackenzie."

"Oh my god, *Beck Ryder*," Ainsley—*not Ashley, dumbass*—says. "I'm wearing your underwear."

"Me too. High five." Beck holds out his palm, and Ainsley slaps it. I'd be disturbed, except I'm wearing Beck's underwear too. After his boy band days, he went on to be a fashion mogul, and his underwear's fucking comfortable.

Which I won't be saying, because while I'd like to shed my V-card, I'd also like to keep my man card.

I nod to his girlfriend, and then turn to her friend, and *whoa.*

Hel*l*o.

Mackenzie's in a short pink sundress, with legs for miles, plump breasts, and a soft blush in her cheeks under wide blue eyes made up enough to be striking without being overdone. Her blond hair is flowing in waves about her shoulders, hanging down to her collarbones and the top of her *Fiery Forever* button pinned to the strap of her dress, which is fucking adorable. Her lips are like cotton candy, and more color is creeping into her cheeks the longer I stare.

I jerk my gaze back to Ryder's girlfriend. "Sarah, was it?"

She smiles, all warmth and happiness, and extends a hand. "Yes. So nice to meet you. Mackenzie and I spent some time with your sister while she was visiting Lila a few months ago."

My sister. Common ground. "You met Parker. Did you meet her phone?"

Sarah laughs. "Not personally, but Lila's shared a few pretty epic text messages. How does a person get autocorrected that badly?"

"Raw talent." I turn my hand to Mackenzie and force it not to tremor. "Mackenzie. Nice to meet you too."

She makes an odd squeaking noise, looks at my outstretched hand, and then jumps when Sarah nudges her.

She thrusts her hand into mine and stutters, "You too."

An electric force shoots up my arm and explodes fireworks out of my nose while her voice niggles at the back of my memory. "Have we met?"

She shakes her head.

Violently.

"Mackenzie's a little shy," Sarah says quickly.

I'm still shaking her hand.

25

"Mac might be shy, but she's also the biggest Fireballs fan ever born," Cooper interjects. "Right, Mac?"

She nods.

If her eyes get any wider, they're going to pop out of her head.

Awkward happens. Ask me sometime about how my brother met his wife, and then about how my sister met her husband. Then ask me about how many hours I've spent in children's hospitals talking to patients and their families who've also gone mute when I walked in the door, or told me embarrassing stories, or asked me inappropriate questions.

Hell, I did the same thing to Hugo Bertelloni—my favorite baseball player *ever*—when I got to meet him at baseball camp when I was twelve.

So it's second nature to try to put everyone around me at ease.

I squeeze Mackenzie's hand gently. "Glad to be part of your team this year."

She makes another noise and snatches her hand back. "Yep."

"Brooks, can I get a drink?" Ainsley says, and I realize she hasn't been talking to Cooper and Beck like I thought.

She's been watching me watch another woman.

I jerk my attention back to her. "Yeah. Yeah, let's go see what's in the kitchen."

"Sarah, I can't do this," Mackenzie whispers as we turn away, and *that voice*.

If I haven't met her, I'm supposed to.

I know her voice. Swear I do.

The crowd of my teammates and their dates has swallowed her and Sarah when I glance back.

Ainsley's tugging my hand.

Right.

I'm here *with a date*.

To *get laid*.

I squeeze her hand back, feeling like a bit of a tool for using the same motion on my date that I used on Mackenzie, who I'd really like to talk to a little more.

Or a lot more.

Or possibly strip naked, lick from head to toe, and—

And one woman at a time, jackass.

I have a date.

A date who can talk to me without freaking out, which should be number one on the list of requirements to make it into my bed.

Speaking of my bed—time for my A game.

I smile at Ashley—*shit*. I mean Ainsley. "Beer, wine, margarita, or sex on the beach?"

She smiles back and settles her hand on my chest. "Definitely sex on the beach."

Oh, hell, yeah.

This is happening.

Tonight.

5

Mackenzie

HE HAS A DATE.

Brooks *has a date*.

And when Sarah off-handedly says *Ainsley seems nice*, I realize the Fireballs are about to lose their brand-new power slugging third baseman, because I'm *positive* he's planning on sleeping with her.

He has to be, doesn't he?

And it's not like I can be around all the time to stop him.

Which means I need to talk to someone.

I need to talk to a very specific someone *right now*.

"Do you know where the bathroom is?" I ask Sarah.

Beck points me toward the nearest mansion. "Through the kitchen and around the corner, past the mascot posters."

Ugh. Damn mascot pictures. I *hate* the new mascot options.

Sarah frowns at me. "You okay on your own?"

"It's only the bathroom." And I'm sweating like I'm exercising with ski gear on in hundred-degree heat.

I force a smile and head off, weaving through players that would normally leave me consciously in a coma—swear it's a thing—and looking for a familiar face.

Lucky for me, he hasn't gone far, and he's not surrounded by other players. Just a bunch of women.

Women.

How can he be thinking about women at a time like this?

I grab his arm, and his brows shoot up over his bright blue eyes. "Hey, Mac. What's up?"

"I need to talk to you," I whisper.

Brooks is over near the fire, laughing at something his date said, and I don't want him to see me.

First, because shaking his hand did weird things to my insides, and while he's a virgin, I'm not, and I know *exactly* what those things are. And second, because I'm mildly terrified that he'll recognize me from last night.

Cooper, thank god, jumps right into action. "You bet. Here. The laundry room in my building's quiet. Is that okay? I mean, if you can't talk there—"

I grip his solid arm tighter and tug. "Where?"

Yep.

Turns out I can talk to anyone if I'm properly motivated, though now that Cooper's leading me into a house, up the stairs, past bedrooms *where the baseball players sleep*, and closing the door to the laundry room, blocking out the noise of the party and leaving us in a very, *very* small confined space, I'm noticing that my deodorant has failed and my boobs are sweating and these heels were only a good idea in that I'll look like a million bucks when the EMTs find me.

My dads will be so proud.

"What's up?" Cooper asks.

Babe Ruth bless him for being so good about this after I've been a total spaz around him for almost two years now. "Hold on. I don't think I can say this if I'm looking at you."

"Okay." He turns his back, and now I have a view of Cooper Rock's ass, and anyone who tells you all baseball players don't have the best asses has zero taste.

"Gah. No, I have to turn around."

"Should we both stay turned around?"

I spin, stare at a shelf of laundry detergent with four different brands and types of detergent over the dryer, which is blinking that a load is done, which means I'm standing basically next to a baseball player's underwear, and I blurt it all out. "Brooks Elliott is a virgin."

Yeah.

I said that.

Cooper chokes on air. Pretty sure he's laughing. Or trying not to, since silence settles heavy and thick almost immediately. It smells like dryer sheets in here.

Maybe I can rub my armpits with dryer sheets. That would be more effective than my deodorant.

Clearly.

"I...that...huh," he finally says.

"It's a superstition thing," I continue in a rush. "I can't tell you how I know, but I have multiple sources that have confirmed that if he has sex, he won't be able to hit a ball, and *I need the Fireballs to win*."

"What sources?"

"I can't tell you. But it's the truth. Ask Sarah. Or Lila. They were both there." And they were, at the cookout in Copper Valley last fall where Brooks's sister, Parker—one of Lila's best friends—drunkenly confessed that she was sure he was a virgin. "But don't let them tell you how they know either."

More silence covered by the hum of the party music sneaking through the walls.

I don't know if he's contemplating that I'm a few papayas short of a fruit basket, or if he's realizing that this is actually life and death of our favorite team that I'm talking about.

"You know how important it is that the Fireballs win this year." My chest is getting tight. Too much talking to one of my idols. And Cooper is definitely idol-able on the field. Even being on the worst team in baseball, he wins awards for his glovework and his bat, and I think he might be my top competition for most loyal Fireballs fan ever.

"Dude, yeah, I...I guess I never thought *this* would be the first thing you'd ever say to me. But it makes sense."

"He's trying to get laid," I add.

"That's understandable. I mean, thirty years with no sex... I'd be climbing the walls. Or I'd have a really big right forearm."

"*He can't.*" Yeah, breathing is definitely getting harder. And no amount of reminding myself that Sarah's probably right, and I need to *do something different* to contribute to my favorite team's cosmic success, is helping with the impending hyperventilation. "He can't score if he gets laid."

"Technically, if he gets laid, he's scoring, but I see—whoa, hold up. Do you need a paper bag?"

"Yes." I gulp air. I am such a basket case. "No."

"Aw, Mac, I'm just a guy."

"Your brother told me. And your sister. But you're *Cooper Rock*."

"I sometimes fart in the shower and blame it on Torres."

"*I know.*" And now there are black dots dancing at the edges of my vision, and my breath is coming in what should be huge gulps, but instead feels like dainty little sips of air-tea.

Get a grip, Mackenzie. You can do this. You HAVE to do this. "*Please* help me. You can't let Brooks have sex. *You can't.*"

"Shit. Here. You need to sit somewhere, and I need to go find you a paper bag."

He grabs my elbow and tugs, and I trot along while he leads me out of the laundry room.

I'm in the hallway outside where *all of my heroes sleep.*

Yep. Not gonna make it. "How's my lipstick?" I pant. "Will the paramedics judge me?"

Cooper pauses, coughs, his eyes twinkling, and then guides me into a bedroom down the hall after pausing outside the first bedroom we pass.

Oh my god.

Am I in Cooper Rock's bedroom?

"Here. Sit. Breathe. I'm texting Sarah—wait. Give me your phone. If you can't talk to me, maybe we can be text friends."

I shove my phone at him. Once he's gone, I'll label his contact information as something like Gomer Aloysius Perdywagon, and then I'll be able to pretend I'm not texting with Cooper Rock.

I hope Brooks—and the whole team—appreciates the lengths I'm going to in order to save his game this year. If anyone can turn the Fireballs around, it's Tripp and Lila and this coaching staff they're building, and wouldn't *everyone* regret it if Brooks getting laid was the one thing that kept the team from the post-season?

"Okay. My number's in there under Fiery the Dragon, and I texted myself from your phone so I have your number too. I'm gonna go find Sarah."

I squeeze my eyes shut even as a little voice whispers, *you did it, Mackenzie! You talked to him!* "Don't let Brooks have sex."

"Look, Mac, I want to win as bad as everyone, but there's a code, you know? You can prank a guy a few times, but you can't cock-block a teammate repeatedly for no reason."

"*Winning* is the reason." I am such a disaster. Normal, rational people probably don't enlist the help of professional baseball players to interfere with a man's sex life.

But *it's the Fireballs*.

You try growing up the daughter of two drag queens, dealing with all of the crap that comes with having nontraditional parents, because kids can be total assholes no matter how much you learn about love and acceptance and the beauty of originality at home, and then tell me you wouldn't go to extreme lengths to help a team that gave you an escape from the mocking and teasing and made you feel like a normal kid who belonged some-where, even if that *somewhere* was a fandom.

There's nothing like the unity of the true-blue fans of a team that never wins.

Wearing a Fireballs jersey made me feel connected to some-thing bigger at a time when I desperately needed it. Still does. I can walk down any given street, pass someone in Fireballs gear, and there's this instant connection, like *yeah, man, I feel your pain, but we're in this together. We're not alone.*

In my teenage years, when I turned into that shit kid myself who decided that my dads sucked and that they were trying to ruin my life—not because I had two dads, but because doesn't every teenager feel like that?—it was baseball that brought us all back together.

"Please?" I say to Cooper. "Please stop him. I could quit my job to stalk him, but I only have so much in savings and only so much more in credit, and even I know that's crazy talk to spend eight months going into debt just to cock-block a baseball player. Plus I'll probably get arrested."

He sighs. "I promise I'll look into if he's trying to sabotage the team. You—stay. Okay? Stay here, and I'll be back as soon as I can find Sarah."

He leaves me in the room, and my breathing evens out almost instantly.

But you know what?

I did it.

I talked to Cooper Rock.

High five to me.

And if I did it once, I can do it again. And maybe that *will* be good luck for the home team.

But maybe not right now.

Right now, I'm good with continuing to hide in this bedroom, and sit on the bed where I know a baseball player sleeps, and practice not freaking out about it.

I know I'm irrational. I know it's nutty. I know they're just people.

But I want to believe in heroes.

I don't know how to be normal around my heroes. It's like, I want to know they exist, but I don't want them to see how dorky I am underneath the silent thing.

I have issues. I know. *I know.*

I hear voices in the hall, and they're not Sarah's voice, or Beck's voice, or Cooper's voice.

Nope.

That's Brooks Elliott's voice.

"Don't come in here," I whisper. "Please don't come in here."

The door's wide open.

He'll see me if I don't move.

And so I do.

All while whispering *don't come in here.*

Completely in vain.

6

Brooks

I FEEL like a dick while I lead Ainsley to my room. She's nice, but I have to keep mentally correcting myself from calling her Ashley.

And I have a meatball in my conscience.

Is she THE ONE? Are you sure? Are you really sure?

I shake off the mental commentary and point to the picture of Duggan Field that someone hung in the hallway. "You ever been?"

"No, but I'd love to someday." She smiles at me, and I realize her eye makeup is uneven.

Yep. I'm judging if I want to sleep with a woman on how even her eye makeup is.

I'm the dick. I am definitely the dick.

I'd kick a guy's ass if he ever told me my sister wasn't good enough because her eye makeup was uneven. And given who my sister is, odds are good she's got way worse miscoordination going on any given day than mismatched eyelid paint.

Damn good thing her husband adores her for all of her quirks.

Clue number seventy-five that I shouldn't bang Ashley —*Ainsley,* dammit—is that I'm thinking about my sister.

Concentrate, Elliott. Would she be sleeping with you if you weren't a pro baseball player? You're getting laid and she's getting something out of it too.

My balls perk up and give a big ol' *Hell, yeah!* at my internal justification, and I slip my arm around Ainsley's waist as I lead her into my bedroom.

As soon as we're inside the white-walled room hung with seascape paintings, she eyeballs the two double beds, then turns and slips her arms around my neck. "You have a roommate?"

I don't—I haven't had a roommate since my rookie year, but I got last pick of rooms when I got here.

But if the idea of getting caught turns her on, I can run with that. "He's pre-occupied with a poker game."

"Strip poker?" She wiggles her brows, which makes me squint at that space where I can tell her eye shadow is uneven. Is one side a different color brown than the other?

Dammit. I have issues.

She presses her lower body to mine, and *hallelujah*, my dick doesn't care what's wrong with her makeup.

I wiggle my brows back at her. "We could skip the poker part and go straight to the stripping."

"I like that plan."

Her fingers thread through my hair. One of her rings catches and she rips out a few strands, and I swallow a yelp of pain as she leans in to kiss me with cold, wet lips.

"Mm," I groan.

She pulls back. "Oh my god, did I hurt you?"

"I—no. That was—that was nice. That was my *I like it* noise."

My *I like it noise?*

Fuck.

I reach over and kill the lights, which plunges us into total darkness instead of giving us mood lighting.

"Ah, sorry." I flip the lights back on.

Her brows crease like she knows this isn't normal, and *what the fuck is wrong with me?*

Screw it.

I strip out of my shirt.

Ashley's—*Ainsley's* eyes go to my chest. She licks her lips and rubs a rough hand over my pecs.

What does she do? Is she a dishwasher or something? Or a

doctor? Or does she need to see a doctor for whatever's wrong with her hands?

Shut up, Elliott, and fuck the woman.

"You have a lot of muscles."

"Wanna see the biggest one?"

"Oh, hell, yeah."

I reach for my belt buckle.

And then the humming starts.

I meet Ainsley's eyes.

She blinks.

A lot.

Dude, that's what's going on. She only put mascara on one eye.

"Is that you?"

I shake my head. Abruptly, it stops.

But now I have "Take Me Out To The Ball Game" stuck in my head.

She laughs awkwardly, and I think about my sister. Again. While I'm supposed to be making out with this hot chick who wants to stroke my chest and help me with my belt.

"Is it true what they say about the size of a baseball player's bat?" Her fingers are making nimble work of the button on my jeans now, reminding me that while I've never gone all the way with a woman, she obviously has.

With a man, I mean.

Not with a—I'm going to quit thinking now.

Her hand is slipping into my boxers and my dick gives a startled squeak as her cold, rough fingers squeeze him. "Oh, it *is* true."

The humming starts again, this time, the national anthem.

I jerk away from Ashley—*Ainsley, dammit*—and drop to the floor, checking under the beds with my semi-hard junk half-out of my boxers.

Nothing except my luggage.

But the closet—

The closet holds a blond-haired, wild-eyed, hot-as-fuck chick who's not supposed to be in the bedrooms. "Hide-and-seek!" she gasps while I make quick work of zipping my pants.

"What?"

"I'm playing hide-and-seek with Cooper Rock!"

She's flushed from the edge of that pink dress over those gorgeous breasts, up her slender neck, all the way to the tips of her ears and her hairline, and she's panting in a way that's making my dick harder than it was while Ashley had her hands on it.

Her.

Mackenzie.

I want to bang *her.*

I angle closer. "Is this a private game of hide-and-seek?"

"Yes! No!"

She's an adorable ball of sexy, and I can't help smiling at her. It's pure instinct. So is the ugly flash of jealousy at the idea that Cooper's using my bedroom for sex games with Mackenzie.

Who could barely talk to him half an hour ago.

Jesus.

Does the asshole have no honor at all?

"Do you *want* him to find you?"

She half nods, half shakes her head, which means her face basically moves in a circle, and there I go, smiling at her again.

I touch her arm, because I can't help myself, and my cock strains behind my zipper. "You don't have to play hide-and-seek with anyone you don't want to, okay?"

She fans her face and nods.

That wide-eyed thing—she's not here because she wants to be. *Ah, hell.*

What has Rock talked her into?

"You want to go find your friends?"

More rapid nodding. Faster fanning.

"Hot flash," she squeaks.

"Yeah, let's go find your friends."

"If you're leaving, do you care if I go talk to Darren Greene?" Ashley asks.

Fuck.

Fuck.

I'm here with a date.

I fling a glance back at the woman I was about to have sex with before I completely forgot she was here. *Ainsley.* Her name's *Ainsley.* And she's giving me dagger-eyes.

Pretty sure I deserve that. Probably a lot worse.

You're better than this, idiot.

I pinch my eyes shut. "Greene's married and his wife is pregnant. I'll be right back." I pause. Realize I'm leaving a woman in my bedroom with all of my valuables. Wonder what my two brothers who were once in the military would say about that. Then wonder what every baseball player I've ever known would say about me being dumb enough to leave a woman in my room. "Actually, here. You want to meet Luca Rossi?"

She looks longingly at my bed, then follows us out.

"I secretly love you," Mackenzie whispers.

Ainsley gives her the same *you're such a weirdo* eyeball that I've seen assholes give my sister one too many times. "You have issues."

And suddenly I'm seeing red.

And not because I've gotten cock-blocked two nights in a row.

Clearly, we all have issues.

And mine is apparently more than the fact that I'm baseball's oldest virgin. Possibly *only* virgin.

The damn meatball was right.

I have zero taste in women.

And even if I did, I don't currently deserve any of them.

7

Mackenzie

BROOKS ELLIOTT SMELLS like the ocean, and it's making me want to go dance on the beach under the moonlight.

With him.

Except *not* with him, because I can still barely talk.

But you did talk! my inner cheerleader reminds me.

As soon as we exit the house, his date veers off to talk to Luca. The look she's giving Brooks suggests she's *not* going to be heading back to the bedroom with him anytime soon.

Totally worth all the humming. Another high five for me.

"Fireballs' biggest fan, eh?" Brooks nods to my breasts, and I realize he's actually looking at my *Fiery Forever* button—isn't he?

Or is he?

Is he checking out my breasts and pretending he's looking at the button?

After I cock-blocked him?

No.

Definitely not. He wouldn't do that.

He would *not* hit on me, because first of all, he was just trying to score with another woman, and second of all, the universe would basically implode if a baseball player truly hit on me, because I am the biggest dork in all of existence when I'm around my idols.

Yet, even though we're surrounded by players and their girl-friends and wives and dogs and wanna-be flings, I feel like we're entirely alone.

And the weirdest thing is happening.

I'm breathing okay. And I can almost talk like a normal human being. "Number one." I tap my button. "Always number one."

Maybe Sarah was right.

I need to get over myself and *do this*.

It's not like the team can get any worse than last year.

Oh, shit. Oh, hell. I need to knock on wood.

Dozens of freaking baseball players, and not a single wooden bat in sight.

"You know Tripp and Lila?" he asks.

"Through Sarah." Need some wood. *Need some wood.*

And I'm not talking about the wood in Brooks's pants. Which *no one* will be knocking on under my watch.

Maybe him hitting on me would be a good thing? Because I definitely won't sleep with him.

Ever.

My team needs that much from me.

He tightens his grip on my arm as he pulls me out of the way of a cluster of women leaping back from a spilled drink near the firepit. "You have strong feelings about the new mascot costume?"

Double-triple dammit, does he know that was me last night? "Anyone who cares about the Fireballs has strong feelings."

"*Wait.* Are you the one leading the charge on social media to bring back the dragon?"

"Fiery. For. Ever."

He pauses and studies me like he's trying to decide what I'd do in the name of my favorite mascot, then smiles, and *oh, god*, he has the cutest smile. With one side of his mouth hitched a little higher than the other, eyes beginning to crinkle in the corners like he's spent thirty years on this earth doing nothing but smiling, and his light brown hair mussed, though I refuse to think about *why*.

"You let me know if you need any help. I might be new, but I like the dragon best too."

The tension that built as he started his questions melts away, and my shoulders sag in relief as I nod vigorously.

Yep.

Totally going to swoon.

Even knowing he's trying to sabotage the team by getting laid, I am *not* immune to him offering to help in my quest to bring back Fiery.

I still won't sleep with him, but maybe I could lead him on a little so he only wants to hit on me?

No. Bad Mackenzie.

Not only would I like to not die of hyperventilation, but my dads and Sarah would probably like that too.

Probably. "Do you want a Fiery Forever button?"

"Duh." He winks. "Don't tell anybody, but I helped the meatball escape last night."

I suck in a surprised breath, because first of all *no, he didn't*, which I know, because *I was there*, and second, I can't believe I got away with it.

"My hero," I manage faintly.

"I don't know who thought that thing was a good idea. I mean, is it a meatball, or is it a giant round flaming turd? It should be on hemorrhoid commercials, not representing a base-ball team."

"That's *exactly* what I told Tripp and Lila!"

We share a look, and *oh my god, I'm sharing a look with one of baseball's hottest sluggers.*

"Mackenzie!"

A different feeling floods through me as Sarah breaks through the crowd. I wave, then throw myself at her for a hug.

She's laughing as she squeezes me back.

"I got lost playing hide-and-seek with Cooper," I blurt.

Hide-and-seek.

Sheer genius, or complete madness.

Probably both.

Either way, I've managed to stop Brooks from making a huge mistake without also revealing myself as the same person who jock-blocked him last night.

Sarah pulls back, glances at Brooks, then at me, and she's known me for way too long, because I can see realization dawning.

Her lips twitch. She tries to squeeze them together, but I know what's going on.

She knows.

She knows I was keeping him from getting laid.

We've been best friends for over a decade. And while I didn't know until two years ago who her parents are—hello, Hollywood royalty—she knows when I'm plotting something.

"Curfew," Beck says as he joins us. He claps Brooks on the shoulder. "Rest up, slugger. We're counting on you. Thanks for a great party."

Brooks is staring at Beck's junk. "Is that...a steak in your pants?"

We all look at Beck's pants. Both pockets are bulging.

"The steak's under his shirt." Sarah taps one of his pockets. "Pretty sure these are cookies."

"Hey. This one's vegetables." Beck taps his other pocket.

"He eats a lot," I tell Brooks, like it's natural for me to explain the habits of an underwear model to a baseball slugger god.

Brooks winces. "Yeah. I know. Sister. Huge fan."

"Like the kind that knows my underwear size?" Beck asks.

"I need to go see a guy. About a thing. And not talk about your steak, vegetables, cookies, or underwear. Ever. Again." Brooks gives me a half-smile. "See you around, Mackenzie. Let me know if you ever want tickets."

He turns and saunters away, and did I say Cooper Rock has a great ass?

Because he has *nothing* on Brooks Elliott.

Holy. Butt. Cheeks.

"You talked to baseball players!" Sarah whispers as she tugs me to follow the crowd of women leaving the party.

Ashley—or was it Ainsley?—is a couple people in front of us, so I slow my steps and pretend I'm checking my pockets to make sure I didn't leave anything, except my dress doesn't have pockets.

So basically, I look like I'm checking my hips to make sure I didn't add any extra pounds.

"Hey, Mac, you feeling better?" Cooper Rock says behind us.

I jump.

Then nod vigorously.

He meets my gaze.

Glances back to where Brooks is entering his house.

Then slides me a grin and a wink. "Good. Nice chatting. Thanks for that laundry trick. Later, taters. I need my slugger sleep."

Sarah pulls me behind a palm tree near the driveway. "Mackenzie, did Cooper Rock help you cock-block Brooks Elliott?"

"I'm not listening to this." Beck turns his back on both of us and pulls his steak out from under his shirt. It's wrapped in aluminum foil, and he peels back one corner and lifts it to his mouth. "There's a code."

"Cooper smelled good so I asked what detergent he used," I lie.

Sarah winces.

Beck makes a noise and takes another bite of the steak.

"But I talked to Cooper Rock! With words and everything."

She's shaking her head as she pulls me into another hug. "*And* Brooks Elliott. I'm so proud of you!"

Beck holds out a fist. "Give it up, Mac."

I bump him. My heart's doing that erratic thing where it's fine one minute and racing the next, and I should probably get checked out to make sure I'm not having a heart attack.

Sarah pets my hair as she pulls back. "You feel okay?"

"As well as I should."

"Did you talk to Brooks about the virgin thing?"

"Ninety-eight percent positive it's true." And if not, it should be. He's super awkward.

Like, how does a guy get to be a god on the field but can't even talk to a woman in private? First the janitor last night, and tonight—well.

It's none of my business.

He could talk to me, but it's not like he's trying to score with me. I'm the weirdo who was humming baseball songs in his closet, and there's no way those vibes I was getting off him mean he was hitting on me, and even if they do, I already know he has zero taste in women.

He just wants to get laid.

I happen to have the right equipment.

Cooper has a point—it has to be hard being a thirty-year-old virgin. But if he held out for New York this many years, he can give the Fireballs a single season.

My phone dings with a text.

It's from Fiery the Dragon, which means it's really from Cooper.

I'm looking into that thing. What kind of donuts do you like? I'm having them flown in from my brother's bakery. Meet me on the beach in the morning, and we can have another conversation where we don't look at each other while you tell me what you learned.

Sarah taps my phone. "You told Cooper."

"Someone on the team needed to know."

Her eyes are round, like she's not sure if she should be horrified or extra proud of me that my first conversation with a baseball player was about the state of use of another player's penis.

"I know, okay? I know it's crazy. But after I told Cooper, he put me in Brooks's bedroom, and then Brooks came in with that woman while I was hiding in the closet, and I let him get half-naked. And they touched. And kissed. And she had her hands down his pants before I started humming. If he can't hit for crap tomorrow, then we know it's true."

Beck shifts uncomfortably and takes another huge bite of steak.

I might be going too far. It takes a lot to make Beck uncomfortable.

Sarah's face is contorting. "Humming?"

"Please don't ask more about the humming. Plus, he called her the wrong name at least once, so he shouldn't be sleeping with her anyway." I stick my lower lip out like a toddler, then jerk my head toward the driveway. "Can we go? I really want to get to the ballpark early tomorrow, and I need to make new signs first."

"And you're meeting Cooper Rock for breakfast."

"Not alone. I couldn't deny Beck donuts. Especially from Cooper's brother's bakery. So, you're coming with me, right?"

Beck shoves more steak in his face, which could either mean he's really hungry—basically his default setting—or it could mean he's avoiding the question because he doesn't want to take part in plotting another man's cock-blocking.

Sarah frowns. "If the team wins tomorrow, are you prepared to have breakfast with Cooper every day this season?"

"That is *so* not fair."

"Mackenzie. You know I love you. But this is possibly going a little too far."

She's probably right.

But I'm saving judgment on if I'm being crazy until tomorrow.

If Brooks hits it out of the ballpark again, then fine.

I'll let Cooper decide what's best for the team.

But if he strikes out all day, Operation: Guard Brooks's Innocence is *on*.

8

Brooks

I'M STUDYING a profile on one of my dating apps at breakfast when Cooper Rock drops a pile of donut boxes on the table in front of me. "Banana pudding donuts, flown in from home. Life-changing. Who's the hottie?"

"She's a pass." Mostly because she's all put together, which means she's probably lying about something. Also, I can't stop thinking about a hot mess in a pink dress and a *Fiery Forever* button. I shut the app and decline the donut. "You really eat sugar before a game?"

"This here's a once-in-a-spring-training special. Have to have a banana pudding donut to remind me what I'm fighting for. Then it's back to light beer and plain chicken and no butter on my broccoli."

"Eat the donut," Trevor Stafford tells me.

Darren Greene pokes his head in the back door, his pregnant wife, Tanesha, glowing next to him. "Donuts?"

"Donuts, man."

"I love donut day. Elliott, man, lucky you got here when you did, or you would've missed donut day."

Soon, the dining room is crowded with the entire team. The handful of new guys—like me—are being indoctrinated in the donut tradition. Cooper's rationale works on all of us, and even I give in and eat a donut.

Don't usually care one way or another about bananas or banana pudding, but that's a damn good donut.

Cooper's chest puffs, and he pulls out his phone. "Donut selfie!"

We pile in, knowing it'll be on the team's Instagram page within the hour.

"This is tradition?" I ask Stafford, who's next to me.

He nods between moans as he bites into his breakfast.

"Ever think you need a different tradition to win more games?"

"Don't touch the donuts. Touch anything else, but the donuts are off-limits."

"Because they're good luck?"

"No, because they're fucking delicious. Rock brings them in three times a season—once during training, once for the all-star break, and once after a sucky, sucky loss. Then we get together at his place in the mountains after the season and have his family cater for us for a week while we mourn."

I bite into my donut again. Banana pudding oozes out the side, and I lick it off, because it's stupidly good.

I can get any kind of donut I want back home in New York, but even I have to admit that this one's special. It's like you can taste the love baked into it.

Taste the love?

Christ.

It's a wonder I still get endorsement deals for muscle cars, chainsaws, and whiskey.

"Can't do it after the season this year," Cooper says. "My brother's finally getting hitched."

Darren looks up from his own donut. "Thought his wedding was in early November."

"Which means he'll be busy tying the knot and leaving for his honeymoon when we bring home the championship."

Silence falls over the team.

I might not have been here long, but even I can read what's going on here.

Be better this year? Yeah. Probably.

There *is* all that shit we did at "the club" the other night.

But the Fireballs making it all the way to the post-season?

No way.

We're not *Major-League*-ing our way to championship rings, plus the analogy doesn't even fully hold. Building this year? Yes. Going all the way?

I'm not betting my virginity on it.

Darren slowly pushes back from the table. "All the way," he says softly.

"All the fucking way," Rossi chimes in.

"All the damn way." Stafford stands and pumps a fist. "We're going *all the damn way*."

Cheers go up around me, and I get a knot in the pit of my stomach while I join in.

All the way.

Yeah.

Easy for them to say.

They're *all* getting laid. Or at least have the opportunity.

Me?

All I have are gloriously filthy dreams.

Last night, starring an accidentally hilarious, overly-awkward blonde who inadvertently cock-blocked me from a closet.

Probably because I introduced her to the woman I was making out with by calling her the wrong name.

Jesus.

She must think I'm an asshole.

Actually, I probably am an asshole, even if I know all Ashley —*Ainsley*—wanted was to sleep with a baseball player.

"Beach run!" Cooper crows.

Everyone groans.

He laughs.

"Fucker does this every year." Stafford shoves me toward the stairs. "Gets us sugared up, then says we need to go for a run together."

"You get a compound every year?"

"No, but donut day is donut day, no matter where we're staying."

I look back in time to see Cooper shoving two donuts into a white bakery bag. "Last one to the beach is a rotten egg!"

Can't help liking the sadistic bastard. Between his brand of

51

crazy and his energy levels, he's too much like my brothers for me to *not* like him.

Right down to carrying that bakery bag of donuts all through the whole run.

"What the hell are those for?" I ask him as we're all collapsing post-sugar-fueled morning workout. The coaching staff showed up to oversee us, and some of them joined us on the run, but none of them have touched the donuts.

He grins at me while his breathing evens out. "Invited some lady friends for a late breakfast on the beach."

Now *that's* good news.

"Don't get too excited, Elliott. Not enough time for nooky before weights, but this is just the warm-up, right?"

I grunt.

He lifts a brow like he's waiting for me to say more.

I lift a brow right back. In my decade in pro ball, I've never once asked a teammate if he gets laid the morning of a game, and I have no intention of starting now. Some might talk about if banging is good luck or bad luck, but no one outright asks.

Most of the team are heading the three blocks back to the compound, but a few stragglers are sitting along the beach or taking pictures while the sun makes its lazy trek higher in the sky.

"You don't want to be here," Cooper finally says.

I stare at the water and don't answer.

"I get it, man. Sucks to be traded to the worst team in baseball. But this team isn't the same team it was last year. New owners, new management, new coaching staff, new fans…fuck the curses. Fuck the haters. Last year, the year before—none of it matters. We're gonna fucking *win*."

He's so insistent, it's hard to not believe him.

There's power in belief.

So much power in belief.

I stare out at the surf rolling in. "You've never wanted to play for another team?"

"I grew up an hour from Copper Valley. I was born a Fireballs fan, and I'm gonna die a Fireballs fan. They're gonna scatter my ashes in the infield one day, and say I was the greatest Fireballs player that ever lived. I get a ring out of my time here, that's the icing on the cake." He shrugs. "Guessing you feel the same about New York. Home team love, right?"

"Something like that."

"I get it, man. I'd be fucking broken if I got traded away from my home team. But give us a chance." He looks behind us, grins, and leaps to his feet. "Hey, Mac. Thanks for coming. You ready to try this for luck?"

I scramble to my feet too, shoving my hands in the sand as I do, leaving me with sandy hands that I can't dust off fast enough while Mackenzie approaches.

She's in skintight jeans, a Fireballs jersey, and a Fiery the Dragon hat, complete with her *Fiery Forever* button. Her lips are painted pink again, her hair tied back in a ponytail, and her feet are bare.

My dick immediately leaps to attention, and I go from semi-hard to uncomfortable and having to block my junk when she shoots me a hesitant glance and a small finger wave after she hands Cooper a bag of buttons.

Fiery Forever buttons.

I might not be happy about playing for her team, but I've gotta admire her dedication. She loves baseball and she loves her team.

How can you not respect that?

Fuck, when's the last time I would've handed out New York team buttons to people because I wanted to, instead of because management put them in my locker and suggested I do it?

"Mac's good luck," Cooper tells me. "She's gonna eat a donut during warm-ups today too."

"And take one to Beck." Her voice is small and hesitant, and she keeps dropping her gaze like she's staring at the sun.

Fuck.

She *is* staring at the sun.

I shove Cooper and make him move until the sun's not behind us so she doesn't have to squint anymore. "You're coming to the game today?"

She nods.

My heart does a boogie dance, and I cringe to myself, because *boogie dance*?

No wonder I've never been laid. "Good seats?"

She nods again.

"If security gives you trouble about the donuts—" Cooper starts.

"I know. Call Lila."

He beams and holds out a fist. "You're talking, Mac."

"Trying new things."

"Superstitions, man. Gotta stick with what's working and take the leap to change when it's not. Appreciate all the help we can get."

She nods again. "I like winning."

"Right? Whatever it takes." He turns to me. "You got any superstitions?"

I stare at him a beat. Is he hinting at something? Does he know? All I've ever said to my teammates who get too curious— and few do—is that I don't date during the season.

Cooper's grin is turning into a smirk. "You *do*. C'mon, Elliott. Spill. What can we help you with? What gets your bat swinging?"

"Nothing I can talk about without cursing myself."

"Jarvis says the same thing, but I got eyes. And I've got his back. You need help with anything, say the word. That's what teammates are for."

I will *not* be asking Cooper Rock for help with my virginity.

Keeping it *or* losing it.

He glances at his bare wrist, where a normal person would keep a watch. "Whoa, gotta run. Have to ask Coach something. Thanks for taking Beck a donut, Mac. You're a peach."

He turns and jogs off like we didn't already do three miles on the sand.

And now it's just me and Mackenzie.

And my hard-on.

And the near-certainty that I've been set up. Maybe Rock's a good wingman after all.

She brushes her ponytail out of her face as a gust of wind picks up. "Play good today."

"You busy after the game?"

Smooth? No.

But then, neither is she, and I like that about her.

She's real.

It's not like I'm going to take advantage of her and push myself on her if she's not interested. Annoying as it was that she interrupted me and Ash—Ainsley last night, even I can admit that doing it by humming "Take Me Out To The Ballgame" was freaking hilarious.

I like hilarious.

Gonna need a lot of hilarious to survive this year.

She's not answering. Just squinting at me, even though the sun's more behind her, lighting her up like she's the all-star baseball god and I'm an awkward geek trying to score with a woman out of my league.

Let's be honest here.

If it weren't for my bat, she *would* be out of my league. Pretty? Check. Friends with actual stars? Check. In possession of two delicious breasts and one most likely smokin' hot pussy? I'm gonna go out on a limb and check that box too.

Her silence has me clearing my throat uncomfortably as I realize she doesn't want to have to turn me down on an offer to hang out. "Right. You're hanging out with your friend. I—"

"I'm free. But I don't know—*aah!*"

She suddenly dives out of the way as a frisbee whizzes past inches from her ear. The donut bag goes flying, and she lands on her shoulder in the sand. I spin around as a group of guys in their early twenties come hustling our way. "Hey! Watch out, numb nuts."

"Cranky-ass," one of them mutters as he darts past me.

"Go get laid," a second says.

Mackenzie squeaks, and I leap into action, squatting beside her and reaching out to help. "You okay?"

Our sandy palms connect, then our gazes lock.

Apparently I'm a sucker for blue eyes, because I can't look away. Hers are bright as the sky on an early afternoon game in mid-July, when the heat's on to keep our place in the standings, and while she's jittery, there's unabashed belief in the intensity of her silent plea. *You can do it. You can do it for my team.*

It's the theme of the day.

We can do it. The team can do it.

I don't want to be the asshole holding everyone back. But after this many seasons in the big leagues, and my entire adolescence before that indoctrinating me in the ways of the game, it's hard not to be jaded, and it's hard not to believe in curses, and it's hard to have to help a team other than the team I was supposed to retire from in another five or ten years.

And it's hard to keep—well, being *hard* with no relief aside from my own fist in sight.

Her hair whips around into her face again. I reach for it the same time she does, making our fingers connect and sand tumble off both of us.

"Here." I hold her ponytail back from her face in one hand while I pull her to her feet with my other.

Her eyes go round. "The donuts!"

We both turn. I instinctively start toward the bag before she grabs me, and we scramble back.

An angry horde of seagulls is attacking the white bakery bag, ripping it to shreds and fighting over the donuts inside.

One squawks at us. Mackenzie scurries back another three feet, right into one of the guys playing frisbee.

"Watch it, lady," he snaps.

I step toward him, but Mackenzie yanks on my hand and squares up to the jerk with lightning flashing in her eyes. "I hope a seagull poops on your head."

He blinks.

She cocks a hip. "What? You've never heard of karma? *You don't own this beach.* So quit acting like it. Your mother would be horrified, and if you have no respect for your mother, I hope the crabs on the beach aren't the only ones you encounter today."

I'm grinning as she starts marching away, our hands still connected, leaving me to follow her or make one of us trip on the beach again.

She has sand all up and down one side of her outfit, and I realize with a jolt that she's wearing a Cooper Rock jersey.

Oh, hell.

It makes sense now. Rock wasn't giving me a chance to talk to Mackenzie on my own. He's probably lurking around the corner laughing his ass off watching me try to flirt with a woman he knows I don't have a chance with.

I freeze and glare at her back. "You want to date Cooper."

She turns on me. "*What?* No. No times a million. I can't date a god."

My eye twitches. "Cooper Rock is *not* a god."

She gasps and snatches her hand out of mine. "How *dare* you."

"What? He's not."

She closes the distance between us and pokes me in the chest with a pink-tipped finger. "Do. Not. Insult. Cooper. Rock."

This anger building inside me is probably irrational, but irrationality isn't enough of a reason for me to tamp it down. "You *do*. You want to date him."

She sucks in a breath like she's about to let me have it, because who the hell am I to have an opinion about who she dates?

I was trying to screw another woman while she was in my closet yesterday. She has no idea I'm even interested, and why should she?

As soon as she opens her mouth, though, she abruptly clamps it shut again. Two big nose-inhales and exhales later, she stops staring at my chest and lifts her gaze to mine.

Christ, those eyes.

They're hypnotizing me.

Or maybe I should've gotten laid years ago. They're just two eyeballs. Every human has them.

Hers are more like soul-sucking windows to another universe where I want to live, rather than simple eyes.

Wow.

I don't know if I have issues, or if my issues have issues, but that was fucking sappy.

"Play good today." She spins and walks away.

"That's it? You're not going to verbally eviscerate me? Not going to defend Cooper the God? You want his phone number?"

She doesn't stop. Not until she reaches the edge of the parking lot, where she bends and picks up a pair of custom Chucks with the Fireballs logo on them, and then keeps stalking to a small coupe.

Something niggles at the back of my brain, something that I can't quite identify, but something definitely suggesting I probably shouldn't get involved with the Fireballs' most obsessed, superstitious fan *ever*.

But I can't stop watching her.

Who is she?

What does she do when she's not at the ball field?

Is she here for all of spring training?

Does she live in Copper Valley? She must, if she's the team's biggest fan, right?

Is she independently wealthy, or does she have a day job? Does she have nutty siblings like I do? What does she do for the holidays?

I've met a lot of people in my career. A lot of obsessed fans. A lot of superstitious fans. Hell, I'm a special level of obsessed and superstitious too.

I've never met anyone exactly like Mackenzie.

Or maybe that's my dick talking. He's not usually turned on by the uber-fanatical, yet here we are, both of us wanting to get closer to her.

As I start to head back to the compound, I feel something land in my hair.

A seagull squawks overhead, and all the guys playing frisbee crack up.

"Hey, asshole, my bird shit in your hair!" one of them calls.

I grit my teeth and start walking again.

I've gotten cock-blocked two days in a row, and now pissed off a woman I'm inexplicably attracted to. I'm playing for a record-setting team with more losses than practically any other professional club in all of sports history. I'm not where I wanted to be in my career or personal life now.

But you know what I do have?

I have training to do and a game to play.

I have a fucking *job*.

So that's where I'm going.

I'm going to channel all of this frustration and go do my damn job.

Brooks

I'M SO SCREWED.

It's been ten days, and the Fireballs are mediocre, which might as well mean they still suck, and while I'm not exactly in a slump—I've been on base in more games than not, even if it took me a few games to get there after the party incident—I'm also not getting laid.

Not winning. Not scoring. Not banging.

With catching up on all the team photos and videos and promo spots that need to be filmed for between-inning entertainment, plus having one-on-ones with the coaching staff—all the things that are normally done *before* the games start in spring training—I haven't had the kind of free time we usually get in the build-up to the season.

Then there are all the media calls.

So damn many media calls, because the Fireballs is the team *everyone* is watching this year, thanks to management's massive, unrelenting public relations campaign, which is also eating into the free time that usually comes with spring training. And in all of my interviews, I put on my happy face and talk about opportunities and playing good ball and not believing in curses, because that's what the job requires.

Baseball's been a job for a lot of years now, but this year, it's wearing on me.

It's wearing on me so bad, the two nights I could've gone out to a real club, I crashed early instead and jacked off while thinking about blond hair and blue eyes and pink lips.

Don't ask about the nights I went back to the *other* club.

So far, that's not doing anything for the team either.

It's spring training, Rock keeps saying to anyone who'll listen.

Any other year, I'd agree with him. Spring training is when the coaches open the doors to guys from the minors to show what they've got and try to score a spot in the show. It's when we test up-and-coming talent, and it's when it's normal to blow out one team one day, and then get blown out yourself the next.

But it's the Fireballs.

The worst team in baseball.

Even with all the changes in the off-season, we've only won three of the last ten games.

It's keeping me up at night—along with my lack of interest in sex with a woman at the moment, which is the one thing I should be able to go out and enjoy right now, for fuck's sake, and I don't like it.

But tonight, I'm putting it all behind me.

All of it.

Tonight, I'm on my way to the beach house that Tripp Wilson and Lila Valentine, team co-owners and soon-to-be husband and wife, have rented for the season. They're hosting a cookout and the air outside their little villa is filled with the scent of grilling meat and the sounds of laughter.

Family's invited, and some of mine arrived in town today. They beat me to the cookout, because they didn't have to have a heart-to-heart with half the coaching staff after the game to discuss why I'm not hitting the ball better.

Long before Lila got involved with the Fireballs, she was friends with my sister and brother-in-law, Parker and Knox. She was at their wedding. All of my brothers hit on her, naturally, because she's a redheaded bombshell. I keep texting to ask Parker if she's here more for Lila than she is for me, which keeps getting me hilarious autocorrected messages that are probably meant to question everything from my manhood to my family loyalty, but actually suggest Parker's incubating a family of turtle-squirrels in her ear.

Life would be dull without Parker's phone.

Also in town from my family?

Trouble.

Of the best kind.

My brother Rhett's a former SEAL. He hung up his night vision goggles to marry Parker's friend Eloise, who's a tatted-up punk chipmunk crossed with a nymphomaniac. The two of them made a side-trip to Copper Valley on the way down, since they're both sort of self-employed these days and could juggle their calendars to find me an apartment up in Virginia for the regular season.

Both Parker and Eloise are pregnant, much to my mother's utter joy, though I have my doubts about how thrilled she'll be once Rhett's kid starts talking like Eloise.

But Eloise isn't the first person I hear when I reach the crowded tropical veranda.

No, that's a voice that niggles at the deepest recesses of my mind and makes me stop short, because I know that voice. Swear I do. And not from pulling her out of my closet and getting yelled at by her on a beach ten days ago.

That voice sets my nerves on fire and makes my pulse buzz, and I shoot a look at Cooper Rock, who's hovering near her.

Fucking Cooper Rock.

Guy gets more action off the field than half the rest of the team put together.

"You need to remove that echidna from voting *right now*." Mackenzie's voice is stronger than I've ever heard it, and I wonder if she talks to all baseball owners like this. She's definitely not shy with an audience of players now, which makes my blood pressure spike as I wonder if she's one of the women Cooper's been banging in his off-hours, and how much she's been around the team for all the progress she's made.

"Right now?" Lila asks with a smile. She's clearly undisturbed, but then, since she hit the team like a hurricane a few months back, ticket sales and press coverage are way up.

"How is a thing with a four-headed penis family-friendly?" Mackenzie's in a vintage Fireballs T-shirt with Fiery the Dragon plastered to her chest. She points to the muscled beast on her breasts, even though she could point to the buttons on both her hat and her shirt now, and hello, cock twitch. "Fiery's family-friendly. He doesn't even have a penis because he's not real. But this echidna? *A four-headed penis.* This is the sort of thing you research *before* you declare it a finalist in a mascot contest."

"Wait, a four-headed penis?" Ah, there's my sister-in-law. Eloise naturally has the voice of a six-pack-a-day smoker. She leaps into the conversation as she normally does, which is to say with all the energy of a squirrel on a five-hour energy shot. "Can a person get surgery to get a four-headed penis? Don't get me wrong, Rhett's thunder stick is my favorite toy, and it puts mortal willies to shame, but a four-headed dick? Dude. Wow."

I catch sight of Parker, my awkward strawberry blond sister, squeezing her eyes shut and muttering something to herself. Knox is wincing beside her, and there's Rhett with them too, smiling proudly under the military buzz cut he's kept despite being officially done with SEAL life.

Mackenzie points at my sister-in-law while she turns a triumphant look to Lila. "See? *That's* what people will be talking about all season if you insist on keeping that awful mascot option."

Only Tripp Wilson appears horrified.

Poor guy's obviously never had the Eloise experience before.

"You're the drummer," he mutters to her, which cracks me up as I approach their group. Parker and Eloise are half of a girl band that plays the juice bar scene in New York, and apparently Eloise's reputation precedes her.

"I bang a lot," she confirms. "A. *Lot.* Wanna watch? Your brother did."

"Eloise. He did not." Parker gives Rhett a glare that's either demanding he shut his wife up, or at least quit enjoying listening to her talk about banging so much. "Also, *children are present.*"

Eloise points to her stomach, where her baby bump isn't showing as much as Parker's is yet. "Duh."

"I mean children of normal parents who would prefer *not* to have their kids' vocabulary full of the world's worst innuendos and euphemisms before they head to kindergarten."

Eloise frowns like Parker's words don't compute. She has

short spiky hair, more tattoos than the Fireballs team combined, and more piercings every time I see her.

She's also a top-notch hacker who can do some crazy-scary things, but practices her skills exclusively in the name of social justice and only does illegal shit when it's for a good cause.

She fits Rhett.

I'm happy for him, and also insanely jealous that he's getting some every night.

And some freaky *some* at that.

"We're not canceling the mascot contest," Lila says to Mackenzie. "Those videos Meaty keeps sending of his adventures after running away are solid gold."

Mackenzie frowns.

"And the work of someone unhinged," Tripp chimes in. "We should've called the police."

Now Mackenzie's eyeballing him with something dawning, and not something good, but Lila waves away his concern. "Replacing that costume is worth every penny. No publicity is bad publicity, and Meaty's up in the standings since he disappeared. I'm thinking the duck needs to go next. You think echidna penises are bad? Google duck penis sometime."

Tripp chokes on his drink, and the two owners share a secret look.

Dammit.

I want a secret look-sharer. Is that too much to ask?

"I know about duck penises. That's why I'm wearing this." Eloise rips her shirt open.

"Not in front of the children." I avert my eyes, because she's flashed me one too many times. Usually on purpose.

Rhett shoves me in the arm. "She's dressed, dumbass. Also, good to see you, baby brother."

I risk a glance with one eye, and *phew*.

She's wearing a shirt with the duck mascot on it under her button-down. "Firequacker will win."

Parker pulls open her button-down. "Meaty the Meatball's better. And Lila knows about your hacking problem, so don't even try to rig the voting. She'll know it's you, and she'll disqualify your favorite mascot if she senses cheating."

"None of it matters. Fiery's coming back." Mackenzie pushes her breasts up, and I can't look away.

I need to so I can pummel every one of my teammates who have also turned to stare, but *god*, she has great breasts.

"Mac's right," Cooper says. He unbuttons his jersey—our invitations dictated jerseys over mascot shirts and jeans tonight for all the camera crews grabbing PR footage around the backyard—and he, too, is wearing a Fiery T-shirt.

Along with a *Fiery Forever* button.

It's like they planned this.

My temper is rising in direct proportion to my dick's interest in Mackenzie.

Maybe that fucking meatball was right, and the problem isn't sex, but sex with the wrong person. I should kiss Mackenzie and see if that helps.

Yeah.

I like this plan.

"Meatballs," Rhett says. He rips his shirt off to display two giant flaming meatballs tattooed to his chest in the middle of the rest of his ink. It doesn't fit. At all.

So it's probably temporary, but it's still horrifying.

Eloise strokes him. "Your balls give me a lady boner."

"This is exactly what's going to happen if you let that meatball win," Mackenzie says. "Ball jokes *all the time*."

"And she can get worse," I offer.

"So much worse." Without warning, Eloise tackles me with a full-body hug, which means she climbs me like she's a spider monkey. "Wait till you see the sweet pad we found you in Copper Valley. Start growing your porn 'stache now. I already ordered a collection of lava lamps to match the bedroom."

Rhett gives me the stink-eye like it's my fault his wife likes to climb men.

I hold my hands up in plain sight, only smirking because I know there's no fucking way he let her get away with hooking me up with a place that requires lava lamps, and even if he did, it's not like I'll be there that much.

We travel half the season, and despite what my agent says, I give New York two months before they're negotiating to get me back. "Not my fault I'm hot and climbable. Getting soft, Mr. Retired."

Yeah, I'm gonna end up with eels in my bed for that.

Worth it.

His eyes turn into nuclear missiles that he aims at my crotch. "You're lucky you're her least favorite."

Parker smacks him behind the head. "Shush. You be nice. Brooks needs to get his bat back, not get picked on."

"Oh, is it beatings time?" Eloise pats my head and leaps off me.

"No. No beatings." We *all* say it.

"Of any kind. And not in public this time," Parker quickly adds, because it's necessary with Eloise.

My sister steps around her friends to greet me with a hug that she has to go up on tiptoes for. "Miss you, you little pain in the ass."

"Miss you more, old lady. How's my first niece?"

"Niece *or nephew*. We're not telling. Have you met Mackenzie? She's awesome. We spent some time together in Copper Valley back when Lila was dealing with her uncle's estate last fall. Oh my god, it's the echidna!"

We all look as she points at the landscaped yard. Tripp's two little kids are dashing around with their shaggy brown mutt, and now the three remaining mascots are traipsing in through the back gate.

But the mascots aren't alone.

"Puppies!" Cooper says.

A collective *Awww* goes up among all my teammates as puppy after puppy dashes into the yard too.

Lila smiles, and she and Tripp clink glasses while the four cameramen turn their view to the baseball players abandoning the veranda to check out the puppies.

And no, I am not immune.

It's *puppies*.

Fluffy puppies and big puppies and little puppies. Brown puppies and black puppies and spotted puppies.

A dozen freaking roly-poly, floppy-eared, adorable-as-fuck puppies.

I never had a dog—I was the youngest, so I basically *was* the dog.

"Smile for the cameras. And jerseys off in ten for mascot shirt photos," Lila calls.

"Puppies are the fucking *bomb*," Eloise declares.

Lila shakes a finger at Rhett as he starts to follow Eloise to the puppies. "Shirt back on, Mr. Elliott."

"Aw, Lila, let him pose with the echidna first." Parker grins at all of us. "It would mean so much to Eloise to be near all her favorite penises at once."

"And now I'm weirdly sad that the new Meaty costume isn't ready yet," Lila murmurs.

Mackenzie props a fist on her hip. "Fiery. Forever."

"Keep it up, Mac. Never give up hope." Tripp holds out a palm, and she slaps it.

"You *can't* use Meaty," she tells Lila. "The Fireballs are almost winning without him."

And that much is true.

The team hasn't been blown out by as many runs this year as they were last year. At least, not in every game. And technically, we've even won a game or two more than the Fireballs usually do.

"Dada! *Doggy!*" Tripp's little girl launches herself at him, all blond curls and smiles. As soon as he scoops her up, she lunges for Lila, who catches her with a laugh. "*Doggy!*"

Fuck, I want a family. Something to live for off the field. And it's not about getting laid.

It's about needing *more*.

Nothing like getting traded to the worst team in baseball to remind you how much you don't even love the game anymore.

It's a job.

The thing I do because I don't know what the fuck I'd do if I wasn't doing it, and also the thing I do because I'm usually damn good at it.

Or maybe that's the sexual frustration and lack of team spirit talking.

Out in the sandy yard, Cooper's rolling around with a golden retriever puppy. Trevor Stafford is tossing a baseball to a puppy that's barely bigger than the ball. Robinson's making a wiggly thing with floppy ears kiss Glow the Firefly, who gets so excited he shakes his ass and knocks over Francisco Lopez, who's probably hamming it up for the camera crew that's capturing everything.

But Mackenzie's sticking to the veranda.

"You don't like dogs?" I ask her.

Her brows knit together. She slides me a quick look, then glances away like I'm still not one of the players she can talk to.

And that pisses me off too.

She *is* sleeping with Cooper. He talked her out of her pants, and now he's talked her into talking to him and *only* him.

Three billion women in the world, and I'm seeing green over one who's quirkier than half my family put together.

I have issues. And it's not only that I can't hit a damn baseball.

I shake my head and turn to join the rest of the team, hoping the puppies can lift some of my funk, when she inhales softly.

"I used to foster puppies. But it got hard having to let them go when they found their forever homes, and even harder when I couldn't foster them all, and I had to give it up. You should go play with them. Maybe they'll pull you out of your slump."

Rhett slips to my side. I thought he was out in the yard with Eloise, but he still has those stealthy SEAL moves. Dude can climb buildings. Used to climb into Parker's apartment whenever we thought she had a guy over to scare the piss out of him.

Still does sometimes, because we like to keep Knox on his toes. Just because he's married to Parker now doesn't mean we're not checking in to make sure he keeps being good enough for her.

"This a normal kind of slump?" Rhett asks.

I shift a glare to him. "I don't have slumps."

"Used to."

He's not smirking. If I were him, I'd be smirking.

But I'm getting the SEAL face. The one that says he knows there's a problem. He knows what it is. And he doesn't know how to fix it, but he's going to figure it out no matter how many buildings have to burn.

Mackenzie's squinting at my brother. "When did he have slumps?"

"Whenever—"

I cut him off by punching him in the arm, which does more damage to me than it does to him since he has boulders where his biceps go.

"C'mon, Bazookarooka. You want help getting out of the slump, you gotta be honest."

"And you need to shut your fucking trap when you don't know what you're talking about."

He knows. *He fucking knows* I'm a virgin.

Anyone who tells you being the baby of a family is the best clearly doesn't have three older brothers and a Parker.

Though I'll never regret that her phone once called me *Bazookarooka*.

"Brooks, if there's something we can do—" Lila starts, but Tripp clears his throat weird, and she blushes and looks away.

I look at Rhett.

Then Mackenzie, who's also turning red.

Lila.

And Tripp.

Fuck.

Fuck.

Do they *all* know?

"I'm fine. Just getting warmed up." I fake a cough. "Florida allergies."

"Daddy, Jupiter finded a lizard!" Tripp's son, the older of his two preschoolers, dashes up onto the veranda with a wiggling green thing in his hand and a tiny brown puffball bouncing along behind him. But where James stops at Tripp, the puppy lunges for my boot like it's a Big Bad to be defeated.

I squat and pick it up, because it's the best kind of distraction from a conversation I'm not having.

Its fur is wiry brown curls, and as soon as I get him up to my face, he licks my nose.

Eloise jogs back over and punches me in the arm. "Now *that's* the kind of action you need."

Rhett slips an arm around her shoulders and clamps his hand over her mouth.

"We're thinking Glow, Firequacker, and Spike should go on a mission to find Meaty," Lila announces.

"But only under direct supervision," Tripp adds quickly.

"Or you drop the mascot contest and bring back Fiery." Mackenzie's watching me, and I'm trying to pretend I don't know it.

What's worse?

Standing here having everyone not-subtly change the conversation from discussing my virginity in relation to my hitting slump, or suspecting it's not the first time they've had this conversation?

If they know—if they all know—then who else knows?

And *how?*

Was it Lila? Did *she* steal that meatball costume for publicity? It didn't sound like her. It sounded like—

Fuck.

Me.

I suck in a surprised breath and look at Mackenzie.

"You've met Parker before."

"She has the b-best phone."

"Say *you'll never be able to hit a ball again.*"

Her face instantly goes redder than the amount of blood I'd like to shed. "Why would I ever say that to you?"

"Pretty damn sure you know why."

The puppy squeaks and pisses on my shirt. *Shit.* I'm squeezing a dog because I've realized the nutcase I can't stop thinking about is the same fucking nutcase who cock-blocked me in a damn meatball costume.

I scratch him behind the ears and cradle him gently to my face. "Sorry, Coco Puff."

The name just comes out, and when he licks my nose again, I'm a goner.

He's a squirmy, happy little runt, wiggling in my palm and smiling as he pants, and I named him.

He's as good as mine.

I look past Mackenzie, because as far as I'm concerned, she doesn't exist anymore. *Jesus.* The closet. The humming.

Was that chick with the "boyfriend" at the restaurant last week her doing too? Is this all one giant set-up to make sure I don't get laid?

I pin Lila with a *don't fuck with me and don't tell me no* look. "I want this dog."

"They're all from a local shelter. Shouldn't be a problem."

"He matches your carpet," Eloise says behind Rhett's hand.

"She means the shag carpet in your bedroom." Rhett's brows knit together. "That still sounds like I'm talking about your pubes, doesn't it?"

"Daddy, what is pubes?" Tripp's son asks.

"Picture time!" Lila announces. "And maybe we get a little pickier about which family you bring next time, Brooks?"

Fine with me.

And Coco Puff.

He's my only family now. I'm disowning the rest of the cock-blocking, secret-telling, back-stabbing traitors.

Mackenzie

OPENING DAY SHOULD BE a federal holiday, especially when opening day happens at home.

But since it's not, I'm using one of my valuable remaining vacation days to lead protests against the new mascot options at Duggan Field.

A girl's gotta do what a girl's gotta do.

Sarah joins me at eight in the morning. We're both in Fiery hoodies, because it's chilly, and while I thought maybe we'd get eight people to join us, it's closer to eighty and growing by the minute.

"I'm so proud of you," Sarah says as we march down Luzeman Lane, the street between Duggan Field and Fireballs headquarters, named after the greatest Fireballs player to ever play the game.

He was in his fifties when I went mute at meeting him the one and only time my dads tried to take me to a fan event. They have the picture framed at home—Andre Luzeman giving me a side eye while I stood there doing a guppy impersonation when I was sixteen. My hair was fabulous and my jersey was stylin', but I was totally dorktastic.

Learning to talk to the players last month for spring training was weird.

But they won more games than they lost in Florida, so you're dang right I need to keep talking to them.

It's working, even if Brooks Elliott has done nothing but glare at me the two times I've seen him since the team got back to Copper Valley a few days ago.

But he's hitting the ball again, even if it's mostly pop-outs and foul balls. And he started an Instagram account for Coco Puff, which is the cutest thing I've ever seen, and it's also making me miss my old foster dogs.

Not the heartache—never the heartache—but the joy of having a dog around.

I wonder if he's bringing Coco Puff to the game today.

Probably not.

A puppy would probably make a ton of messes in the clubhouse, and it's newly renovated. Plus, who's going to watch him while the players are playing?

We're marching both through the front courtyard and around the block and past the players' entrance in case any of them want to join us. It doesn't hurt that I really want to see the team. Cooper's been texting regularly—mostly funny baseball memes every few days and occasionally a random mention that Brooks isn't seeing anyone—and he tells me that all the players fully support my efforts to bring back Fiery.

I had to send another case of buttons for the teams' friends and family members to wear.

I still haven't confessed to anyone that I have the meatball costume. And don't ask how I got it through airport security. You don't want to know.

My dads know though. I'm hiding the costume at their place, because Sarah never goes there, because why would she? I wouldn't go to her parents' place randomly and unannounced either.

Plus, my dads have been helping me take the new videos that I'm feeding to Tripp through a burner phone often enough to discourage the Fireballs' video and marketing team from putting their new mascot costume to use.

"We're gonna win this year." I link my arm with Sarah's and lean in for a shoulder-bump. I'm freaking proud of her too.

Two years ago, we were both uber-shy dorks hiding from the world in our own ways. Now, she's dating a superstar, no longer paranoid about the paparazzi who captured every gloriously awful moment of her awkward childhood—her parents are Hollywood royalty—and she's balancing time with Beck with running her science blog and working part-time for an environmental engineering firm.

And I can talk to baseball players.

We reach the corner and turn to start the march back, only to bump into two massive guys who completely block the sidewalk.

Block?

More like overflow.

I have to look so high up to see their faces that my neck hurts, and recognition makes me sputter in surprise.

Copper Valley's two most well-known pro hockey players—identical twin beasts—are standing there in Fiery the Dragon T-shirts and *Fiery Forever* buttons, one with a protest sign that reads *Fiery is Best, Bring Back the Dragon Mascot, Meatballs Taste Yummy*.

Oh my god.

They're protesting in haiku.

"You're Mackenzie?" one asks.

I nod.

"The Thrusters believe in you, lady. We'll get that dragon back." He holds out a meaty fist.

I bump.

The other twin grunts and bumps my fist too.

"You call if you need anything." The first one hands me a slip of paper with his number on it, and the entire Thrusters hockey team files past us, all of them wearing my buttons and bumping my fist while they loop back to continue the protest route.

Their goaltender even brought along his pet cow, who drops a patty while the cops overseeing the protest watch.

"Your friend is totally badass, Sarah," the team's captain says when I don't immediately reply to his *hey, Mackenzie, nice job*.

I can talk to hockey players. They're not baseball gods.

But the unexpected support of their entire team has me a little choked up.

We're starting the second hour of the protest, with news crews showing up because the street and the courtyard are overflowing, when I catch sight of Brooks pulling into the team's parking lot.

He climbs out of his Land Rover behind the fence, and even though he's wearing sunglasses, I swear he looks straight at me.

You could say things got a little awkward once he realized how many people knew about the virgin thing at the cookout.

He didn't confirm it, but he didn't deny the hints that were hanging heavy in the air that night either.

And I still don't like the way he looked at me when he told me to tell him he can't hit a ball.

Unsettling might be a good word for how that left me.

Or possibly *so paranoid I have an escape route if the cops show up at my apartment.*

Sarah and I keep walking our path amongst the protesters, who start shrieking with excitement as they realize the players are arriving.

"Brooks!"

"Elliott! Over here!"

"Can I get your autograph, Brooks?"

"Oh my god, marry me?"

Sarah smiles at that last one. "Don't worry, I doubt he takes her up on it," she whispers.

"I'm not worried."

Instead of heading for the players' entrance, he walks to the fence and greets a few fans, signing baseballs and protest posters through the chain link.

"Mackenzie," he calls as we walk past.

I almost keep walking, because he's not calling *me*.

But Sarah grabs me and stops me. "Don't clam up now. The team needs you."

"He's not—" I start, but when I turn, he *is*.

He's lowered his sunglasses, and he's looking straight at me.

My knees get a little wobbly, because this is unexpected.

Also, his hazel eyes are really, *really* hot when he's peering at me over his sunglasses like that.

And I might have been having dreams about him having a four-headed penis the size of Mount Rushmore after listening to his sister-in-law talk a little too much about his brother's penis.

For the record, I did *not* get a glimpse of the goods the night I was hiding in his closet.

And good thing, too, because I want him to *not* have sex, even if I'm getting warm in all the right places from him looking at me like that.

I draw up across the fence from him. It's a chain-link number, about eight feet high, so we're definitely separated.

One side of his mouth quirks up.

It's not friendly, even if he *is* wearing a *Fiery Forever* button on his jacket.

"How's Meaty?" he asks.

My eyes bulge.

Everyone around us turns to stare at me.

"*Fiery*, you mean?" Crap, my stutter's back.

He holds my gaze without speaking for three long beats where he silently telegraphs that no, he means *Meaty*.

You know my secret. I know yours, that smoky smirk says.

He pushes his sunglasses back up onto his head. "Yeah. That's what I meant."

A news crew is pushing in, and I am not going to hyperventilate at the fact that he could completely blow my *Save Fiery* campaign and probably get me arrested at the same time.

This is worse than that moment at the cookout where I thought he'd figured me out, because now I *know* he has.

Probably I need to come clean with Tripp and Lila.

Hey, guys, funny story that ends well, haha…

"Brooks! Brooks, how are you feeling before the game?" the reporter calls. "Are you coming out to protest for Fiery? How are you liking Copper Valley? How's your puppy? Do you have any family in town for opening day?"

He stares at me. Even though the sunglasses, I know he's staring at me.

Mostly because he mouths *Meaty* before he gives the crowd a wave and turns to walk away without answering the reporter's questions.

Brooks

A MONTH AGO, I was happily secure in the knowledge that there were younger guys with hotter bats on my team, but that I was still necessary, especially as a veteran presence, and that I needed to stay in top shape—mentally, physically, and virginally—to keep the baseball gods happy and to keep my paychecks rolling in.

Today, I'm leaving Duggan Field, almost five hundred miles from the team I thought I'd retire from. I hit a single today, but I made a stupid error on the field in the second inning that cost us our home opener, and now the fact that the Fireballs are still losers is squarely on my shoulders.

As is the fact that I've lost sight of why I ever loved this game in the first place.

Why would I pick a career where I'm basically done before I'm thirty-five?

What next?

Teenage me, who thought I could spend every day swimming in piles of money, was an idiot. I don't do boredom well, and I'm realizing that an endless stretch of boredom might be upon me sooner rather than later if I don't figure out how to hit the ball again.

There are coaching jobs. Front office jobs. Scouting jobs.

But fuck, I'm tired of baseball.

I'm looking forward to hanging out with my puppy in my porny apartment. Eloise wasn't kidding about the carpet, and she sent a case of lava lamps, fake mustaches, and extra-bushy glue-on chest hair to accompany the toys for Coco Puff that I swear are sex toys and she insists are actual dog toys that just *look* like sex toys.

It's not like I need a happy apartment here. Given the way it's started, I'm here one season, max. Maybe not that long. It's good to live in a place where I won't get attached.

Plus, all the paisley wallpaper and olive green kitchen tile are making for stupidly rockin' Instagram pictures with Coco Puff.

He's such a hilarious little dog. And so happy. He grins all the time, and he has some problem with his teeth that makes his tongue hang out crooked, hence the reason he was in the shelter.

He was the weirdo of his litter, and nobody wanted a designer cavapoo dog who dribbled more water on the floor than he got in his mouth.

But he's so damn happy all the time.

Hard to be down when you're around that.

His puppysitter tells me he only tinkled on the carpet once, but hit the puppy pad or the fire hydrant outside the building every other time. I get the run-down of his nap schedule, when he ate, and which toys he played with, and then ask the obligatory question, because she's in her mid-twenties, cute, and single, and fuck it.

Why not try to get laid? "You want to stick around for dinner?"

She laughs. "Thanks, but I don't date baseball players. Cooper would flip his lid, and the last thing we need is *both* of the team's power hitters struggling. Or one of them in jail."

I blink at her. "Cooper."

"He didn't tell you? I'm his cousin. And he's not picky about much, but he's definitely a pain in the ass when it comes to his female family members getting involved with his teammates. Or anyone, really."

No. No, the fucker didn't tell me, and it's only Coco Puff attacking my shoelace that keeps my temper from spiking into the red zone.

She swings her bag over her shoulder. "I'm also a damn good

puppysitter, so don't think he got me this job just because he's my cousin. Actually, this is the first time he's ever gotten me a job. He must really like either you or me. Also, I think you got another package from your sister-in-law. I left it on the counter. She's special, isn't she?"

She takes off after promising to be back tomorrow five hours before game time, and I grunt and grumble to myself while I climb onto the floor and roll around with my itty-bitty, brown, curly fluff-ball, snapping pictures of him to send to my mom and selfies of us for Instagram.

I've been too busy playing with Coco Puff and avoiding unpacking to work on Operation: Get Laid, but my Insta comments suggest that once I'm back in the game, I won't have any trouble.

Provided I quit getting puppysitter recommendations from my teammates and take care of the *other* half of my cock-blocker problem.

Pretty sure I handled it before the game though.

I'm not proud of how pale I made Mackenzie when I said *Meaty* to her, but if she thinks she's going to screw with my life, then she needs to know I can screw with hers too.

And we're not going to talk about how my pulse did the Macarena when our eyes met. Just because she's hot doesn't mean she's not the wrong kind of crazy.

"You think Daddy should date?" I ask Coco Puff, who yips excitedly, chases his tail, and then collapses on the ground with his back legs splayed so cute, I have to take another picture of him.

I could slide into a few DMs on Insta, but I'm not subjecting my dog to any random crazy that hasn't been vetted, so instead, I pull up one of those dating apps I registered for earlier this month.

The first one flashes a red warning. *Account disabled.*

When I try to get a new password sent to my email, instead, I get a nastygram from the company telling me I've used their site inappropriately and I'm not allowed back in.

"What the hell?"

The second one doesn't even pull up. I get the white screen of app death.

The third won't acknowledge my email address, user name, or send me a new password.

By my fourth failure, I know exactly what's going on, and I switch over to my text messages.

BROOKS: DAMMIT, Eloise, WHAT THE FUCK DID YOU DO TO MY DATING APPS?

RHETT: Hey. You want to pick on my wife, you call her by her real name. Hot Crazy Pants.

BROOKS: *middle finger emoji*

KNOX: Was this supposed to be a private message?

JACK: Definitely not. We all need to know the state of baby brother's innocence.

PARKER: Pickleroni cheesemuffins.

ELOISE: *GIF of woman curtseying and a flashing YOU'RE WELCOME*

BROOKS: Dammit. Yes, it was supposed to be private. FIX. IT. NOW.

ELOISE: Dude, I am saving you from yourself. That pickleroni in your pants? He needs to sit and stay, because I can't let you finish your career in the slump of all slumps. You need to go out ON A BLAZE OF FUCKING GLORY. Like the kind of blazing glory we'd see if we set Rhett's ass on fire, because that's also glorious.

. . .

PARKER: Chicka-chicka vroom vroom *trackpad emoji* *sperm emoji*

GAVIN: Dating apps? Why do you need dating apps? Doesn't your agent set you up with women you fake-date so people don't know you're a virgin?

JACK: *EGGPLANT EMOJI* *"NO" symbol emoji* *laughing clown emoji*

BROOKS: I hate you all.

KNOX: Hold up, Bazookarooka. Look, I don't know how you feel, but I've read a LOT of romance novels, and I can imagine how frustrating it is to be baseball's oldest virgin. That's like, the uber-ultimate worst sacrifice the universe can ask of you. But are you sure contact with attractive women is the actual problem? What if it's that you've been trying to bang the WRONG women?

BROOKS: Don't start spewing meatball philosophy at me. I am NOT in the mood.

ELOISE: Not being in the mood is a good thing, baby brother-in-law.

JACK: *meatball emoji* *WTF emoji*

PARKER: What the goobledeedoo is masturbator phyllo dough?

. . .

81

Parker: ELOISE. F-I-X M-Y VAGINA-llama-dingdong.

Rhett: I bow to the master. Crazy Hot Pants, I don't know how you keep making Parker's phone better, but you're getting all the meat stick you want tonight.

Brooks: *GIF of an asshole*

Rhett: Oh. Right. Sorry for rubbing it in your face that I'm getting some and you're not, Bazookarooka. But my wife's right. We can't let you end your career in the slump of all slumps. You need to get out on that field, kick ass, take names, and be part of the Fireballs' record-breaking winning season. YOU ARE GOING ALL THE WAY. You just need to see a witch doctor to get rid of whatever curse you got from the chick you made out with in Florida.

Eloise: Shouldn't have let her touch your pee-pee.

Brooks: Pee-pee? PEE-PEE? Are you the same woman who nick-named Rhett's dick TARZAN THE WONDER SCHLONG? And you're calling mine a pee-pee?

Eloise: I have some limits.

Parker: *laughing emoji*

Knox: *The Princess Bride GIF of Valerie screaming LIAR!*

Gavin: Eloise, you created a computer virus that wiped the word "limit" from all online dictionaries.

. . .

Rhett: Babe... They're right. You really don't have any limits. But Brooks, yeah, compared to me... you've got a pee-pee.

Brooks: Again, I hate you all.

Eloise: You know that Mackenzie chick that you think stole the meatball? I know where she's at tonight. Want the address?

Brooks: Why the fuck would I want her address? She's the original cock-blocker.

Eloise: That makes her good people for you to hang out with. She can help you.

Knox: Brooks, dude, she is the MOST superstitious person I've ever met. If anyone knows how to break a superstition, it's gonna be her.

Parker: Slick slick clit in a banana-jama peanut butter haiku.

Parker: *knife emoji* *computer emoji*

Eloise: Have faith in your brilliant and sexy sister-in-law, Bazookarooka. If nothing else, going to see her will remind you that you hate her more than you hate us. Also, I sent Coco Puff a present. I hope you both like it.

SHE FOLLOWS UP WITH AN ADDRESS, and I glare at it while Coco Puff rolls over on his back and gives me puppy dog eyes. It's like

83

he's saying, *How can you be unhappy when I'm adorable and want belly rubs?*

"I'm not going to see Mackenzie," I tell Coco Puff.

He yips, then growls, then swishes his entire lower body in the brown shag carpet while he wags his tail.

"Don't you start too. She's a thief. And a cock-blocker. And she's getting away with all of it."

His tongue hangs out happily and he barks in agreement.

"Don't tell me you approve."

He yips and rolls over, then leaps to his feet and attacks the blue rubber dildo-toy, which makes me think about that night at "the club" that we don't talk about, and about how utterly useless it was given the game today.

"You know what would serve them all right?"

He cocks his head and lifts his ears at me as an idea takes shape, and holy hell.

That *would* serve them all right.

"Puppy wanna go for a ride?"

Coco Puff goes banana-pants, yipping and turning in a circle and accidentally peeing all over the brown shag carpet.

But I'm grinning while I get it cleaned up, put him in a Fireballs jersey and the surprisingly tasteful collar Eloise sent for him with his name embroidered on it, then tuck him into his doggy car seat for the ride across town.

Two birds, one stone.

I have a plan.

Mackenzie

I'M RUNNING LATE for dinner with my dads, but I'm not too worried. They are, after all, the men who taught me to be fashionably late to everything, which means I'll still be twenty minutes early.

I stumble into Periwinkles with the birthday present for Dad, and Dame Delilah claps her hands at the hostess stand. "Oh, Mackenzie, that wrap job is exquisite." She slips around the stand to take my elbow, gives me cheek-kisses, and runs her manicured fingertips over the gold wrapping paper on the present. "We saved you a seat by the stage. Come come. Queen Bijou and Lady Lucille are on in twenty minutes. And your friend is already here. *Hello,* hotness. I approve, baby. I approve."

My dads adopted me when I was two—my biological mom was Papa's sister—and I basically grew up here at Periwinkles. We still do Christmas backstage with everyone who doesn't have other family to spend the holidays with, and there have been many an off-hours party here for every reason from *just because* to *someone had a hard break-up* to *Mackenzie got her braces off on the same day the Fireballs won by four runs.*

I got drunk the first time here. I had my hair done for prom here. And I learned everything I know about superstitions from

Dad—aka Queen Bijou—by watching his pre-show routines and rituals in his dressing room here.

We were an accidental family, but this is as much home to me as my apartment downtown, three blocks from the ballpark.

And my home has now been invaded by a broad-shouldered, arm-porn-displaying god hellbent on destroying my favorite team.

"Here you go, sweet cheeks. Evianna's taking care of you tonight. You know what to do if you need anything." She winks and lowers her voice. "And I do mean *anything*. But tell him he's swinging too soon and needs to keep his eye on the ball."

Brooks Elliott is seated at my table, one ankle crossed over his knee, stroking his puppy with his long fingers and looking like a king surveying his kingdom. He's in a dark polo, jeans, and he's managed to encase himself in some kind of magic cloud of pheromones.

I momentarily go mute, but almost as quickly remember that *I can do this*, and I set the present on the black tablecloth and seat myself in the cushioned red velvet chair beside my current obsession.

He shouldn't be here.

Am I ashamed of my dads?

No. Not a chance.

But you're damn right I'm protective of them. I don't know what this man's doing here, what he knows about my personal life, or what he wants.

He obviously wants something or he wouldn't be here. And if he thinks that dropping hints that he knows who my dads are can give him an upper hand, he'll be so wrong, he'll be on a train back to New York with his career in tatters before I'm done with him, and yes, I can accomplish that in two minutes or less if I have to.

"What are you doing here?" I growl.

Yes, me. Mackenzie Montana. Growling at a baseball god.

Do *not* fuck with my family.

He gives me the innocent eyes. "I missed you."

His puppy barks, then says *Fuck this shit*, and the man of both my dreams and my nightmares and I both blink at Coco Puff.

"Did your dog just cuss at me?" I ask.

Coco Puff barks again. "Asshole!" he adds.

Brooks squeezes his eyes shut, mutters, "*Dammit, Eloise*," and tries to unbuckle the collar.

Coco Puff yips and strains to get away. "Pussy-licker!" he says.

His collar.

He has a custom cussing collar.

Courtesy, apparently, of Aunt Eloise.

I choke on a laugh, and Brooks turns those gorgeous hazel eyes on me. In the reflection of the low light aimed at the stage, the frustration in his expression seems less irritated and more smoky and seductive and full of promises I know better than to let him offer.

Not that I have any trust right now that his intentions are good. It takes more than a cussing puppy and seductively mussed brown hair to get me to put my guard down.

Plus, he's not flirting with me. He's not.

He's irritated.

I square my shoulders. *Eye on the big picture, Mackenzie.* And the big picture is that the Fireballs need to win. "Dame Delilah's right. You're not keeping your eye on the ball."

"Oh, I've got my eye on the ball. I've got my eye on the ball *right now*."

I swallow.

He has his eye on *me* right now.

My tongue doesn't want to work again, and I'm struggling to keep up this farce that the look in his eyes is irritation.

Dammit. "No," I force out.

"No? You haven't even heard what I want yet. And you'd do anything for the team, wouldn't you, Mackenzie?"

"What. Do. You. Want?"

"I came here to ask for help."

I blink.

Coco Puff flips over onto his back in Brooks's lap and stares at us upside down, begging someone for belly rubs, which Brooks handles with those long-fingered hands without looking away from me.

"You...want help?" I ask.

"I need to hit the ball again."

Coco Puff yips. "Motherfucker!"

"And you think I can help with that?" Suspicion has me

glancing around to see who's here and close by in case this goes wrong.

Like I wouldn't leap in front of any of these ladies before letting them risk a nail at my expense. But I'm a little out of my league when pro baseball players come into the drag club where I grew up.

Brooks spreads his hands. "Who else to ask about fixing superstitions than the team's number one fan?"

That was entirely too complimentary. "You were hell-bent on sabotaging your own career last month, and now you want *my* help saving it? What changed?"

"You know *anyone* who likes to lose?"

"My dad loses on purpose in Monopoly."

"Duh. It's Monopoly. You lose, you don't have to play anymore. I lose on purpose too. But that's not why I'm here."

"No?"

Coco Puff gives me a *don't use sarcasm on my daddy* glare and barks. His collar calls me something I can't repeat and makes the couple at the next table gasp.

Brooks ignores all of it, his attention still trained on me. "I'm giving up my superstitions. Which means I'm going to get laid. *And* I'm going to hit the damn ball."

"And quit making errors at third?"

His cheek twitches. "And you're going to help me."

"Um, no, I'm not."

"Yep. You are."

"Nope."

"You want what's best for the Fireballs, don't you, Mackenzie?"

"Yes, and what's best is you keeping your pants zipped. Period."

"Or maybe what's best is me finding some balance, and I've been out of balance for so long that I need to have lots. And lots. And *lots* of sex. All the time. Everywhere. In every position."

Babe Ruth help me, now I'm picturing him banging me over that motorcycle that I know he rides sometimes, and I'm getting hot everywhere. My toes. My breasts. My pussy. My cheeks.

Brooks Elliott should be banished from saying the word *sex*.

Especially around me.

Because I *cannot* let him have sex, even if I'm now getting visions of everything from roses on beds to acrobatic things that shouldn't be possible.

"With all the women," he adds.

I see red.

I see red so hot and fast that it only belatedly registers that Evianna's practically leaping over tables to get to us. "Mackenzie, darling! Look at your hair, sweetheart. Those curls are to *die* for. You need a water, baby? Tequila? Chocolate éclair?"

Chocolate éclair is what we all call the bouncer who's been here half my life, because the big, burly guy both loves chocolate éclairs and also is as soft and sweet as one on the inside once you get to know him. "Can I get those fried Brussels sprouts with the bacon and cheese, and a milk shake?" I reply without taking my eyes off Brooks.

Evianna sucks in a breath. "It's artichoke dip night."

I have never not ordered artichoke dip on artichoke dip night, so her shock is understandable. "I'm experimenting."

She touches the dragon brooch pinned to the silver sequins over her breast. I couldn't talk the ladies here into *Fiery Forever* buttons, so they're wearing dragon brooches instead. "Change happens, baby. You change your mind on Chocolate éclair, you know the sign."

"What kind of milk shake?" Brooks asks. "I like milk shakes."

Evianna lifts her nose. "It's not on the menu tonight."

That's actually true every night.

I get milk shakes.

No one else does.

He breaks eye contact with me to look at her, then back to me.

I don't blink.

"Iced tea?" he says.

I shake my head. "Drinks are only for people who are staying. You're not."

"What if it's what I need to hit the ball again?"

"Then maybe you should keep your pants zipped and do what's always worked for you before."

Evianna chuckles. "Proud of you, baby girl. Back in a flash. Gotta tell Chef how important these Brussels sprouts are."

Brooks flashes a curious look at her as she leaves, and I don't have to watch to know she's going to ask Chocolate éclair to come check on me in two minutes. Brooks's gaze settles back on me, and it occurs to me that he wasn't using that smolder on the woman back in Florida he was trying to score with.

My heart hiccups, and I don't know if it's a fear-hiccup, an excitement-hiccup, or an *I fell through to an alternate dimension* hiccup, which kind of makes the most sense, because I'm a disaster attempting to cock-block this man, and he knows it.

Why would he be hitting on me?

He pulls a dog treat out of a bag hanging on the edge of his chair and hands it to Coco Puff. "You're pissed that I know about Meaty."

"I have no idea what you're talking about."

"You stole Meaty."

"I hate Meaty, and he's leading the mascot standings right now because of all those videos of him enjoying his life away from the Fireballs. Your hypothesis makes zero sense."

"Interesting. I could say the same about your hypothesis that I need to keep my pants zipped."

"Mine's proven. Yours isn't."

"I'm going to have sex." He rubs Coco Puff's little belly, still staring at me intently. "And I'm going to start with a woman I'm *very* attracted to."

Did someone suck all of the oxygen out of this room? And also all the brain cells out of my head? That would explain my simultaneous lightheadedness coupled with rage at whoever his mystery woman is.

She's going to ruin my team's chances of making the play-offs, and I'm going to cry.

I get it. It's not fair that he has to keep it in his pants for his team when other guys can do things like wear the same socks all season or meditate while holding the ashes of their first baseball bat. "You can't even give us one season? Just one? What's a few more months? Besides, you don't even know who this woman is. You're making her up."

"I'm not. And I didn't say I was *happy* about being insanely attracted to her. Or that I'm going to enjoy it."

"Then why bother?"

"Because when you give in and let me bang you, you're going to *know* it happened. And then you're going to watch me walk onto that field the next day and hit a fucking grand slam."

Oh my god.

He's talking dirty to me. My inner baseball lover is swooning at the idea that a baseball player would need to sleep with me to hit a grand slam.

He'll be rounding the bases while I spontaneously orgasm in the stands at knowing I gave him a grand slam, and he'll round third, point right at me, blow a kiss, thrust his hips in a promise to do it again, and my nipples will get so hard that they'll fall off, but we'll still meet in the locker room afterward and he'll let me sniff his glove before he bangs me while wearing his dirty, sweaty game jersey.

Ultimate. Sexual. Fantasy.

A horrified gasp flies out of my mouth. "You're trying to trick me into staying away from you!"

"Don't we wish," he murmurs.

"We? Are you talking about yourself and your penis like you're two separate entities?" For what his sister-in-law told me about his brother's penis, I could believe it, because I think it's far more likely the family's genetically blessed than that one brother got all the penis.

Which I am not thinking about.

He gestures to his puppy. "I was talking about me and my dog. But if you'd like to get acquainted with my—"

"*No.*" I hold my arms in front of me and cross my fingers. "We are *not* sleeping together. *Ever.*"

"What if a psychic told you it was the only thing that would turn my game around?"

"You can't pay a psychic to tell you that you have to get laid. That goes against the psychic code of honor."

"This is happening, Mackenzie. You and me. Turns out, being attracted to crazy is genetic. You *have* to. You have to do this for your team. You have to do *me* for your team."

He's bearing down on me now, those bright hazel eyes on fire, smelling like pine and leather—baseball bats, balls, and gloves—and a little like puppy breath, and *oh my god*, how has this man stayed a virgin for thirty years?

How do women not fling themselves at him every time he breathes?

"No," I force out.

Would I sleep with Brooks Elliott if he weren't a baseball player?

He's something of a dick, but that puppy—and he's not hard on the eyes—and I am not immune to the heat simmering in the air between us.

It's highly likely.

Sleeping with him isn't marrying him. And while I'll sleep with a dick if he's good enough, I won't marry one.

But he *is* a baseball player. The stands at Duggan Field were full today, which is awesome, but they have to stay that way through the end of the season, or my team will be in danger of being forcibly moved out of Copper Valley by the baseball commissioner, who has to do the hard things sometimes, even if he's publicly stated he wants to support Tripp and Lila and all the Fireballs fans in Copper Valley.

Which means it doesn't matter what I'd do if he wasn't a baseball player.

What matters is what I *have* to do for the love of my team.

I glare at him. "I'm not sleeping with you."

"But you want to."

"And this won't work. You can't chase me away by threatening to make me want you."

"Good. I also happen to like a challenge."

He smiles.

Smiles.

With his eyes crinkling a little at the edges, and that slight lopsidedness to his lips, and honest to god amusement dancing over his rugged features, and it's like I've discovered the Milky Way is full of baseballs instead of stars, and I can't stop staring.

I'm hypnotized by a happy Brooks Elliott.

Which is the only reason I don't see what's coming until his lips are brushing mine.

An undiluted shot of adrenaline surges straight to my clit and makes my legs go numb with sheer pleasure.

All because of one simple, easy kiss that *needs to stop right the hell now.*

But I'm not stopping him, because it's taking all of my concentration to not grab onto his polo with both fists and yank him harder against me and show him how *this* woman likes to be kissed.

Must. Not. Take. His. Innocence.

His lips taste like bubble gum, and his rough stubble is hot as hell. And don't ask what happens to my body when he runs his tongue over the seam of my mouth.

Let's just say I need to change my panties.

But somewhere in the lusty haze of *oh my god, this kiss is going to break me* is the distant reminder that if I think this kiss will break me, it's nothing compared to what it'll do to Brooks's game.

And the Fireballs need *everything* this year.

I dig deep to channel my inner superhero and wrench myself away. "Bad. Bad baseball player," I gasp.

Coco Puff barks. "Eat my dick!"

"Oh, this is going to be a problem," I hear Papa murmur from behind us.

A problem?

A problem is snow on opening day.

This?

This is asteroids hurtling toward earth like giant gods in the sky are having batting practice.

And yes, that might sound extreme, but I've been lying.

This isn't about the Fireballs not being forced to move out of Copper Valley if the new owners' plans don't work. And it's not about simply *not losing*, and not being the worst.

I want my team to go all the way.

I want them to win it all.

And for that, they need *every* player fully committed.

Which means that even though I'm pointing a finger and ordering Brooks out of my dads' club, I'm making plans.

It's not enough to cock-block him.

I have to make him believe the Fireballs can go all the way.

Brooks

I SHOULD NOT HAVE KISSED Mackenzie.

But I did, and now I have to deal with the consequences.

First consequence?

I should tell you it's forcing myself to meditate on all the ways I'm going to smack the shit out of the ball today despite kissing a woman I'm insanely attracted to. Home run every at-bat. Diving grabs at third. Firing rockets to first. Being the leader in the dugout for the Fireballs that I was for New York.

But it's not.

No, the first consequence is that as soon as I finish rubbing one out in the shower the next morning, I remember the feel of her lips on mine, that subtle taste of cotton candy and Cracker Jacks, the beat of the background music flowing through me, the snap and crackle in her eyes, and I'm hard as steel once more.

I groan and fist myself again while the hot water pummels my back.

Why is it always the crazy ones that are so damn hot? I'm starting to understand what Rhett sees in Eloise.

Which should be a turn-off, except I'm not picturing my brother and my sister-in-law while I pump my dick.

No, I'm picturing a blond vixen with a dragon splashed across her gorgeous breasts. And I'm not just picturing her throwing daggers with her eyes at me while I left the drag club last night, which, yes, is hot as fuck too.

The daggers, I mean.

Why is it so sexy when a woman's pissed? Is it the challenge of making her un-pissed? Or is it the passion?

Fuck.

Passion.

What's harder than steel? Because that's my dick right now as I picture Mackenzie naked, riding me, her breasts jiggling, losing all control at the feel of my cock inside her. I jerk harder, gripping myself to the point of pain, while my balls squeeze so tight that I can feel it in my toes. Can balls permanently cramp from getting too tight?

I've never been inside a woman, but I've read a few romance novels. I can imagine it. And right now, I'm imagining Mackenzie's pussy as a hot, tight, silky, wet channel wrapped around me from root to tip, gripping and stroking me with her body, and I groan out loud while a second orgasm rips through me, leaving me panting and sagging against the cool avocado green tile of my shower wall.

How?

How is she the one that I can't stop thinking about?

And *why*?

What the hell's wrong with me?

Probably that you've never gotten laid, idiot.

Whatever it is, I need to get out of this shower before I have to jack off a third time. I've never not taken care of my own needs with my hand, but at this rate, I really will be dealing with a lopsided forearm problem before long.

Coco Puff prances around my ankles when I step out of the shower and dry off. The bathroom's so steamed up, I can't see even a hint of my reflection in the mirror.

Not that I want to.

It would be all self-loathing and bitter disappointment.

I push the door open, and why does it smell like pumpkin spice and bacon in my apartment?

Coco Puff goes nuts, yipping like Santa Claus came in March, his fucking collar spewing profanities since he won't let me take it off, and he takes off down the hall. Maybe my puppysitter reconsidered dating. Or she got here early. Or maybe my mom's in town.

"Oh, sweet puppy! Look at you in your jersey! You're all ready for the game tonight, aren't you?"

Coco Puff barks, and his collar screams out a good "Motherfucker, damn right!"

I freeze.

That voice.

My cock leaps to attention. *Again*.

And fuck the clothes.

She wants to be here? Just as good that I'm only in a towel. Hell, I should drop it.

I pause.

Huh. That's brilliant.

Dropping this towel is the best idea I've ever had.

I finger-comb my hair, fluff my junk, and stride out of the bedroom buck naked. My toes squish in the brown shag carpet, and the scents of pumpkin spice and bacon get stronger as I emerge into the kitchen, where Mackenzie's bent over, rubbing Coco Puff's belly.

All I can see of her is her ass in brown dress pants, and despite the fact that her pants match half my linoleum, the sight of that heart-shaped butt is definitely causing more blood to surge to Mr. Happy.

Fuck.

My hand and my dick are well-acquainted, and it's probably good that I wouldn't have a hair trigger if she decided to jump my boner right now, but I don't know if I'd be able to finish the job after two rounds of choking the chicken.

Her ass wiggles, and never mind.

I would *absolutely* be able to finish the job.

Even if one of those candles she's lit around my apartment was singeing my ass hair, I'd be able to get off with Mackenzie.

I clear my throat. "Morning, sexy pants."

She squeaks and leaps up, sending her long hair flipping back over her head.

Her gaze goes down to my morning salute.

Snaps back up.

Pink floods her cheeks, matching the tones in her patterned

blouse and the tips of her fingers, which are flying to her lips. She spins, turning her back on me, and *fuck*.

She's in pink stilettos too.

Pink. Fucking. Stilettos.

I'm dead.

Pick me up off the floor and send my body back to New York.

Those stilettos killed me, and if my dick strains any harder to get close to this woman, it's going to fall off.

Coach is right.

I need a fucking therapist.

"Morning," she sputters. "I wanted to make sure you ate a good breakfast this morning, because champions should start the day on a good note. There's bacon in the oven. How do you like your eggs? Coffee? Or tea? There's not enough about your personal information on any of the sites I found for baseball groupies, and your cabinets are a little bare."

I don't bother asking how she got in. Crazy does what crazy does.

But I do make sure to brush against her as I head to my freezer for my protein pancakes.

She visibly shivers.

I yank open the freezer, grab the box, and turn to face her again. "Cold?"

She focuses her eyes on the ceiling. "Yes."

"Want to cuddle?"

"No. I have to go to work. But since you're wooing me, I thought I'd give you a few tips for getting into my pants. First things first, I like sleeping with winners. So if you want to bang me, you have to hit a home run."

She says *bang,* and my nuts wind so tight I feel like I've been racked in the jewels. "Work? You have a job?"

"I'm a sanitation engineer for the city."

I blink. "So you're like…smart."

"I can do math in my head, yes. And discuss the city's program to reduce landfill emissions at length. And also handle being yelled at when people get mad that their trash wasn't picked up on Christmas day, because my extension and the customer service extension are very similar."

"Why don't you work in baseball?"

"The restraining order."

I snort. That's easy enough to believe.

She scowls at me. "That was a joke." Her gaze dips to my hard-on, and she jerks her head back up so she's staring at the ceiling again. And then her eyes crinkle as she squints at one particular spot up there. "What...?"

"The dicks on the ceiling?" I study the artwork too. "Eloise said they were here when she and Rhett signed the contract for me, but I think she probably drew them herself. Especially the one with four heads. Speaking of, you planning on stealing the echidna next, or has Duggan Field security foiled you?"

"I don't have a clue what you're talking about." She turns to the oven while the timer still has two minutes on it, bends over —*god*, that ass—and pulls out a tray of perfectly crisped bacon, which, yeah, is also a complete and total turn-on.

It's *bacon*.

She flaps a hand at me. "Stand back if you don't want to get hot bacon grease on your pee-pee."

"My *pee-pee?*"

"I mean, I see why your sister-in-law calls it that, but if you're proud, then you do you."

"You could give up the act anytime."

Coco Puff yips in agreement, and his collar translates. "Shithead!"

He's overexcited and probably needs to go for a walk.

Which means I probably need to get dressed, but I'm enjoying the hell out of making Mackenzie uncomfortable with my nudity.

And the more I think about it, I wouldn't turn her down if she decided she wanted to ride the pony.

It'd be a memorable way to lose my virginity, and while she's batshit crazy, she's not unattractive, even if my original goal was, as she suspected, to make her think I was going to woo her so she'd leave me alone, since clearly, she'd never be able to resist the full Brooks Elliott wooing experience.

Which I'm still planning in my head, because I've spent the last dozen or so years of my life actively *avoiding* wooing women.

I need to call Knox. Get some advice. Guy's read every romance novel ever written, and he knows that if he tells anyone I'm asking for help, I'll use his nuts for batting practice.

Mackenzie goes digging in my cabinets. I should probably put a stop to this, but I like watching her stretch up on her tiptoes and reach for a plate like she lives here. There's something innately graceful about her movements, and I'm charmed.

I don't want to be, but I am.

She turns, catches me staring, and darts a quick glance at my very happy, very proud dick again before turning back to the bacon. "Do you know the Fireballs have *never* won a championship and have only gone to the post-season three times? And even then, they've never won a pennant either?"

"Yep."

"Wouldn't it be amazing to be the guy who helped push them there?"

Right. We're the fucking *Bad News Bears*. "Why does this team matter so much to you? You don't play. You couldn't even talk to any of us on the team without having a stroke a month ago."

She turns and faces me head-on. "You seriously have no idea?"

I lift my brows. "Oh, you mailed me a Mackenzie manual? Security must've thought it was a threat and trashed it. I'll have a talk with them."

Fuck, she gives good glare. It's calling to my hard-on, coaxing it to the breaking point.

"Do you even love the game anymore? Or is it all the paycheck for you now? Baseball is *life*. It's a place where people aren't trash engineers or bullied kids or weirdos. We're all equal when we're cheering on the same team, and *some* players still remember that. But apparently not you."

It's been a long time since anyone called me a shit to my face.

I don't like it.

More, I don't like that I probably deserve it, because she's right.

I don't love the game anymore. Not the way I did before it became a paycheck.

Mr. Happy is turning into Mr. Sappy, and one glance south, and she'll know she's getting to me.

But the weirdest thing is happening.

Amidst all the shame slashing through my chest, there's something else welling up.

I want to know who bullied her. And why.

And then I want to make them pay.

She pokes me in the chest. "Duggan Field is my *home*. We

almost lost it last year, and I will *not* stop until I know it's not in danger anymore."

I ball my hand into a fist to keep from touching her, which is all I want to do. All I *need* to do.

A person doesn't get as fanatical as Mackenzie about a friggin' *game* if they're not running away from something else. "You really think the new owners will let anything happen to the team?"

"They traded for *you*, didn't they?"

Ouch.

She squeezes her eyes shut, then turns away. "I have to go to work. If you don't get a hit today, I'm calling a guy my dads know who knows how to motivate people. And don't freaking fumble an easy line drive again."

She leaves me standing there buck naked in the kitchen, my hard-on drooping, while Coco Puff squats and pees on the brown and yellow floral linoleum, barks, gets translated to "Twatwaffle," and I realize something has to change.

Unfortunately, that something is me.

1 4

Mackenzie

NIGHT GAMES in March are freaking cold, but the weather won't stop me from hitting the ballpark tonight.

I have season tickets on the third base line, and Sarah's with me, and we're going to win.

Dammit.

We have to.

We have to.

"Totally naked?" she asks over a bag of caramel corn while we watch the guys warm up.

"Not even a sock."

"And?"

"And what?"

Her dark eyes sparkle with mischief. "And did you like it?"

"It doesn't *matter* if I liked it. It matters that he keeps his pants zipped so he can hit the ball. We need every single player doing every damn thing they can to win. *Every. Single. One.*"

My seats this year are four rows back from the field, right on the aisle, halfway between third base and left field. Most years, I've resisted season tickets, because the Fireballs win more when Sarah and I watch the game at her house.

But she sold the house recently since she's living full-time with Beck now, who not only renovated the terrace of his penthouse to make it friendly for Sarah's beehives, but also convinced the city to set aside part of Reynolds Park for an apiary—with funding for the necessary staff coming from his pocket, naturally, because that's what Beck does.

So between Sarah's house being unavailable, because even though I have a key still, I don't want to get arrested by the new owners if I randomly show up for baseball games, and also this year being about trying new habits and patterns to help my team, here we are.

Darren Greene's in left, tossing the ball with Luca Rossi, the Fireballs' new center fielder who's played for like half the teams in the league, while we wait for the first pitch and national anthem. At third, Brooks is out there fielding balls and warming up with the rest of the infielders.

The guys are in their thermal shirts under their uniforms. Tripp and Lila are out on the field talking to the team manager, wrapped up in Fireballs jackets, with Lila in a stocking cap too.

My loaded fries are already cold, which is fine, because I'm ready to pull on my Fireballs gloves and I don't want to get cheese all over them.

The three mascots suddenly run out of the dugout. Glow the Firefly grabs Lila's hat and makes a mad dash for the opposite dugout, his giant glowing butt swishing, while Firequacker the Duck steals Tripp's phone from his hand and darts and weaves, acting like he's going to throw the device into the stands.

And while both team owners take off chasing the first two mascots, Spike the Echidna puts a big claw to his mouth—the universal symbol for *shh*—and tiptoes to third base.

None of the players are paying any attention to the mascots, until Lopez, who's playing shortstop, starts to grin as he tosses Brooks the ball.

I can't see Brooks's face.

I don't have to.

Because suddenly I realize what's coming.

I bolt to my feet before I realize I've moved. "Bad echidna!" I yell. "*Bad!*"

I'm thundering down the steps to the edge of the field, hollering, "Bring back Fiery! Bring back Fiery!" when Spike snags Brooks's hat.

Brooks spins around. He points at Spike, who's rapidly

retreating as the crowd takes up my chant and I realize Spike *wasn't* going to yank Brooks's pants down.

Heat floods my face at my overreaction, and then heat floods my chest when the weirdest thing happens.

He *smiles*.

Brooks is actually *smiling* at the mascot contender stealing his hat.

Spike acts out giggling, which is hilarious for a terrifying creature with claws that could put someone's eye out.

Brooks tucks his glove under his arm and gestures the echidna back to third.

Spike shakes his head, holding Brooks's hat high in the air.

Or as high as a man in an echidna costume can, anyway.

Brooks taps his fist against his palm.

Spike tilts his head.

"C'mon," Brooks calls, loud enough for his voice to carry over into the stands. "You a chicken?"

The *Bring Back Fiery* chant has died as quickly as it started while everyone watches the Fireballs' newest acquisition and its current third-place mascot option have a stare down.

Brooks taps his fist on his palm again.

Spike tucks Brooks's hat into his back pocket, then does the same.

And the two of them launch into a rock-paper-scissors battle while Trevor Stafford sneaks out of the dugout behind the echidna.

Not that it's much of a battle.

Spike can't bend his fingers, so he's playing *paper* every time.

Brooks still plays *rock* twice, and yeah, my heart is melting a little at knowing that he's letting the mascot win a couple rounds.

"Is Trevor going to de-pants Spike?" Sarah whispers beside me.

She's barely gotten the words out before Stafford yanks on Spike's pants, and the mascot's furry bottom flashes for all the world to see.

Brooks flashes Stafford a thumbs-up. Stafford grabs Brooks's hat and jogs it out to third.

And when he turns back to continue warming up, he's smiling.

Smiling.

Like he's happy to be here.

It's more potent than seeing him in all of his birthday suit glory, and confirming for myself that yes, the Elliott brothers are *all* blessed in the penis department.

"Sarah?" I whisper.

"Yes?"

"He's really cute when he's happy to be playing for the Fireballs."

"Are you saying that because he's a baseball god, or are you saying that because you'd go to dinner with him if he asked?"

"I am *not* having dinner with Brooks Elliott."

"You made him bacon."

"I'm guarding his innocence and making sure he didn't have a woman in his apartment. Plus, if he falls in love with me, he won't want another woman. This is psychological warfare for the greater good of winning."

She lifts a brow.

She knows he crashed Periwinkles last night. She knows I'm hypersensitive about people being dicks to my dads, and I don't know if he knows who my dads are, or if he knew why I was there, but I know I didn't want him there in that drag club.

And that, more than anything, is why I won't be going on a dinner date with Brooks Elliott.

Go to dinner with him to keep him from taking anyone else?

Yes.

But it won't be a date.

Because I am not sleeping with Brooks Elliott.

Period.

15

Brooks

I HIT a home run in the third game of the season.

It's barely a homer, but it's a homer, and it puts us in the lead in the bottom of the fifth.

Two outs later, I'm heading to third with my glove when a new video of Meaty flashes on the jumbotron. I pause to watch, because *what the hell?*

Meaty's walking into a damn Italian restaurant.

Where they serve meatballs.

The crowd gasps.

Rossi pauses on his way out to center field and looks up at the screen. "That'll solve the Meaty problem," he mutters.

Just as Meaty's opening the door, two massive, very familiar dudes come running. "No! Meaty! Don't do it!"

Rossi barks out a laugh.

I squeeze my eyes shut and mutter a curse.

What the fuck is Mackenzie doing hanging out with hockey players? Some of those guys are assholes. And single.

Not the massive twin tanks lifting her—I mean, *Meaty*—onto their shoulders and dashing her down the street, away from the chef chasing after her with a meat cleaver. I know those two personally. They're married. They're also obnoxious, but they won't hurt her.

But other hockey players? The single ones?

I don't trust them.

Rossi's still laughing. "I love those guys."

He can love the hockey players all he wants. I'm gonna have a talk with them. Mackenzie's too much of a nut to be trusted not to get herself into trouble.

"Dude. Elliott. What's with the scowl?"

I shake my head. "Don't want the meatball to win."

He hoots again and jogs away.

And three innings, one mascot dance-off, and four rounds of the wave later, the game ends with us up by one.

First win of the season, and it's because of my bat.

Jesus.

No pressure, Elliott. No fucking pressure at all.

After the game, we all have a quick dinner, and then it's time to load up for a trip out west. We're boarding the plane when Cooper thrusts his phone at me. "Dude. Is that really your bedroom?"

I glance down at the picture of Coco Puff on my bed, beneath the gaudy pink unicorn chandelier with the giant blue dildo horn that I swear Eloise had installed, even if she denies it. "Jealous?"

"Fuck, yeah. You must have master sleeping skills to not worry that's gonna crash down on you in the middle of the night. Like, you'll be the guy whose body's found half-decomposed and impaled by a dildo. You'll make the baseball hall of fame for sure for most ignominious death ever."

"Did you just say *most ignominious death*?"

Darren snorts and rolls his eyes while he drops into a seat. "His sister got him a word-a-day calendar for Christmas, and he's been insufferably intolerable ever since."

"Only on days the words are good. Like when they're *nincompoop* or *recreant*."

"What the fuck's a recreant?"

"A dick."

He looks at me pointedly.

Like he's calling *me* a dick.

Probably is.

If he's not, he should be.

And it makes me smile, because the thing about realizing

you're being a dick, and then deciding not to be a dick anymore, is that now, I have something to prove.

I have a team to win back.

And you're damn right I'm gonna do it.

Why, you ask?

Something about being reminded that no matter what team I'm playing for, there are kids who look up to me like I'm a hero. Hell, there are adults who look up to me like I'm a hero. Baseball —the game I fell in love with when I was four years old—is bigger than I am.

I can mourn my old team, and I can still text my old teammates.

But baseball?

Baseball's about the game.

Not the player.

It means different things to different people, but that doesn't change the fact that I owe the fans my all.

Doesn't hurt that Mackenzie came over and made me bacon again this morning.

She took off before I could kiss her again, but she was there. She rubbed Coco Puff's belly. I almost asked her to stop in and play with my dog while I'm out of town.

It's because she bakes good bacon.

Yep. That's my story.

Cooper sits, and I take the seat in front of him. Luca Rossi drops into the row next to me, then turns to look at Cooper. "Hey, Rock, you really getting your brother to bring his goat down for a de-cursing?"

I tuck my phone in the seat pocket and shake my head at both of them while I dig into my travel bag for my noise-canceling headphones. "I thought the ducks already did that. And...the other stuff."

"There's no such thing as too much de-cursing," Darren chimes in from the row ahead of us.

He's probably right.

Mackenzie implied the same thing this morning. *"Whatever you're doing, it's working, so keep doing it."*

"Like kissing you?"

"Your dog just peed on the carpet."

I smile to myself. She's damn fast when she's on a mission to leave my apartment.

And I might've had too much fun torturing her this morning.

Once the team and staff are all on board, the plane takes off, and I switch on Wi-Fi for one last check of messages before kicking back to get some rest.

Yeah, I'm lying.

I'm texting Meaty.

Eloise did her computer woowoo magic and got me the burner number that Mackenzie's using to send videos to the Fire-balls' front office.

BROOKS: If you really want to bring Fiery back, you need to commit some heinous crimes. And stay away from the Berger twins and the Thrusters. They're trouble.

MEATY: Who is this?

BROOKS: Spike. The Echidna. Remember me?

MEATY: If you're really Spike, you can tell me what's the last thing we did together before I ran away.

BROOKS: We admired that drawing of my penis on the ceiling.

MEATY: WRONG. We gave Firequacker a flushie, but only because *YOU* made me do it. It's *YOUR* fault I had to run away. I know I was next on the flushie rotation.

BROOKS: You have quite the imagination.

. . .

MEATY: I'm a meatball. I have ground sausage for brains.

BROOKS: Do the Thrusters know you're made of the remains of their mascot?

MEATY: That's exactly why I had to run away. I love the Fireballs too much to let their mascot be the remains of another team's mascot.

BROOKS: Wow. This just got sad.

MEATY: It's BEEN sad. Who's watching your puppy, by the way?

BROOKS: I'm an echidna. I don't have a puppy.

MACKENZIE RESPONDS with a picture of me.

Sitting on this very plane.

Texting with her.

I jerk my head around. Rossi's got his eyes closed and his seat leaned back. Darren's smiling at his laptop and talking quietly, earphones on, video chatting with his pregnant wife.

And Cooper Rock is snoring with his phone loosely clutched in his hand.

I turn around in my seat, reach over the headrest, and smack his knee.

He pretends to startle awake. "Huh? What? Dude. Elliott. Some of us are trying to sleep."

I *know* he took my picture.

But if I tell him Meaty sent it to me, and he doesn't know Mackenzie stole the costume, will he rat her out?

If he *does* know it's her, then he knows I'm texting her too.

Fuck it. I don't care what he knows. I only care that he tells me. Right now. "Mackenzie Montana. Talk."

He grins. "Aw, Elliott's got a crush."

"She's a nutjob."

"She's good people."

I arch my brows.

He crosses his arms. "She *is* good people. She volunteers to help clean up parks all over the city. She's the one who convinced management to hire Addie for our batting coach. And she talked her dads into doing a Fireballs day at their club. It's good luck to have the drag queens on your side."

My brows furrow. I'm not tracking.

Cooper leans toward me like he's ready to grab me by the collar and shake. "Don't you dare be a dick about Mackenzie's dads."

"Why would I be a dick about—whoa. Wait." *That's* why Mackenzie was at Periwinkles? "Mackenzie's dads are drag queens?"

"Yeah. Duh. Queen Bijou and Lady Lucille."

"Some people are dicks about that," Rossi says without opening his eyes, and it pisses me off that *he* knew about her dads when he hasn't been with the Fireballs that much longer than I have.

Wasn't she basically mute around all of us a month ago?

"We kick those people's asses." Darren's shut his laptop on his video call with his wife, and he, too, is watching me.

Like I'm going to be a dick about anyone's family. "Did you all meet my sister-in-law? Have you forgotten who wins the award for weirdest relatives?"

"Just so we're clear." Cooper leans back and grabs his phone again. "I'd hate to have to make my brother's goat bite your ass before a game. You play mostly okay."

I sink back into my seat.

Queen Bijou and Lady Lucille.

The headliners at Periwinkles. Owners of the club.

Growing up with non-traditional parents couldn't have been easy. Is that why she was bullied?

I look back at Cooper. "Quit texting people my picture."

He smirks in his fake sleep.

And I pick up my phone again, because this is suddenly more than teasing an annoying—and annoyingly attractive—woman who's cock-blocking me.

. . .

Brooks: You need help burying a body? I have a teammate volunteering to be fake-murdered so that we can get you locked up and bring Fiery back.

Meaty: I can't get locked up until I've secured the top vote and the other mascots have been sent to Mascot Heaven.

Brooks: Wait. You WANT to win?

Meaty: No. I want NONE of the mascots to be good options so that the original mascot can come back, but to do that, I have to eliminate all the competition first. By beating them.

Brooks: That's crazy devious and brilliant for someone with sausage for brains.

Meaty: I have layers.

Brooks: So you're also part ground beef?

Meaty: And onion and oregano. I'm delicious.

Brooks: Maybe I'll get to eat you one day.

THE TEXT STRING GOES SILENT.

I wait a full ten minutes, and when she doesn't text back again, I send her a GIF and sign off.

Season's barely gotten started, and you know what else?

That fucking meatball was spot on.

I *should* wait to have sex with a woman I'm interested in.

I'm not going anywhere. She's not going anywhere.

I have plenty of time to get to know Mackenzie Montana and all of her layers.

16

Mackenzie

THE FIREBALLS ARE GONE for a full week. I'd be upset that they're starting the season with back-to-back away series, except they're playing in California, where the weather is much nicer, which is easier on the players, even if the game times are so late that I get a dirty look from my boss a few times for rolling into work exhausted.

I have a normal weekend partially hanging out with my dads, partially hanging out with Sarah, and partially sneaking the meatball costume out to Cooper Rock's hometown in the Blue Ridge mountains for a stroll into his brother's bakery.

It's well worth the hour-long drive outside the city to visit with the Rocks—yes, I can talk to Cooper's whole family, who owns half the town, even though it's only recently that I can talk to him—and I load up with take-out for bingeing on at home all week. The Crow's Nest's donuts are second to none. The banana pudding at The Crusty Nut is the stuff of fantasies, and Anchovies, the pizza place, does something magical with their sauce.

Even better, Desmond—aka Dame Delilah—is driving us in his hybrid SUV since I can't walk as Meaty and also take video of myself, and also since my peapod-size car is a little recognizable, so there's plenty of space for all the goodies that I bring back.

While he drives us home, I pull out my burner phone to text video footage to Tripp and Lila. But before I can upload the video, I realize there's a message waiting for me from "Spike the Echidna."

Exactly like there has been every day this past week.

Today's is simple.

It's a picture of the fortune out of a cookie.

Your dog will bring you great joy.

And beneath it, Brooks has added a little message.

In bed.

I crack up, which has Desmond lifting a brow at me as we arrive back at my apartment building.

He's incognito today, dressed in street clothes, because Dame Delilah stands out in a small town, even a town as friendly and welcoming as Shipwreck, whereas Desmond as a man is nothing more than your average gay black man in an official Fireballs polo accompanying a flaming meatball down the street.

Considering Beck has a weekend house in Shipwreck, there was no reason to make people curious about the man with the meatball. And I couldn't take my dads, because they've come with me a few times and might've been recognized.

Desmond puts the SUV in park and points to my burner phone. "They're going to trace that phone back to you one day."

"And when they do, I'll point out how much good I've done for all of the Fireballs' extended fan family. Plus, you've got my back."

He sighs. "We do, baby girl. That we do."

My dads are off tonight, so I head to their place to watch the game together. We eat our traditional meal of weenie-mac while the Fireballs lose, and we collectively decide we're never eating weenie-mac with baseball again.

Overall, though, while the Fireballs are still losing more than they're winning, there's definitely more talent on the team, and every shot of the dugout shows them talking to each other, and once, the camera caught Brooks putting sunflower seeds in Cooper's helmet while Cooper wasn't looking.

One at a time.

He'd eat a sunflower seed, catch Cooper not watching, and then he'd slide Lopez a grin and drop a seed into Cooper's upside-down helmet.

The whole bench knew it.

And every one of them kept a straight face like they had no idea what Cooper was talking about when he grabbed his helmet and got a rain shower of sunflower seeds.

Epic. Perfection.

I might've teared up at the idea that Brooks is warming up to being a team player.

Monday morning, I head down to my car at a normal, healthy hour—thank you, afternoon games on the west coast—and as I step off the elevator, someone's checking out my car.

Not unusual—it's basically the coolest car in existence. I drive a SmartCar, and it's completely decked out in Fireballs colors, with the logo splashed on the side, and a Fiery hood ornament.

That's right. I found a place for a hood ornament on a SmartCar.

The curious onlooker turns, and I lose my breath.

Brooks Elliott is stalking me. And oh, god, he has a baby sling for Coco Puff. This tall, broad, thick-muscled, corded-forearmed, fine-assed baseball player is carrying his teeny tiny puppy in a baby sling, and my vagina has jumped ship.

Fireballs who? Let's do him!

Our eyes lock, and his lips tip up in the corners. "You didn't show up to make me bacon."

Coco Puff barks. His collar shouts out "Ass-licker!"

Brooks rubs his little head with a single finger. "We won that last home game after you made me bacon."

Did he just—

He smiles, a real, full smile that brings sunshine into the underground parking garage and makes the concrete smell like roses, and he *did*.

He used me against myself.

I plant a hand on my waist. "I also petted your dog. Maybe that's what helped."

He puffs his chest, putting Coco Puff closer to me. "You can pet my dog anytime you want."

Gah, that voice is offering me the opportunity to do *so much more* than pet his *dog*. "I'm going to be late for work."

"Two of the three games we won on the road, we had bacon with breakfast."

I mutter a curse that would make a hockey player blush, but

not because I'm upset about being late for work, since of course, I'm going to make Brooks bacon.

It's more that I'm struggling with the idea of having to actively resist him. Of being near him.

He better not smell like baseball.

"Fine. You can come upstairs and I'll make you bacon. But *only* so we can test if it's good for the team."

"If we lose today, you can come back to my place tomorrow to see if that makes a difference. Right, Coco Puff?"

The puppy yips and licks his fingers. "I love pussy!"

He smiles down at his dog with the smitten love of every pet owner perfectly matched with his best friend.

Couldn't he have fallen in love with a snake or something? I could way more easily resist a man with a snake. Or one with a pet lizard.

Instead, he's in love with a puppy with a cussing collar, and it's very much working for me. "Why don't you take that thing off?"

"He won't let me. He likes being a foul-mouthed creature of destruction beneath the fluffy exterior."

I could so easily fall for this man.

I climb back into the elevator, this time with Brooks and Coco Puff, and by the time we reach my floor, the scents of leather and pine have invaded my nose and I've fallen a little more in love with those little brown puppy dog eyes.

And I do mean the eyes on the puppy, and not the hazel beauties on the man, which might also be working some unfortunate magic on me.

When I unlock my apartment door, I refuse to hold my breath and await judgment. If he says a *single* thing about my décor, I'm fully prepared to fire back with all the questions about *his* place.

His lips twitch when he glances around, but he doesn't say a word, so I let him live, and I head to the kitchen. Coco Puff joins me, leaping at the Fireballs towel hanging from my red oven handle.

Brooks doesn't appear in the kitchen until I'm putting the remaining half-package of bacon back in the fridge.

He sniffs. "Pizza?"

Yeah. Can't open the fridge without the whole kitchen smelling like everything I brought back from Shipwreck yesterday. "Nuh-uh, buddy. You said bacon. You want pizza, get your own."

"You ever worry that your bobbleheads will come to life one night and eat you in your sleep?"

"You ever worry about living to see the rest of the day?"

Coco Puff growls and leaps on a dust bunny under my cabinet. "Fuck-turd!" his collar translates.

Brooks cracks open my fridge, lifts his phone, and snaps a picture of the pizza box.

"What are you doing?"

"Taking notes on pizza to try."

"You can't—" I stop myself, because I can't tell him that he can't get Anchovies' pizza here in the city. And as soon as we start talking about where he *can* get it, he'll know I went to Shipwreck, and whenever Tripp and Lila decide to broadcast Meaty's latest adventures around the world, his suspicion will turn into full-blown knowledge.

It's one thing to banter back and forth on text and know he *suspects*.

It's another to give the man I irritate on a regular basis the full knowledge.

"Crow's Nest? Are those—those *are*." He snatches one of the bakery bags from my fridge and peers in it before I can stop him. "You got donuts from Cooper's brother's bakery."

"I go up there with Sarah and Beck all the time. Beck's weekend house is right next door to Cooper's house. Have you ever been? There's this legend about how the town was founded by Cooper's great-something-grandfather, who was a pirate who loaded up his treasure in a covered wagon and drove out here to hide from the po-po. And they have this pirate festival, and everyone goes digging for the treasure, and—"

"Are you sleeping with Cooper, or are you only talking to him to convince him to help cock-block me?"

Well. Nothing like getting straight to the point, is there? "Cooper's cock-blocking you? Jeez. I thought there was a code. And were you the same guy who said you were going to sleep with *me* first, or are you one of those guys who says that to every girl to see who jumps you first?"

His hazel eyes narrow while he lifts a donut out of the bag and bites into it.

My eyes bug out. "That's my donut!"

Banana pudding oozes out the donut and onto the corner of his mouth. When he licks it off, my stomach bottoms out and my breasts get heavy and my clit tingles.

Eye on the prize, Mackenzie. Eye. On. The. Prize.

And I don't mean the man eating the donut.

I mean the Fireballs' winning. I point at him. "Did you eat a donut that morning in spring training? The morning before you couldn't hit a ball?"

"You really want to blame that on the donut?"

"We have to look at *everything*, because knowing *one* thing that stops you from hitting a ball doesn't mean we've identified *everything*. And don't think it's escaped my notice that the Fireballs win every time you get at least a double."

He takes another bite of my donut and makes a contemplative noise. Then he glances down, and all of his features soften into utter adoration for the curly-furred puppy that's gotten the towel off my oven rack and is barking and cussing at it while alternately smiling happily with his crooked tongue.

Brooks has *got* to stop acting human, or I'm going to forget one of these days that he's a baseball player whose habits and routines need to be fostered for peak performance.

I gesture to Coco Puff. "Do you take him to the ballpark?"

"He has a puppysitter." I get a dubious eyeball, like that's my fault.

So I give him the *what's your problem?* eyeball back.

"Cooper's cousin," he clarifies. "Who also won't sleep with me, because she's Cooper's cousin."

So apparently funny is blue, because that's both hilarious and infuriating—the part where he casually mentioned he tried to sleep with *another* woman, I mean—and now, with the two emotions put together, I'm seeing purple.

He snorts like he's suppressing a laugh, and I stifle a growl while I dig into my utensil drawer, looking for something else that I can toss to his puppy.

I riffle through my collection of Fireballs-themed pasta servers, spatulas, wooden spoons, and jar openers until I find what I'm looking for.

It's a silicone mold of the New York logo that one of my coworkers gave me as a joke a few years ago.

Who knew this would come in so handy?

I toss it on the ground. "Here, Coco Puff! Here's a new toy for you!"

Brooks isn't laughing anymore. When I risk a glance at him while the faint scent of bacon sneaks into the kitchen, he's not scowling either. "You get bullied growing up?"

That sound you hear? That's the brakes screeching on this conversation while my heart leaps from zero to sixty at the same time.

No one talks about my family, my childhood, and my *growing up* unless I ask them to.

I try to sidestep him, but we're caught in a dance of *which way are you going so I can go the other way?* and it's not working right, and I can't get away from him. "There's too much different about this morning than the last mornings in your apartment. It's not going to work. We have to go back to the porn cave tomorrow, and I take zero responsibility for what happens today. Good or bad. Do you know how to use a hot mitt and get your own bacon out of the oven, or do you need me to go ask Mrs. Miller across the hall to come in and take care of the poor helpless baseball player?"

He goes left with me. I go right. He goes right.

And I *still* can't freaking get past him.

He finally grips my elbow to stop us both. "You grew up there? At Periwinkles?"

"Don't think being a big bad baseball player with that baseball butt and that—that—that *smile* is going to save you from me kicking your ass if you don't shut your mouth *right now*."

"You've met my sister. And my sister-in-law. You think I'm going to mock your family?"

My heart's pounding so hard it's cramping, and my defenses are dialed up to eleven. "I think you're pissed at me for caring more about my team than about your understandable wish to score with a woman, and people get irrational when they're in a dry spell."

Plus, he also knows I stole Meaty.

He's basically hitting me in all my weak spots.

I don't like it.

"What if I'm not pissed at you anymore?" He studies me like he's staring down a pitcher, and I don't like that either.

"You came here to make me late for work, and you ate my donut, because you're not pissed at me anymore?"

"There's a difference between being a cock-blocking asshole for the joy of being a cock-blocking asshole, and being a rabid fan who wants what every other fan wants."

"You think I'm *reasonable* now?"

"More like *almost understandable*. Reasonable is pushing it." He releases his grip on my elbow to slap the wall, and all the bobbleheads in the next room nod in agreement as the walls shake.

Gah, that grin. He needs to put that grin away, because even while my pulse is hammering and I'm poised to fight him if he so much as hints that there's anything wrong with my family, I want to bask in that grin like it's the first rays of sunshine at the North Pole after a long, drawn-out winter.

Coco Puff jumps on his leg, and he bends to pick the cavapoo up in a single hand. "I think we can find common ground and help each other out."

"Why?"

"*Why?* I'm offering you a truce, and you want to know *why*?"

"Yeah. Duh."

He sighs while he stretches his neck first one way, then another, eyes on the ceiling. "Because it feels like the right thing to do."

"Is this your new tactic to get into my pants?"

"Do you want it to be?"

"*No.*"

"But what if sleeping with the *right* woman is what takes my game from exceptional to greatest of all time? What if the team *needs* you to sleep with me?"

Yep. He's the asshole. "Out. No bacon for you. You're done."

"I'm being serious, Mackenzie. What if you're my *one*?"

As if that's possible in *any* dimension. I'm the freak who makes my best friend go to the bathroom every time he's up to bat. I've cock-blocked him directly twice, and probably indirectly several more times. Also, I say goodnight to my Andre Luzeman bobblehead every night, for luck.

There's not a man on the planet who wants my kind of crazy, especially one who knows I'll never sleep with him so long as he's wearing my team's uniform. "I have Tripp Wilson on speed dial, and if I call him and tell him you're harassing me, he'll fire you before he calls the cops on me for anything you think I may or may not have done with a mascot costume."

He makes puppy dog eyes at me. Then lifts Coco Puff to double the puppy dog eye effect.

"*Gah*." I slap my hands over my eyes. "Out. *Go away*. Get out. And go do your damn job and freaking *win* today."

I spin to my oven, shut it off, snag the towel from the floor as a hot pad to pull out the bacon, and toss it in the trash.

Pan and all.

I'll dig the pan out later—of course I'm not going to throw the whole thing away. I'm a freaking trash engineer, and I know better than anyone how important it is that we don't make unnecessary waste.

Except the hot pan is melting the garbage bag, and if plastic melts all over my pan, I'll never get it off. "*Gah!*" I shriek again.

I grab the whole thing with my bare hand, and pain sears up my palm.

Brooks leaps over, snags it from me and tosses it back in the trash, and drags me to the sink, where he thrusts my hand under cold water. Coco Puff squeals nearby, and for once, his collar is spot on. "Oh, shit!"

Tears prickle my eyes, because *fuck*, my skin's already puffing up, and the cold water on my burnt skin smarts.

Brooks wraps a hand around my waist, leaning his body against mine while he holds me there, smelling like pine and grass clippings, running water over my booboo.

The pain recedes from my palm in direct proportion to me embracing this feeling of all of that baseball god surrounding me.

When I'm watching a game on TV, the guys are these fit athletes running the bases and swinging bats and throwing balls.

When I'm at Duggan Field in person, they're a little bigger in stature, but still, they look kinda normal.

But when I'm here, basically wrapped up in Brooks Elliott, it's one hundred percent obvious how big baseball players are. He has to be at least six-two, and he's broad as a bat is long.

His thigh against my ass is solid muscle, and I know exactly what that is poking into my lower back. I can't smell the bacon anymore, and I can't even feel the water running over my hand and spilling up my wrist.

We stand there in silence, me attempting not to hyperventilate at how close he is—or, you know, throw myself at him since it's been a while since I've been this close to a man that I'm attracted to—and him firmly holding my hand under the running water.

We're about to enter awkward territory when he finally speaks.

"New York is home. Being here—for me, it's the same as asking you to give up the Fireballs and fall in love with a new team all over again. I'll do my job, but being happy about it—it's taking time."

And there goes any lingering anger or distrust.

Poof. Just evaporates.

All because that makes so much sense, my heart hurts for him.

Could I survive having to root for another team?

Not without a lot of emotional trauma and pain. His being traded here is to him what Copper Valley losing the Fireballs would be to me.

And here I am, standing in the way of the one thing he wants to ease that pain.

I am such an asshole.

He twists my palm and pulls it out of the water, bending over to inspect the skin and giving me a whiff of whatever it is he uses in his hair to make it so perfect like that.

"You have any burn cream?"

I nod.

"You need help with it?"

I shake my head.

Coco Puff is whimpering and jumping on my leg. He's so small, it's like being attacked by a leaf in the wind.

A very profane leaf, but still a leaf.

"I gotta get to the field. There's a thing."

There probably is. The new management and owners have reinstated community outreach, and the guys are meeting VIPs every day before games. And by VIPs, I mean kids from the children's hospital, veterans groups, breast cancer survivors, little baseball players from lower-income neighborhoods with pro dreams, and so on.

The only rich, famous, and powerful people getting access to the Fireballs right now are the ones who pay to watch the game from the stands, the ones coming to sing the national anthem or "Take Me Out to the Ballgame," or who know the guys personally and hang with them anyway after hours.

Brooks lifts Coco Puff back into his sling, kissing the puppy on the head and getting a lick on the nose in return. "Do you want me to call or text anybody?"

I shake my head again.

He's not looking at me. He's looking past my shoulder. "I—sorry, Mackenzie. Just…I'm sorry."

He ducks his head and retreats from the kitchen.

And I finally find my voice. "It's not your fault."

It's *my* fault.

My fault for, well, being crazy.

Something needs to change.

And that something is me.

Mackenzie

My hand is still aching at lunchtime, but I'm going to live. I've seen curling iron burns worse than the blisters on my palm. It's making typing at work around the bandages a pain in the ass, but I deserve the pain.

I needed the wake-up call.

And now that I've had it, it's time to face the music.

I'm sitting at a table at Chester Green's—no relation to Darren Greene, if you're wondering—because it's the hangout for all the hockey fans in Copper Valley. The Fireballs don't have a similar establishment.

They used to, but it shut down for lack of business about four years ago.

If my lunch meeting today goes south, I'm hoping the hockey fans will have my back. A few of them have already stopped to ask if I'm the chick angling to bring back Fiery the Dragon, and asked for *Fiery Forever* buttons of their own, so this was definitely a good choice.

My pulse is operating at warp speed, and my hands are getting clammy, which isn't the best feeling on my burn blisters. I'm about to start biting my nails when Sarah walks through the door.

Sarah.

My eyeballs go hot, and I sink low in my seat. Maybe she won't see me. Maybe she's grabbing take-out from the bar. Maybe—

Maybe she's headed directly toward me with *you are in so much trouble* written in her frown.

I lunge across the table and cover the open spot with my hands, banging my injured hand hard enough that I stifle a yelp of pain. I don't have a purse, so I can't block the seat with that. And the weather's warm enough today that I'm not wearing a coat, so I can't use that either.

"Business meeting," I spit out when she stops in front of me.

She frowns and touches my bandage gently. "What happened?"

"I grabbed a curling iron. I'm fine."

Her brown eyes search mine, and after a moment, she sighs the same sigh I've heard her mother make all the times Sarah's refused a *little* more makeup before going out with Beck for the evening.

She pulls the chair out. "I'm going to let *that* one go, because I'm here to negotiate something else with you."

Uh-oh.

This isn't part of the plan.

"I really do have a meeting," I insist. "They'll be here any minute."

"I know. Lila sent me." She points to the baseball sitting next to the stand-up drink menu in the center of the table.

It's the sign I texted to Tripp that I'd use so he'd know where to find me to negotiate the return of the Meaty costume.

And there go my eyeballs getting hot again.

Shame isn't an unfamiliar emotion. I don't *like* it, but Papa always tells me to embrace it, because it's what makes me a normal, rational, good person.

I drop my eyes to the table. "I want Fiery to come back."

Sarah scoots her chair around the table so it's next to mine, and she wraps her arms around my shoulders and squeezes. "You are my favorite nut on the entire planet."

"Are they mad?"

"Honestly? I think they've suspected it all along. Tripp wants to put security on you the next time you go out as Meaty. Lila only wants the costume back because she'd like to let Meaty have a few outings to other cities. Like Minneapolis and Atlanta."

I blink at my hands in my lap, and I swear my bandage on my right hand blinks back at me. "You mean where the Fireballs have their next two away series?"

"Yep."

"I really hate the meatball, but he keeps growing on me every time I wear the costume. And now I've accidentally made him extra popular."

"Your *Bring Back Fiery* pages have half a million followers across all your social media accounts. I think you could influence the voting for the duck or the firefly just as effectively."

"Can I have those costumes too?"

"I'm not authorized to promise you that."

Look at that. I can still laugh about something.

She lets me go as our server stops at our table, and she orders for both of us without hesitation.

It's a game day, which means I'm having a soup and salad for lunch so I can binge on whatever feels right at the ballpark tonight.

As soon as our server leaves, she points to my hand again. "What really happened?"

"Brooks came to my place to ask for bacon, we had a fight, and I got stupid."

"A fight about what?"

"My dads."

Was it a fight?

Or was it me being a paranoid crazy person?

"He figured out who they are," I explain. "And…"

Her eyes soften, and she hugs me again.

I don't have to explain.

She's been there with me.

All of my relationships have ended one of two ways. Either my boyfriend meets my dads and freaks out, thinking they're going to try to dress *him* in drag too, or my boyfriend meets my dads and goes so far overboard trying to prove he's okay with them being drag queens that everything gets awkward.

I have yet to meet a man with romantic interest who can accept that my normal isn't his normal.

Beck's been cool, but he's Sarah's soulmate, so of course he is.

Same for his buddies—most of whom toured the world with him in the boy band Bro Code back in the day, and who have seen a *lot* of things more atypical than my family situation.

But all of them are like brothers to me, and even if I had a crush on any of them, I know what they see when they look at me.

The baseball-obsessed freak who always turns into a goober whenever one of her baseball idols is around.

"Is Brooks still insisting you're going to sleep with him?" Sarah asks quietly.

"Not this morning. This morning, he said he needed me to make him bacon since I did that before the Fireballs' last winning home game. But…" I pull out my burner phone and flip open the text messages to show her everything we've talked about this past week.

Plenty of innuendos. Plenty of flirting.

She scans them quickly, and every time she starts to smile, she catches herself and frowns again.

I grab the baseball in my left hand and rub the stitches. "It's hard to believe any of that's real when I know he hates me for cock-blocking him."

"Are you still planning on cock-blocking him?"

I shake my head. "I'm done. If he wants to ruin his season… well, there are twenty-four other guys on the team, and Tripp and Lila know how to trade him away as easily as they know how to keep him. And it's not like we're breaking records even with him helping. Plus, that woman in Florida had her hands all over him, and he can still hit a ball."

"I don't think that woman in Florida was the woman he was supposed to be with."

"Well, duh, but they were still touching. And kissing. And I'm done talking about this, and if he wants to go have sex with a different woman every day—or even every hour—then that's his business, and not mine. Not anymore."

It hurts to admit defeat, but I have to move on. I can't subject my family to a man who's only interested in me to chase me away, because Babe Ruth only knows what else he'd do in the name of getting rid of me. And no matter how attractive I might find him, and how much the idea of him being intimate with another woman hurts, even irrationally, I won't be the one to sleep with him first.

Not when that would make me responsible for whatever happened to his game next.

I take the phone back from Sarah, and I type out a message in the text string with Brooks.

I lift it for her to read.

She nods.

Hugs me again.

And then sits there with me while I hit *send*.

My heart hurts, but I know it's the right thing to do. And I need to start doing the right thing, because I can't live with myself anymore knowing that I'm trying to cheat the superstition system.

Brooks

I'M BEATING the shit out of the ball in batting practice before the game while Cooper and Luca look on. And by *beating the shit out of the ball*, I mean I'm taking mean hacks and hitting the damn thing about four feet in choppy bounces like I'm eight years old again and don't know how to hit a ball, because nothing about my swing is smooth tonight.

I'm surrendering. Sleep with whoever you want. It's none of my business, and I'm sorry for interfering in your love life.

Who do I have to blame for Mackenzie Montana bailing on me?

Me, myself, and I.

I'll own that.

So who do I blame for how shitty I feel about being given permission to go screw my brains out with whoever I want?

And by someone whose permission I don't even need? Who is she to dictate who I bang?

"Girl trouble?" Rossi calls after I completely whiff on a pitch.

Girl trouble.

Jesus.

What the hell was I thinking, going to her apartment to ask for bacon? I find out about her dads, dream up this elaborate story about how she was picked on and tormented her whole life and now is crazypants obsessed with baseball because it's the closest thing she has to normal, and decide I have to see her.

Have to save her.

Have to be her fucking hero.

Except she didn't want to see me.

And now she has burn marks all over her hand from grabbing that cookie sheet.

And she's broken up with me.

Over text message.

We weren't even dating, and she broke up with me.

Cooper slaps a hand on the bar at the edge of the batting cage. "You need to pet Grady's goat. It's good luck. Plus, Sue's the cutest damn goat you've ever seen. For a boy goat."

Rossi looks up from tugging on his batting glove. "Sue's a boy?"

"Grady tried to name him everything from Goat to Assmuffin to Frederick von *Baa*tzalmittens. Only thing he'd answer to was Sue. He's a special kind of goat. I got him a goat house for Christmas."

"High-class, man. High-class."

They bump fists.

I take one more swing, tip it foul, and if it weren't for the cage, I would've taken Cooper's head off.

"Sue's also good at redecorating." He points to the dugout, where several members of his family—including a goat in a Fireballs jersey who keeps trying to pick his own nose with his tongue—are talking with the coaching staff and Tripp and Lila.

"Is that a hint?" I ask him.

"Just saying. My goat-nephew could improve your digs. Unless you like that place. You like that place, let us know, and we'll re-do your locker to match. Anything for a teammate, man. Anything."

Mackenzie should be here.

Not because she'd help insult my apartment, but because the goat's here to take part in a de-cursing ceremony.

She should be involved with de-cursing. Not hard to picture her on the field in tight jeans, a Fireballs jersey, a Fireballs jacket, and those Fireballs shoes.

After seeing her apartment, I'm convinced she has Fireballs leggings in her drawers.

Probably Fireballs lingerie too.

My dick twitches behind my cup at the image of Mackenzie in skimpy Fireballs panties and a matching lace Fireballs bra, like we didn't have happy fist time in the shower right before heading to the ballpark.

While imagining myself licking her all over to apologize for this morning.

"Holy shit, you *do* like it," Rossi says.

It takes me a second to remember we're talking about my ugly-as-fuck apartment. "Lava lamps are making a comeback."

"Dude. You're getting those confused with *llama lamps*." Cooper jerks a thumb toward his family again while I pull my gloves off and step out of the cage. "But what you really need is a goat lamp. Sue's right over there, man. Go talk to him. But don't say a word to my sister or I'll have to put itch powder in your shampoo. You can hit on my brother's fiancé though. She'll have you in a headlock so fast, your neck'll pop. Make sure the cameras are watching first."

Rossi blocks me as I head out. "Elliott."

"What?"

"Somebody in your family sick or hurt?"

I squeeze my eyes shut. "No."

He slaps my shoulder. "Then think about Coco Puff and get the fuck over yourself today."

Great advice.

Especially since my puppysitter is here with the whole Rock family. Naturally. Since she's related to them.

Lila glances my way and gives me the *come here* finger.

I look behind me to make sure she's talking to me. She calls my name, so I jog over. "Yes, ma'am?"

"Don't start that with me. Parker texted. Do you know what this means?"

She flips her phone around and flashes me the message from my sister.

Dingo Bazookarooka hey macarena.

I pull my helmet off and scratch my head. "Yep."

She lifts her brows.

Like I'm going to tell her Parker says my game's in the shitter.

Not that my game *is* in the shitter. I'm hitting stupidly well for letting a woman stick her hand down my pants a month ago, which I assume means either my curse is lifted, or I was so *not* attracted to Ainsley that the universe figures letting her touch my *pee-pee* was punishment enough.

Also, I don't honestly have any idea what Parker's text was supposed to say—her phone's gone from interpretable to complete gibberish—but she's definitely talking about me, and what else would she say?

I clap Lila on the shoulder. "Watch good from that comfy owners' suite."

"Go pet the goat."

"Shouldn't we be petting ducks instead? Wasn't it ducks that were in the guest dugout all winter bringing luck?"

I get the eyeball of doom.

Probably because she knows I know the story about how those lucky ducks on the field attacked her with rabid duck penis. Parker can't keep a secret for anything.

I'm almost smiling as I back away from the team's owner. "You know it's bad for my psyche to get glared at before a game."

"You're already in a pissy mood, so I don't see how this will make anything worse. Go talk to Stafford. If he doesn't have any advice on getting your head back in the batter's box, I hear he also keeps magic gummy bears in his back pocket. Hell, I'd have your mom's cheesecake flown in on game days if that's what it took to get you to hit a few more home runs."

"My mom's cheesecake is terrible."

"I know, but Parker said you always hit better after you ate it. Go on. Pet the goat. Actually, let it lick your face. That'll be a good shot for the cameras."

Santiago, the team manager, calls her name, and she switches directions to head over to talk to him.

And it's not like I can ignore my puppy when he's on the field, so I say hi to Coco Puff. He gets to lick my face. I'd keep him in the dugout with me through the game if I could. Explain the rules of the game. Teach him to bark—and cuss—at the echidna mascot. Store him in my helmet when I'm out on the field.

The goat?

Not a chance. And not only because he's too big to fit in my helmet.

"Who's a good boy?" I ask while Coco Puff pants happily and tries to jump all over me.

It's utterly impossible to not smile at being attacked by puppy tongue. Better therapy than talking to anyone or eating magic gummy bears.

And even though I'm pretty sure that apologizing to Mackenzie for making her uncomfortable would be better for my game tonight—and yes, I know where her seats are, and no, I haven't seen her yet—I'll take puppy kisses too.

"Brooks Elliott," a voice whispers next to me.

A blue-eyed, dark-haired woman is angling closer. "Can you sign my shirt?" She puffs up her chest and points to her left boob. "Right there?"

"Tillie Jean, put that away!" Cooper sprints over, grabs her by the shoulders, and glares at me. "Don't look at my sister's boobs, asshole."

"Can I?" Lopez calls from the dugout.

Tillie Jean rolls her eyes and looks at my dogsitter. "Told you he'd notice."

It's so fucking *normal* that I crack up.

Huh.

I can feel like a total shit over how I treated a woman and still stand out here on the baseball field and laugh.

Cooper's trying to cover his sister's chest with his batting helmet. She spins away from him, trips, and stumbles, and I do the same thing I'd do for my own sister, and I lunge to catch her.

With my dog in my other hand.

Growing up with Parker gave me a lot of practice with helping awkward.

Growing up with my three older brothers gave me a lot of practice with annoying the shit out of people too.

And right now, I'm hitting a personal home run that makes me feel like I'm back in New York, on solid, familiar ground.

I'm grinning while I make sure Cooper's sister has her footing, but only for a split second, because in that split second, I catch sight of someone in the stands.

Someone watching me holding on to another woman.

Shit.

Mackenzie's totally poker-faced, in Fireballs gear from head to toe like normal, but her hand's wrapped in gauze, and her normal glow is missing. It's a punch to the gut.

I broke her.

And I need to fix that.

First, by playing the fuck out of this game tonight.

And second—fuck, I don't know what second is, but I know Firequacker's dashing out onto the field, and my dog does *not* like that duck.

Coco Puff howls.

His collar yells something that isn't fit for broadcast TV.

The goat howls too, and then it charges.

Right at my crotch.

Mackenzie

I'm in a mood this morning.

It's not because I lost my Cooper Rock bobblehead at the game last night, which I *never* do, because *bobblehead*. It's not because I was up too late. It's not because my hand hurts. It's not even because the Fireballs lost last night.

It's because my heart hurts.

And when my heart hurts, there's only one thing to do.

"Lord have mercy, child, if this isn't an emergency, you're grounded," Papa says when he answers the phone.

I'm dancing into my Louboutins—a splurge two years ago at Christmas—and reaching for the new lipstick I grabbed over the weekend as I answer him. "I've been mean to someone, and I need an aura cleansing."

The look on Brooks's face last night the minute before that goat almost took him out of the game—*god*.

He looked like someone told him baseballs come to life and choke puppies to death every night.

And now I'm going to give myself nightmares too.

But I probably deserve it.

Brooks struck out every single at-bat. And Cooper texted to tell me that someone was with him all day, so it's not like he got laid, and also that if Brooks ever touches Tillie Jean again, Cooper's sorry, but the man will die.

So now I'm worried that Brooks and Tillie Jean, who's a lovely woman, might be a good match, which makes my heart hurt, and I've caused so much trauma that Cooper will interfere and no one will ever be happy again.

Yes, I'm neurotic.

I know. *I know*.

Hence, I need an aura cleansing. A fresh start. And to spread happiness instead of insanity.

"Oh, honey," Papa sighs.

I hear Dad saw a log, snort loudly, and then shout, "Dundersticks!" which basically means he's belatedly realized that he's awake.

"Get dressed, Billy. We're having ice cream for breakfast."

"I can wait until lunch," I assure my dad. "But I'm in meetings all morning and wasn't sure you'd check your text messages in time."

Dad yawns loudly. He scribbled over the phrase *morning person* in the dictionary when I was seven, tore the page out, and taped it to their bedroom door after I woke the house up by singing show tunes at six AM.

Papa reminded him where I learned the show tunes, and he apologized for snarling, but he kept the dictionary page taped to the door for months to remind everyone that he's not to be spoken to before his third mocha latte.

"Do you need us to sneak in Jack in a flask too, or is this the smaller kind of aura cleansing?" Papa asks.

I grimace while I grab my purse and dart for the door. Ice cream, Jack in a flask, a dousing in *Kindness* perfume, and a TED talk on the power of karma would probably all be appropriate. "The smaller kind."

And possibly a psychic medium who specializes in being able to see how black one's soul is after putting baseball and winning above all else.

The thought nearly makes me slap myself, because *of course* baseball and winning are most important.

Except logically, I know I'm being irrational.

I *can't* control if my team wins based on which hand I hold my spoon in while I'm eating my morning yogurt at work. No matter how connected I believe we are as a human species, which hand I eat my yogurt with doesn't determine how accurate Max Cole pitches or how well Cooper Rock connects with a ball.

Wow.

It feels like a part of my soul is dying now.

"Mackenzie, baby, are you sure you can make it until lunch?"

"I'm out of vacation days if I want to go to Dollywood with you two at Thanksgiving."

He sighs.

It's not a *you shouldn't have wasted two vacation weeks at spring training* sigh.

It's a *you should get a job with more flexibility* sigh. And I'd consider it—I would—except I like making enough money to continue chipping away at my student loans while I give the other half of my paycheck to Etsy stores that specialize in custom Fireballs gear.

Yes, yes, I also mostly like my job. I *am* decently good at it.

And with that reminder—that I'm good at something *other* than being a baseball fan—I throw my shoulders back, take one last look in the mirror to make sure I'm wearing my game face, and stride to my door like a freaking queen.

"I'm about to hit the elevator," I tell Papa as I swing open the door. "I'll see you at—*aaah!*"

I drop my phone, because there's a very large man poised to knock on my door, which means he's poised to knock on *me* now.

I'm a split second from throat-chopping him and following it with a knee to the nads when Coco Puff yips from inside the cross-body sling, his collar calls me something that makes my dad gasp, and I come to my senses.

Mostly.

"What in the name of Andre Luzeman are you doing here?" I shriek at Brooks.

"Oh, hells, no," Dad says distantly on the other end of the phone. "Who's tormenting my baby girl? He's gonna die. He's. Gonna. Die."

Brooks glances down at my phone, then back up to me. He takes two steps back before I realize he's holding a foil packet in his hand. "I'm trying a variation on the bacon. Brought you breakfast."

Coco Puff yips again. "Turd-sniffer!" his collar yells.

My pulse catches on to the fact that we're not in imminent danger, and the sudden plunge in heart rate makes me go momentarily light-headed.

I sag against the wall. "Stand down, Dad," I say to the floor. "I've got this."

"Billy, you can't drive without pants on," I hear Papa say. "Honey, you still have your—"

There's an *erp* noise, and I sigh while I retrieve my phone and turn my back on Brooks to finish my conversation with my dads, because I know exactly what happened, because it happens at least once a week.

Dad says he can't fall asleep with Papa snoring, so he puts in earbuds attached to a meditation app on his tablet, and then he forgets, and he tries to get up wrong.

Every. Time.

"Papa, can we *please* get him wireless earbuds so he quits clotheslining himself in the morning?"

"Not as long as I get the show of watching him go down like this a few times a week."

I don't have to be there to know Dad's flipping off Papa right now, or to know that Papa's dry humor is hiding his utter frustration with Dad.

"If you didn't snore like a sailor, I wouldn't have to wear ear protection," Dad snaps.

"I'm hanging up," I tell Papa. I have video of both of them snoring, and I don't need to be a part of the argument brewing right now. "I'm fine. And I'm going to work."

"See you at lunch, baby girl."

I grab my door handle, because I need my keys, and—

And I need my keys to get into my apartment to get my keys.

My head drops on its own against the door. Several times.

A fluffy brown puppy with curly fur and sweet baby eyes sneaks between my chest and the door, and a high-pitched voice attached to the arm holding the dog says, "Don't be sad, Mackenzie. Pet me. I make everything better."

I pull back enough to look down at Coco Puff.

He gives me the universal look of *Yes, my dad embarrasses me too.*

"Are you going to pee on me?" I whisper to him.

"There's an unfortunately high chance," the falsetto voice behind me replies.

I sneak a look at Brooks. "Do you always make him talk?"

His cheeks go ruddy. "No."

The big bad baseball player, brought to his knees by a little furball.

The man needs to stop being attractive.

"Here. Eat this. You need me to go get building management?" He shoves the foil packet at me again, looks at my hand, and winces. "How bad is it?"

I, too, look at the bandages on the hand I'm using to scratch Coco Puff behind the ears. "It'll be fine by the weekend. And no, thank you. My neighbor has a spare key."

His hooded hazel eyes study me like he's trying to decide something, and my brain leaps to a thousand conclusions.

There's poison in whatever he's brought for breakfast.

He has a secret identical twin brother who didn't get the memo that I'm done cock-blocking him, so he can stop coming over and pretending that he wants to have sex with me purely for the sake of torturing me with the knowledge that I'm the reason he'll have to retire imminently.

He's not actually a baseball player. He's a secret international assassin who's discovered a plot at Duggan Field to make ducks into radioactive soldiers for a shadow government made up of former bullied geeks who want to change all professional sports by making athletes wear shock collars during the games and be punished for poor play.

He likes me and wants to ask me on a date.

That last one is so ridiculous, I snort softly to myself.

Of all the women in the world, I'm the last one he'd want to date.

His gaze dips to my lips, and my stomach bottoms out.

Brooks Elliott wants to kiss me.

"How do you do it?" he asks.

"Do what?"

"Believe."

I don't have to ask *believe in what?*, because my thumping heart and that intense gaze are filling in the blanks.

Plus, there's only one thing I really believe in.

The Fireballs.

"I can't *not* believe. It would be like not breathing."

"But *how*?"

"I just...do. It's like hope on steroids. I hope. I hope so hard, and so long, it turns into belief, because there's no sense hoping for something you don't believe in. I can't be out on the field playing the game. For one, because I broke my collarbone the one time I tried to play softball, and for two, because if I were to get out there on the field for every game, I'd get arrested for trespassing since, well, see number one. Not a player."

He either wants to laugh, cringe, or he's suppressing a fart. Possibly all three, or at least the first two.

I can acknowledge I'm a little bit crazy. I don't even mind waving that crazy banner in public from time to time. But right now, I don't want Brooks to think I'm crazy.

A small part of me would die if he completely wrote me off as that nutso girl who only wanted to keep him from having sex.

"Since I can't play, I believe. We're all connected, you know. All of humanity. So I send positive vibes out into the world for my favorite team to win, because that's what I can do for them. I can't bat. I can't pitch. I can't coach. So I believe. It's my part. And I'll keep doing it as long as it takes. No matter what."

Yep.

He totally thinks I'm bananas.

I squeeze my eyes shut and open my mouth to tell him I need to go get my spare key, but thinking suddenly becomes impossible, because he thrusts his hands into my hair, and his lips connect with mine, and *hello, good morning, yes, please*.

Not what I expected.

But *oh*.

Oh, this kiss—it's tender and sweet and desperate and hungry at the same time. I gasp against his mouth, and he touches the tip of his tongue to mine, and *more*.

I need *more*.

Or maybe he needs more.

He needs all the belief I can give him.

Believe, Brooks. Believe.

I angle my mouth against his, using my lips and my tongue to infuse as much belief into him as I can. I don't care if he thinks this is simply another point—that I'll be the woman who breaks his game to punish me for stopping him in spring training.

Because *I* know that this is more.

And the way he's gripping my hair, lighting up the nerves on my scalp almost to the point of pain, and the way he's crowding me against the door, his body hard *everywhere*—I don't think he's trying to prove a point.

I think—

I think he *wants* me.

The idea startles me so bad that I jerk out of the kiss, banging my head on the door and squeezing Coco Puff so hard that he squeaks.

Brooks's chest is heaving. His gaze flies to mine while he swipes his thumb over his lips, and *gah*, I want to bite it.

I want to bite his thumb and I want to leap into his arms and I want to kiss him so hard that he can't help but win tonight.

But that's not how this works.

Not for Brooks.

"Breakfast." He bends and grabs the foil pack from the ground. "Eat this. For luck. Please."

He takes Coco Puff, puts the puppy back in the sling one-handed, and shoves the package at me.

As soon as I take it, he turns and strides to the stairwell exit without a goodbye.

The door across the hall inches open, and one of my neighbors—this one a grad student in particle physics at Copper Valley University—pokes her head out. "Were you making out with Brooks Elliott?"

"It…looks like," I stammer.

She eyeballs the foil-wrapped food in my hand. "What's that?"

I peel it back, and inside, there's a sandwich.

A bacon sandwich, with pancakes for bread, and—I swipe a finger over the brown creamy stuff.

Nutella.

He made me a bacon-Nutella sandwich on pancakes.

Be still my beating heart, he made me a *masterpiece*.

My neighbor's still watching.

"Breakfast," I tell her. "It's breakfast."

But it feels like something more than breakfast.

It feels like a *date*.

Brooks

I'M NOT A STALKER. I'm just sitting here on the side of the road in my SUV, watching Mackenzie's apartment building so that I can make sure she gets to work okay.

And so I can see if she's eating her bacon.

That's all.

Nothing stalkerish about that.

"This is totally normal," I tell Coco Puff. "It's all in the name of superstition and winning."

He grins at me and licks my arm.

He tinkled on a fire hydrant as soon as we were out of the building, and I high-fived him for not peeing on Mackenzie.

Who I left standing in the hallway without a way to get back into her apartment.

Fuck.

I'm such an idiot.

My phone dings, and I glance at the read-out with half an eye, then a full eye as I realize what it says.

ELOISE: Why are you sitting outside Mackenzie's apartment building? Are you spying on the crazy chick?

· · ·

Brooks: QUIT TRACKING ME.

Rhett: Don't yell at my wife. Ma made us do it.

Brooks: I'm disowning you all.

Gavin: Thank god. I've been waiting for this day for thirty years.

Parker: Duck duck goose.

Knox: Parker's right. Gavin's sarcasm doesn't work well on text, and Brooks, you can't disown us. No one else will ever love you as much as we do.

Brooks: Half of Copper Valley loves me more than you do, and I haven't even helped their team win yet.

Eloise: You need to lay off the jacking off. Sorry, bud. Only thing that'll help.

Knox: Okay, Hot Crazy Pants, I'm gonna have to stop you there. Wait. Hot Crazy Pants. Hot Crazy Pants. E-L-O-I-S-E. Shit. My phone's doing it now too.

Rhett: Bazookarooka, get home now. I'm invoking Code Dead Brother-in-law. Knox is looking at my wife wrong.

Brooks: You know Eloise is the one who made his phone say that. Also, if you kill him, Parker will tickle you to death.

· · ·

Rhett: Fine. I'll activate my old team. Pigpen's been itching to take him out anyway since the fucker made us all read that Nicholas Sparks book. HE SAID IT WAS A ROMANCE. HE LIED. And now he's making eyes at my wife. He has to die.

Eloise: I love it when you get all pissed at being denied a happy ending. It's so hot.

Jack: *monkey covering his eyes emoji*

Brooks: I'm muting you all.

I TURN my phone off and glance back at Mackenzie's building, then nearly jump out of my skin.

I can't see Mackenzie's building.

Lila Valentine's standing at my window. I hit the button to roll it down, swallowing hard and trying to shove my heart back into my chest, instead of letting it keep hammering up in my throat. "Mornin', boss-lady."

"Why are you stalking Mackenzie?"

I stare at her without blinking. "I'm not stalking Mackenzie."

She lifts her phone again, and there's a message from Parker. It's a photo of a hand-written note.

Brooks is stalking Mackenzie. I'm worried he's going to try to sleep with her and completely destroy his game for good.

I'm torn between an irrational desire to grab Lila's phone and fling it into traffic so no one can ever see that offensive note again, and wanting to high-five my sister for her ingenuity. "Huh. She got around the auto-correct problem."

Coco Puff lunges toward the window and gives Lila the puppy dog eyes that no one can resist. She smiles at him and scratches his ears. "You're such a good boy, aren't you? Is Brooks taking good care of you? Yes? He's spoiling you with treats and love and letting you sleep on his bed? What a good doggy daddy. Maybe next, he can try being happy to be here with this amazing opportunity? Yes? Yes? Would that make you happy, you adorable little puppy?"

"I can hear you."

"I know. I want you to."

"You know my mom's having a voodoo doll made because she's so upset that you took me from her."

She lifts her eyes to mine, and while she might be friends with my sister, she's not going to tolerate my bullshit this morning. "What do you want, Brooks? You can't go back to New York. They were offering you to half the teams they were talking to about trades. You're not doing poorly, but you're not spectacular either. There won't be many other teams who'd take you without also wanting one of our draft picks or partial payment of your contract. Statistically speaking, you've probably already peaked as a baseball player. You're not one of the young guys anymore. So, as your friend, I need to know what you need. How can we help you make this work for all of us?"

I catch sight of Mackenzie's car pulling out of the parking garage, and I crane to see if she's eating the breakfast sandwich I made her. But she turns the opposite direction, and I can't tell.

Dammit.

I'll have to text her.

Lila glances behind her, then looks back at me expectantly.

Hard to miss the Fireball-mobile.

I scrub a hand over my face, realize I forgot to shave this morning, and then drop a hand to scratch Coco Puff's wiry fur. "I was set in my routines in New York. I just—I need a little time to find the new patterns."

I get the eyebrow of *I don't believe you.*

Like I'm the only one who's done this dance lately. "You didn't need any time to adjust to Copper Valley after living in New York for how many years?"

"Oh, I did. I'll own that. But I did the same thing you're doing too, and I got involved romantically in something that could've been a very, very bad idea."

"You don't think Mackenzie's good enough for me, or you don't think I'm good enough for her?"

She purses her lips and looks up at the sky. "I'm trying very hard to not comment on superstitions or thievery right now, because there are some things I like to pretend I don't know. It helps me sleep at night."

Oh, *shit*. She knows.

She knows Mackenzie stole the meatball.

I wait until she looks me in the eye, and then I do something I've done so often as the youngest child in my family that I don't even get a blip in my pulse. I lie through my teeth. "I have no idea what you're talking about."

She doesn't believe me, and I know it. But she drops it. "Whatever you did in New York seemed to work for you. Maybe you should associate with the same kind of people and do the same kind of habits."

"I'm hitting the fucking ball."

"Not like you used to. Parker says your game's off. Tripp says your game's off. And half the guys on the team don't trust you yet."

I'm trying hard to care, because I do, despite what she thinks, but I need to let Mackenzie know that she needs to stash that meatball costume *right now*. "So you think I should get rid of Coco Puff? Lila. That's cruel. At least let me keep my companion for my normal habit of randomly parking on different streets to meditate the morning before every game."

"Also, if you hurt Mackenzie, I won't be responsible for what Tripp and his friends will do to you."

Coco Puff whimpers. Guilt grabs me by the throat. "I don't want to hurt her. I—I'm trying to understand her. To help my game."

Her eyes narrow while she studies me. "I'm so glad Tripp's kids aren't old enough to lie convincingly yet."

"I don't like to suck."

"*That*, I believe."

"Even in the minors, I never played for anyone but New York. This is all new."

"So how are we going to fix this?"

I glance at my phone, where my siblings and in-laws are still continuing what's undoubtedly a hilarious text conversation without me. They'll probably get together for a book club meeting one night this week. Have dinner together at Ma's house once or twice this month. Heard there are baby showers in the works.

I miss a lot of shit during the season. I wouldn't be there for any of this anyway.

But knowing it's happening five hundred miles away instead of in the same metro area sucks.

I lift my phone. "Can your IT department wipe whatever Eloise put on this to track me?"

"Is there *anyone* on this planet who can stop Eloise when it comes to electronics? We're talking about the same woman who launched that dick pic phone virus last fall, aren't we?"

Fuck, that was funny. She bricked a third of the phones in the locker room back in New York.

I don't know how many guys on the Fireballs got hit with the same thing. I might've been actively invited to the de-cursing night at spring training—nope, still not telling what we did with the dildo—but I don't know which of my new teammates is most likely to put bubble gum in my helmet or which one most deserves to have his car parked in center field before a game.

I haven't been to these guys' weddings. Haven't gone on a McDonald's run for fries after a late night of drinking after a bad loss, or helped pour a cooler of Gatorade on Santiago after a win.

"If you're out, if you're done, at least do us the courtesy of telling us," Lila says softly. "No judgment here. We know the Fireballs' record. We know we're trying to do the impossible. And we know it's not for everyone. But I hoped you'd give us a chance."

She gives Coco Puff one more scratch behind the ears and steps back. "See you at the ballpark."

"Lila."

"What?"

"You know what works really well for team spirit?"

She lifts a brow.

I wiggle mine. "Matching pajamas for road trips."

"You're hilarious. Don't make things awkward for your sister and me, because I'm pretty sure you're the one who'll lose if you do."

"I'm serious."

"You want matching pajamas. Matching *Fireballs* pajamas."

Not a question.

A statement pointing out the lunacy of my idea.

"Tell Tripp. Tell Cooper. Then tell me I'm the asshole."

She's giving it serious consideration as she steps away. I can see it in the battle going on in her face.

Good.

I need her distracted. And, despite the fact that she thinks I'm mocking her, I'm completely serious.

There's nothing like everyone looking like idiots and owning the fuck out of it to bring a team together.

As soon as she's gone, I lunge for my phone and pull up my conversation with Meaty.

Mackenzie needs to know that Lila's on to her so she can hide the costume. Or ditch it. Maybe burn it so they can't swab it for her DNA or any stray hairs on the inside of the meatball head.

Yeah.

I'm helping a woman stash a meatball, when I should really be worried about the impact of the meatball missing on the team that's paying my paycheck.

Lila's right.

I have a Mackenzie problem.

But I'm not sure it's a bad problem to have, if I want to get my game back.

21

Mackenzie

MY PHONE WILL NOT STOP BUZZING.
   Not my regular phone. My burner phone.
   It's blowing up with texts from Brooks.

LILA KNOWS. SHE KNOWS you have the costume. Hide it. Get rid of it. Burn it. Then toss this phone too.

MEATY? C'mon, Meaty, answer me so I know you're not in meatball jail.

DID you eat the breakfast sandwich? Oh, shit. Are you allergic to hazelnuts?

IF YOU STILL HAVE THIS phone and haven't tossed it, I need to talk to you. I think I know what's wrong with my game, and I need a crash course in all things Fireballs. I'd ask Rock, but I want the full story from someone who won't make him out to be a god.

• • •

RELATED TO THAT LAST TEXT: Please don't make Rock out to be a god when we talk. It makes my dog irrationally angry.

FINE, it's me. I get irrationally angry because Rock still has his home team, whereas mine didn't want me anymore. It sucks. It sucks worse than being a fucking thirty-year-old virgin. Happy now?

I'M NOT ACTUALLY mad at you. And I don't usually talk this much. And OH FUCK. I need my own damn burner phone, because I think my sister-in-law is tracking mine. SHIT. Eloise, if you're listening in, I will strangle you myself with Ma's leg warmers, because THAT WOULD BE FUCKING JUSTICE.

SORRY, Meaty. Ignore that last message. Also, you should probably get a new burner phone too. Or maybe we can learn Morse Code and talk from the roofs of our buildings. Eloise can't hack that.

SHIT. I just realized she probably can. Satellite imagery and all that.

FUCK ME. If she didn't have the idea before, she does now.

CAN YOU PLEASE CALL ME? I meant what I said about the crash course in all things Fireballs, and it really is vital that I get an outside perspective.

MY DADS HUDDLE TOGETHER, cackling as they read all the messages while we wait for our soup and salads and milk shakes at lunch. The café is a ray of sunshine on what's turned into a gloomy spring day. All yellows and whites with fresh flowers on all of the cozy tables to battle the gray in my soul matching the gray clouds outside.

"And I thought you were a disaster today," Papa says to Dad. "This poor man. He's a train wreck."

"I can see why he's never been laid."

"*Dad.*"

They give me matching *you know we're right* looks.

I frown at both of them. "We're cleansing the auras. Not being shameless gossips."

"And the child becomes the parent," Papa murmurs over his coffee as Dad passes me back my phone. "Also, I thought we were here because you needed an excuse for ice cream."

"I'm serious. I think everything I've been doing to cock-block him is messing with the Fireballs winning. It's a team thing, right? He might be hitting the ball, but they're not winning yet, and it's probably because he's passing on the crankiness to someone on the field, or it's keeping him from bonding properly. I need—I need the guilt to go away."

Dad squeezes my hand. "Will your guilt going away make *him* do better, or will it help *you* do better?"

"I can't put out good vibes for the team if I'm miserable and guilty." And don't ask about how conflicted I am about that kiss this morning.

That kiss is exactly the sort of thing that should be good luck, because *oh my god that kiss*, but I'm terrified it's going to send his not-great start to the season further into the hole.

"You're not the only reason the Fireballs are losing." Papa points to the phone. "He basically says it himself. He's self-sabotaging on some level because he misses his old team, who didn't want him anymore."

"So he's getting a double whammy with me laying the guilt on him, plus his own insecurities. Awesome, Mackenzie. Just awesome."

"Stop." Dad steals the sugar packets I'm arranging in the little holder beside the carnations. "You do *plenty* for that team. You helped one of their awful mascot contestants get to the top of the voting so far, *and* you ate cotton candy until you almost puked because it was cotton candy night."

"We lost anyway."

"But you're doing what you need to do. That's more than anyone else in this city's doing."

"Technically, the whole team is trying to win."

"Would you stop downplaying your role in all of this? Please? Just once?"

Papa smiles at both of us. "Billy, she's fishing for compliments."

"I'm aware, and I'm not going to give her what she wants until she compliments herself. Self-esteem and self-worth come from within. She has to forgive herself before it'll mean a damn thing that we forgive her."

I lean back as our server delivers the milk shakes. My dads both pounce on theirs as soon as she's gone, but I sit and stare at mine.

I don't deserve a milk shake.

I've been messing things up for my team when I really need to stay out of their way. "This is why I shouldn't talk to the players."

Dad scowls at me. "Those players are damn lucky to have you around to brighten their lives."

"Not all of them."

"Repeat after me, baby girl. *Those players are damn lucky to have me around to brighten their lives.*"

"Are they? Are they really?"

Dad heaves a sigh and looks at Papa. "She's being difficult. Fix her."

"I shouldn't have gone to spring training. Then I wouldn't be interfering with the Fireballs."

"Or maybe you're learning where you fit, same as he is." Papa taps my phone. "This is new. Change takes work. You can't get it all right the first time, but that doesn't mean you quit. It means you adjust, and you keep going."

"But what if I never find what works?"

"Baby girl, they're coming off the worst three seasons in the history of the world. No matter what you do, if you do it with your heart, you're going to help. It's your intentions that count."

"My intentions involve perpetually angering a player who's supposed to be the last key to lifting us out of the worst losing streak in professional sports ever."

"Did he have a dog BCV?"

"BCV?"

"*Before Copper Valley.* Keep up, little bit. Did he?"

"I don't think so."

"So maybe the dog's the problem."

I gasp.

Dad gasps.

And then Papa gasps too.

My brows start to crinkle when I realize a shadow's fallen on our table, and no sooner have I processed the subtle scent of grass and pine before a large frame drops into the dainty open chair next to me.

Brooks points at the burner phone on the table, flashing with a new message notification from "Spike the Echidna," and yes, it's in quotes in the contacts. "You're not answering my messages."

This is where I should find my tongue, but my dads and I sit there gaping at him.

He shouldn't be here.

He should be at practice.

And he *really* shouldn't be taking the chance that he'll look at my dads wrong on a game day. Or in the middle of the season. Because if he does, I don't care who he is, I will curse him with yesterday's moldy meatloaf and top it with a hex on his sinks.

And clearly, if hexing his sinks and giving him a few plumbing problems is the best I can come up with, especially given the situation he's already living in, it's probably a good thing that I have a day job.

Coco Puff leaps at my leg while Brooks pulls a notebook from the doggy diaper bag he's carrying. "You need to ash-tray the ascot-may."

"You smoke?" Papa asks.

Dad *tsks.* "Ascots are so last century."

"Did you just speak pig Latin?" I whisper.

"*Yes.*" He scrubs a hand over his face and sighs. "And I promise to not do it again. Did you? Did you…get rid of…the thing?"

"You should learn French, honey-pie," Dad says in his Queen Bijou voice. "Goes over much better with the ladies."

I give him a look.

He plays innocent with his eyebrows, but I know what's going on.

He's testing my current obsession.

"Do any of you know French?" Brooks asks.

"*Ooh la la,*" Dad says as Papa snorts out a guttural "*Ohn ho ho.*"

He stares at them a moment, then turns the full force of his gaze on me. "Your dads can never meet my sister-in-law. Where the fuck are you hiding *the package*? I'll take care of it."

I should tell him the mascot issue isn't a big deal. That I already cleared the air through a mediator, and he has nothing to worry about. "Why would you do that for me?"

You know that moment in a movie, when the sassy, spunky, awesome heroine looks across a diner at the man who's been a thorn in her side forever, sees him helping a little old lady into her chair, and realizes she's misjudged him, and he's basically everything she's ever wanted?

I'm getting the oddest feeling that's what Brooks is feeling today, except I haven't helped any little old ladies into their chairs, or saved any babies from a rabid pack of otters in the park, or even introduced him to the super secret magic trick to hitting a ball out of the park even when he's not in the mood, because I don't actually know that secret.

But he's looking at me like *of course I help people that I like*, and I don't know what to do with the idea that he might not hate me at all for jock-blocking him in the name of the team.

He taps a pen on the notebook. "Fine. We'll come back to *the package* when you're ready. For now, we have thirty minutes. Tell me everything you know about every prank ever pulled in the dugout, starting with last season and working backwards."

"He's a few feathers short of a boa, isn't he?" Dad says softly.

Brooks gives my dads the *apparently, duh* look, then turns back to me. "Or we can start simple. Worst call the umps made last year? How do the fans feel about the whole coaching staff getting sacked last year? Who's got the best dance moves on the team?"

"Oh, honey, Francisco Lopez. No question. Moves like a disco queen."

Brooks looks at me expectantly, like he needs me to confirm Dad's opinion.

"Max Cole has the voice of a lounge singer," Papa offers. "You know the kind. The ones who get a rise out of you without even trying?"

Brooks is still watching me for confirmation.

I stare at him, because what the hell is going on?

He shrugs, scribbles the two names in his notebook, and

notates *moves* for Lopez and *sings* for Cole, then turns to my dads. "What else?"

Dad flaps a hand over the notebook. "What is this?"

"Finals week cramming. I need to know my team. I need history. Connection. Blackmail material. All that stuff you'd know about family."

I'm still staring. If I blink, I'm going to open my eyes back up and find that I'm swooning. "You want to be a Fireball."

He shifts his seat to face me again. "I *am* a Fireball."

That's a morning shot of joe straight to my clit. There is nothing sexier that a man could ever say to me. *Ever.*

Which begs the question—was I terrified to talk to baseball players because I was afraid to make mortals out of my gods, or was I terrified to talk to baseball players because I couldn't handle it if they turned into assholes about my dads and broke the one thing that always made me feel like other kids?

Dad fans himself. Papa grabs my milk shake and puts it in front of Brooks. "Nutella bacon. You need to drink this to absolve Mackenzie of her sins."

My skin flushes. *All* of my skin. And while I could squirm away the aching in my clit, I can't hide a whole-body blush.

Perceptive hazel eyes flash back to me, and he starts grinning. "Nutella bacon?" he repeats.

"Don't get a big head, sweet cheeks. She always orders that."

Oh, that smile. It's getting bigger, and I want to kiss that corner of his mouth that never gets as high as the other. "So you liked breakfast?"

I force myself to sit on my hands, because if I don't, I'm going to reach for his dog, and then I'm going to reach for him, and of everything I need to do for the Fireballs, *not sleeping with Brooks Elliott* is at the top of the list.

Having a crush? I'll live.

Destroying the team by sleeping with him? Absolutely not. That won't be on me.

I clear my throat. "Cooper grew up in this little town called Shipwreck, and they have the *hugest* rivalry with this other town down the road called Sarcasm. If you want to get his goat—I mean, figuratively speaking—you should wear a shirt from the Sarcasm Unicorn Festival the next time you go out with him."

His face twists like he's eating a vomit-flavored jelly bean. "Always unicorns."

"You don't like unicorns? But you have a unicorn chandelier in your bedroom."

"It's a sign that I don't hate you that I'm not telling you about my sister and her husband and their unicorn fetish right now. Sarcasm unicorns. Got it. What else?"

"Lopez stole Stafford's lucky gummy bears before a game last year, and Stafford retaliated by filling Lopez's locker with gummy worms," Papa offers. "Apparently Stafford's afraid of worms."

Dad leans into the table. "Can you tell me about the unicorn fetish?"

"*Dad.*"

"I'm not doing my job as your father if I don't make him uncomfortable, Mackenzie."

"We're helping a professional baseball player find his game. That's it."

Brooks slides another glance at me, and *gah.*

Not the smolder.

Not the smolder.

I tap his notebook. "Robinson Simmons has a niece who was born with Down syndrome last year. He doesn't post her picture on his social media, but he's trying to start a foundation for kids with special needs."

"Trying?"

"Hello, rookie year. His contract's tiny, and he's twenty-two years old. He needs help."

"How do you know all this?"

"You can't just follow the guys once they get to the show. You have to track them in the minors too. Not that I'm a stalker. Stalking would mean knowing where all their houses are and driving by inappropriately while leaving them love notes."

Dad throws his hands in the air. "*One time.* One time, a fan expresses his love for Aretha, and he never lives it down again."

I crinkle my brows at him while Papa chokes on his milk shake.

"You stalked Aretha?"

He looks at me. Then at Papa. "No," he lies.

He *did*. I'm so getting this story out of Papa next time we're alone.

In the meantime, I have more gossip for Brooks. "Emilio Torres is looking at rings for his girlfriend."

"Pretty sure anyone who's seen him attached to his phone knows that."

"She wants a dragonfly in amber instead of a diamond. And she's worried he doesn't know it, and she'd basically turn him down if he doesn't figure it out, because she's dropped seven thousand hints."

"This is me not asking if you're the crazy kind of stalker," Brooks mutters while he scribbles the note, but there's a smile playing over his features.

"And this is me not texting any of your teammates to suggest they fill your apartment with packing peanuts."

"You've seen my apartment. That would be an improvement."

His apartment.

His apartment.

Duh. Of course.

A man can't play good ball if he's not happy at home. And while my superstitions tend more toward the *Sarah has to go to the bathroom every time Cooper Rock comes to home plate* kind, I won't dismiss chakras and feng shui and the benefits of a little aromatherapy.

Forget the milk shake.

I know what I need to do to cleanse my aura and help the Fireballs.

Brooks

I FORGOT what it feels like to be a team player.

My batting average still isn't where I'd like it to be—probably need to see a psychic or ask Eloise for a recommendation to get rid of the residual memories of the woman I made out with at spring training—but we pulled off the win last night against Arizona.

I didn't act on anything Mackenzie and her dads told me about the team, but I'm watching closer, learning my teammates, and getting back in the groove of reminding the younger players when to panic and when to let the bad stuff flow off your back.

Down by two in the third? We still have six innings to score.

Missed an easy hopper up the middle? Set us up for a double play, didn't it?

Watched a video of Meaty touring Cooper Rock's hometown, knowing it was Mackenzie under that costume hugging random strange men on the street?

Probably a good thing Stafford knows how to talk a guy off a ledge too.

What's with you and the meatball fascination? he wanted to know.

I don't like that it's winning was my answer.

He's not an idiot, and he didn't believe me.

But watching the mascots rally the crowd before the bottom of the eighth inspired me, and so Tuesday morning, I decide to continue a tradition that clearly influenced us winning last night.

With a little help.

"I can't decide if you're an idiot or a genius," Luca says to me as we step off the elevator.

"Definitely genius," Stafford pipes up.

"Idiot," Robinson chimes in.

Like Luca, his voice is muffled.

And I'm grinning like an idiot. "Ready?" I ask Stafford.

He nods and knocks at apartment 1302, then steps back, the camera we borrowed from the Fireballs' AV department aimed at all three of us. It's a slick set-up—basically a phone hooked to a stabilizer that he can hold in one hand.

The door swings open, and Mackenzie shrieks and slams it shut again.

Robinson—or rather, Glow the Firefly—turns to face me. "That's not good luck."

I shrug my echidna shoulders.

Cooper—in the duck costume—bangs a padded fist on the door. "Don't write off anything, rookie."

The door opens again, and there's Mackenzie in a knee-length sundress and strappy heels. Her hair's mussed like she's been running her fingers through it, and her pink lips are parted as she breathes rapidly. Pretty sure she slapped on two more *Fiery Forever* buttons, because she only had one stuck to her dress the first time the door opened. "Gentlemen. Or should I say, mascots. What brings you here this morning?"

"They're sad that you don't like any of them." Stafford's doing our talking since mascots aren't supposed to talk, and he's the only one of us not in a costume.

Which is a rule Mackenzie should've known the night we met, but I can make an exception for her. She had good intentions, even if I'm still pissed at the universe for *that* particular curse.

Not her.

Just the universe.

It's complicated.

She purses those lips as she looks between the three of us in costume, and that tiny action combined with her still rapidly rising and falling chest makes my cock ache.

"I don't dislike you," she tells the three of us.

"But you're campaigning to bring back the old mascot."

I put my mascot hands to my face and shake my mascot head like I'm disappointed. Robinson's smacking the firefly in the face. And Cooper—in the duck costume—does a dance move.

Actually—what is that? It's like a cross between the lawn mower and the MC Hammer dance, and he might be a genius, because no one could ever vote for a duck that dances that badly.

Mackenzie's fighting another smile. "I think you three haven't found the right team yet."

"What about Meaty?" Stafford asks. "Would you take him back to the Fireballs?"

"If Meaty wanted to be part of the Fireballs, he wouldn't have run away, would he?"

"Fiery left."

"Fiery *had to go to the hospital*. That's completely different than voluntarily running away."

"Is it?"

"*Yes*. You know Fiery wanted to stay with the Fireballs forever. He's a dragon. He shoots fireballs. And he has way bigger muscles than Glow here."

I poke Robinson, and he belatedly lifts a costumed arm like he's showing off his non-existent biceps.

Then he hangs his head in shame.

Who says none of us will have careers in baseball once our playing days are over?

Cooper tests the muscles on Glow's extra arms.

Glow punches the duck and then feels his muscles, which are even smaller.

"Okay, guys, break up the muscle contest." Stafford reaches into his back pocket with his free hand and pulls out a smashed packet wrapped in foil. "We're here to bring Mackenzie a peace offering, remember?"

She eyes the packet.

Looks at the duck, who flosses. Then at the firefly, who launches into the Macarena. And then at me.

I mean, the echidna, but if she doesn't know it's me, then she's not as bright as I think she is.

I can do the worm, but probably not in mascot costume, so I settle for making a bunch of hand gestures that would probably be rude in certain European countries.

They're pretty similar to the third base coach's gestures for *don't fucking steal second until I tell you to.*

Mackenzie stifles another smile while she takes the packet I fixed this morning. "Is this poisoned?"

Stafford jerks a thumb at me. "Spike thinks he can cook."

"That must be hard with those claws in the way."

"He uses them to flip pancakes."

"Fiery once made me eggs. He cooked them by breathing fire over them."

"Dude, I can't compete with that," Cooper says.

I punch him, because mascots aren't supposed to talk.

Robinson cracks up.

I punch him too.

Mackenzie curtsies to us. "Thank you, kind mascots, for breakfast. I hope we can still be friends after Fiery comes back. You're all very good mascots, but you're not quite right for the Fireballs."

"I hope you're right, Mac." Stafford gives her the thumbs-up. "We have to run. More breakfasts to deliver to the voodoo queen who's been stabbing her echidna doll."

I fake a sudden twinge in my back.

Mackenzie stifles a laugh, and has to try three times to make her face go straight. "Best of luck. Tell the Fireballs to win today."

She waves and steps back into her apartment, shutting the door on all of us.

Stafford lowers the camera. "What would management do if we didn't bring back these costumes?"

"Fire us," the duck says. "They'd fire us."

No, they won't. They're getting too much free publicity over all the mascot antics. "You know they have six extra versions of every one of these back in storage after the meatball incident."

We all look at each other.

I mean, as much as three mascots and a relief pitcher who's sliding a release form under an apartment door can look at each other.

"It's three hours before Stafford has to get to the park," Cooper says.

I look back at Mackenzie's door.

It's not opening. And no small part of me wants to circle back here as soon as I ditch these guys.

But when's the next time I get to semi-anonymously wreak havoc all over a city?

Back when Rhett was in the Navy, anytime he came home during the off-season, he, Jack, Gavin, and I would find a way to get into trouble in New York.

There was that time we glued little green army men to the backs of random benches in Central Park. Then that time we talked the maintenance crew at the Empire State Building into lighting up the windows in the shape of a giant penis. That time we kidnapped Knox after he and Parker hooked up and accidentally lit his pants on fire and singed his pubes when we were merely trying to prove a point about how he'd better not hurt our sister.

What better way to fit in with my new team than to participate in some harmless mischief?

And four hours later, when we all get to the ballpark late, with the mascot costumes returned to headquarters unapologetically stained and a little worse for the wear, having treated half of the city to an even better show than a ball game, I almost feel like I'm at home.

Being a Fireball might not be such a bad thing after all.

Mackenzie

Brooks has made me breakfast every day since The Bacon Incident. I am officially living in an alternate dimension, and I don't like it.

First, because it's been good luck for the Fireballs. We've won four of our five home games since, which means we need to do this every day until it quits working, but we can't, because the team has an away series starting tomorrow, and it's not like I'm going on the road with them.

Which means that not only do I get breakfast companions in the form of Sexy McBaseball Pants and Super Adorable Dog— yes, Coco Puff has a superhero nickname, and yes, as soon as I nicknamed him, Brooks went out and got him a *freaking cape* and shared photos all over Instagram of Coco Puff in his cape at Duggan Field—but I also have to video chat with Brooks while I eat breakfast for the next week.

Have I mentioned that I hate away games?

And that I really, *really* hate that every morning Brooks shows up with that notebook, demanding that I grab him by the scruffy cheeks, stare deep into those hazel eyes, and tell him I believe in him and I believe in the team.

You know what?

Never mind.

I don't want to talk about what this new little ritual is doing to me.

Fiery Forever. Fireballs forever. And sometimes true fans have to make sacrifices.

Mine happens to be falling hopelessly head-over-heels in love with a baseball player who can never get laid if we want him to help our team to win.

Not that it's *love*-love.

I'm pretty sure this is merely an overly developed crush that I have no frame of reference to deal with, because two months ago, I couldn't even *talk* to baseball players, much less voluntarily get up thirty minutes earlier so that I could walk into their apartments for breakfast.

Yes.

Yes, I'm doing this to myself. I'm not waiting in my own apartment for him to come over.

I'm voluntarily going to his for this ritual he's declared is good for his team.

His team. Because he's not sexy enough already. Now he's all-in with being a Fireball.

It's a Sunday, and the game's early, and Brooks has to be packed for the trip, and so it made more sense for me to go to him while he's running around like a headless chicken finishing up last-minute things.

Probably we'll find out this isn't effective when we do our ritual at his apartment, and then—

I sigh while I knock on the door, because if this doesn't work, then I'll be hosting him in *my* apartment every home game for the rest of the season.

It's *torture*.

Even if I can convince myself that these happy butterflies in my stomach are hero worship, and not me actually falling in love with Brooks, they're still there, and I can't ignore them. I feel like my hormones and emotions have reverted to the stage they were at when I fell in love the first time.

With a cartoon character.

Tarzan was *hot*.

The door swings open, and speaking of hot, did he just get out of the shower?

He smells like he just got out of the shower, and his hair's still damp, and now I'm having flashbacks to walking around this apartment with him while he was naked as a jaybird, and yep, there's a hot flash.

"Whoa, you okay?" He puts a warm hand to my forehead, frowning, and *gah*.

This overbearing caretaker thing isn't helping the crush thing.

I leap past him into the apartment, where Coco Puff is playing on the brown shag carpet and attacking a dildo that's as long as he is.

You'd think it wouldn't stop me in my tracks after growing up with my dads, but I'm not at my dads' club where sex toys are stage props, and that dildo is completely out of place in Brooks's apartment.

He follows my gaze. "Eloise."

Ah. That makes sense. "And you kept it?"

"If I don't, she'd send a box of replacements addressed to me at Fireballs headquarters. All that mail gets pre-screened. You hungry? Or are you sick? You don't look so good. I mean, you look great, but in a *the flu's winning* kind of way. Not that you look like death warmed over. You really do look great, other than the whole—never mind. Shutting up now."

And then there's that.

Brooks Elliott is not only a baseball god.

He's also an actual man, with real problems, interesting family, and moments where his mouth starts going and he can't shut it up.

He's this magic combination of hot and adorable, and he doesn't blush or get weird about grabbing the thick pink dildo and teasing Coco Puff with it, and then this giant of a man gets down on the floor to roll around with his growing, floppy-eared, floppy-tongued puppy, and yep.

This is definitely more than a Tarzan crush.

I lift my Fireballs commemorative 50th anniversary tote bag— the one I got off eBay for a dollar-sixty-two from an equally superstitious fan who was sure that her being at the game where they were handed out was what caused the team's epic twenty-nine-game losing streak last year—and I jerk my head toward the kitchen. "Brought a few things. I'll put them in there."

He grins from the floor. "You brought me presents."

I did, and they don't belong in the kitchen, but there's no way I'm setting foot in his bedroom. "Aren't you supposed to be packing?"

"I won't see my dog for seven days. This is more important."

"Fair enough. My dads sent good luck charms."

"Should I be excited or nervous?"

"Excited. Definitely excited."

He rolls to his feet and follows me into the kitchen, which smells like bacon, and where there's flour and eggs and baking powder sitting on the counter and a griddle warming on the stove top.

Like he's going to make me fresh pancakes.

Us.

Make *us* fresh pancakes.

For the ritual. Nothing more.

I thought he had frozen pancakes. I very distinctly remember frozen pancakes being involved the last time I was here, because he opened the freezer—and he has one of those refrigerators with the freezer on bottom, which meant his hard-on was dangling inches from ice, and it didn't shrink *at all*.

Which I very much need to not think about right now.

I set the bag on the only open counter space I can find in the olive green kitchen, and when Brooks crowds into me, I tug it open for him to see.

"What is that?"

"A Fireballs superhero costume."

"Tell me it doesn't involve…" He gestures to his crotch.

"Superhero panties?"

"Yes."

"It definitely involves superhero panties."

He pinches his lips shut and looks up at the echidna dick on the ceiling, but after the normal eye twitch at having a dick on his ceiling, his lips quirk like he's suppressing a smile.

I poke him in the ribs. "Are you a team player or not?"

"I like winning. I don't like having dicks on my ceiling, but I like winning."

The man keeps getting sexier and sexier. "My dads say you have to wear this to batting practice at every away game to cleanse your aura of what's left of that Ashley chick from spring training."

They didn't, but it's fun to watch Brooks go pink in the cheeks. "That wasn't my finest moment."

"And this is your final apology to the universe. How much would all of your teammates love seeing you walk out onto the field in a Fireballs superhero costume instead of your uniform? How many of them are going to want their own Fireballs superhero costume? You're going to be the original Fireball Man."

"*Fireball Man* makes it sound like my nuts are burning."

"Considering what I heard you guys do to one another's personal equipment in the locker room…"

He's smiling when he pulls the cape out of the bag. "Look, Coco Puff. We're twins."

Coco Puff barks, and his collar translates. "Fuckin' A!"

He digs into the bag for the spandex Fireballs shirt that's intentionally two sizes too small. "Where's yours?"

"I can't wear anything besides my Cooper Rock jersey. Anything else is bad luck."

"Is that the same jersey you wore the last three years?"

"It's going to work better this year. We're already winning more than we did last year."

"You started last year with twelve straight losses. Doesn't take much to be better. Maybe it's the *Fiery Forever* button and not the jersey."

He lifts the Fireball Man superhero panties, and we both stare at them.

"Mackenzie?"

"Shh."

"These aren't *panties*."

"The universe picked your punishment. My dads were merely the vehicle for delivering what you needed."

"This wouldn't even fit my dog."

"I'm sure it stretches fine."

I either have the coolest dads in existence, or the very, very worst. It's a toss-up right now.

When they said *superhero costume*, I should've known they'd take the opportunity to switch out superhero panties for an itty-bitty superhero thong.

I gesture to the little pouch of fabric with Fiery the Dragon screen-printed onto it. "He'll look really cool stretched out over your cup."

He tests the elastic waistband, and huh.

It probably doesn't stretch enough to go around his dog.

But I'm not thinking about his dog.

I'm thinking about his modeling that for me. In his bedroom. Surrounded by lava lamps.

Is it hot in here, or is it just my clit? "Bacon! I'll check the bacon."

He's looking at me, and it's a calculating kind of look that could either mean he's also thinking about modeling the Fireballs Man thong for me, or it could mean he's mentally picturing stabbing me with a broken baseball bat.

"Which one of your dads wears sequins?"

My shoulders twitch back involuntarily. "Why?"

"Because a gift this thoughtful demands a proper thank-you."

"You mean payback?"

"That'll depend on if being Fireball Man helps the team win."

I blink. "You—you'll wear it?"

"Won't hurt." He squints one eye at the thong again. "I mean, cosmically. Physically might be another story."

My brains flee my body, dragging along my superstitions with it, and the next thing I know, I'm leaping onto him and peppering his face with kisses until my clumsy attempt at a *thank you* turns into a full-body kiss with me sandwiched between Brooks and the fridge, my fingers running through his hair and his *very* eager hard-on pressing against my clit.

He rocks his pelvis into mine, and pleasure rockets through every nerve in my body.

In this moment, he's not a baseball player, and I'm not a Fireballs fan.

I'm a woman falling more and more for this man who shouldn't want anything to do with me, but who keeps surprising me at every turn.

He knows I'm a little off-center, and he *likes* it.

This little ritual where he has to see me for Nutella-bacon pancake sandwiches?

I don't think it's superstition.

I think it's something else entirely.

And I don't know if that *something* is good or bad, but there's no way I'm breaking this kiss right now to find out.

Whatever happens, happens.

Now?

Now, I'm kissing the hell out of a man I can't resist another minute.

2 4

Brooks

I CAN'T GET ENOUGH of Mackenzie.

Her smile.

Her devious side.

Her belief in the team.

Her belief in me.

The hot, slick caress of her tongue on mine.

Her legs wrapped tight around me and her sweet pussy cradling my dick.

Fuck me, I want this woman like I've never wanted anything else in my life, but if I don't stop kissing her, and we lose the game today, I'll lose *her* forever.

I wrench myself out of the kiss. "I want to strip you naked and lick you from head to toe."

Smooth, Elliott.

That'll help the *don't lose her forever* situation.

But her eyes cross and she tilts her pelvis into me, rubbing me with her body. "Oh my god, yes."

"I mean—*shit*. Mackenzie."

"I don't care." She squeezes her eyes shut. "I know I should, but I don't."

She smells like Cracker Jacks, and she's wearing a *Fiery*

Forever T-shirt, and I want to make love to her until I can't feel my cock anymore, but she needs me to keep my hands to myself.

But—

I slide her to the floor and make myself step away, reaching back and yanking my shirt over my head. "Take your clothes off."

Her cheeks are roses. Her lipstick is all smeared off, which means I'm probably wearing it, and fuck if that's not turning me on more. Her eyes are glittering jewels of pure blue lust complementing the rapid rise and fall of her chest.

And right when I think she's going to bolt, instead, she meets my gaze while her hands drift down her breasts, cross over her belly, and grip her T-shirt hem.

My dick's so hard it could smack the seams off a baseball.

And that's before she slowly lifts that shirt, exposing one tantalizing inch of skin at a time. Her belly's sporting the same rose glow as her cheeks, and I want to know where else she's hot and bothered.

I can't breathe. Can't think. Can't move.

She's not wearing a Fireballs bra.

She's wearing a red lace bra.

She finishes pulling her shirt over her head and tosses it aside. It might've landed on the floor, or it might've landed on the stove and be in imminent danger of catching fire, and I don't care.

She has a Fiery belly button ring.

And I have the hardest hard-on in the history of hard-ons, and the brainpower to go with it. "I want to touch you so bad."

"I fantasize about your cock when I masturbate."

That. Mouth. "Show me."

She bites her lower lip, her electric blue gaze skimming my bare chest and making my skin light up like fireworks after a night game.

And then she trails her pink-tipped fingers over the edge of her lace bra, and I. Am. Dead.

Pick me up off the floor dead of over-arousal.

Pretty sure my dick would like to detach itself and clobber me over the head until it bashes my brains in for all of these years of denying it sex.

It can shut the ever-loving fuck up though, because if my reward for my patience is this woman, then it's all been worth it.

Forget baseball. Forget winning. Forget everything else.

I want this woman whose neck is arching back and whose eyes are sliding closed while she pinches her own nipples through her red lace bra, and I would wait a hundred years if I knew she was the light at the end of my tunnel.

"Mackenzie."

She peers at me through lowered lids. "I want to see you."

I'm not in my ugly-ass kitchen with Mackenzie framed against the backdrop of an olive fridge that's making noises like a dying rhinoceros.

I'm standing firmly in my own fantasies come to life where a crazy-sexy woman with mussed hair and bedroom lips and the breasts of a goddess is slipping a hand into her pants while asking to see me naked.

I strip out of my sweats and boxers and toss them, only hazily noticing my dog's bark and the subsequent "Dickhead!" translated by his collar.

So, so fucking accurate right now.

Mackenzie's gaze drifts to my morning salute, and she licks her lips.

I fist myself, because if I don't, I'm going to ask her to, and I can't.

I can't take that chance. Not if it'll make her feel responsible for anything else that happens the rest of today.

"You would feel so amazing inside me." Her breath is coming faster, and it's not enough to watch her hand disappearing under her leggings.

I want to see her too. "Take them off."

She bites her lip again. Looks down at my dick, which I'm stroking as slowly as I can.

Must. Maintain. Control.

"Show me your sweet pussy, Mackenzie. Show me what you're doing with your fingers."

Show me what I'm missing.

Her fingers are wet when she pulls them back out of her pants and teases me with lowering her pants even slower than she took off her shirt.

Half an inch down one hip. A quarter-inch down the other.

I jerk harder.

She smiles triumphantly, and I make my fist slow.

Torture has never been this enjoyable.

"Do I do that to you, or is it any red-blooded woman?" she whispers.

"It's you."

Her gaze demands my full attention while she continues to peel those tight leggings off her hips and down her thighs, and not even the matching red lace bikini panties can distract me from the demand that I prove to her I'm telling the truth.

She's seen me at my lowest.

Hitting on anything that moved.

Actively hating being here in Copper Valley.

Trying to sabotage her favorite team. The team that *I* get paid to play for. Not her.

"From the minute we met, I haven't been able to look at another woman without thinking of you."

"I'm a hot mess."

"You're a spicy taco with extra guacamole."

She laughs, and what little blood I have left in my brain surges straight to my dick. The sight of her with her eyes sparkling happily and her skin flushed and that wide mouth spread in a smile will fuel my next four dozen jack-off sessions.

At least.

Her gaze lingers on my cock, still fisted in my hand, because I have this erroneous assumption that I won't have a premature issue here if I hold myself still.

She licks her lips again. "You're very big."

"Pent-up frustration."

"Stroke yourself."

"You first, Kenz."

Our eyes lock once more. "Where?" she whispers.

"Touch your pussy. I want to see you touch your pussy."

"Like this?"

It's a good thing I'm already dead, because watching her slide that lace aside, part her legs, and stroke a finger into her blond curls would've finished me off.

"Pinch your clit." I can barely talk, but I force the words out, and I'm rewarded with her doing exactly as I ask.

Her lips part. Her eyelids lower. And a soft moan of pleasure fills my ears as she plays with her nub.

I'm yanking my cock erratically. I can't control my fist, and I don't want to. "More, Kenz. Put your fingers inside yourself."

She groans as she obliges, and watching her jerk her fingers in and out of her wet channel is taking me to the edge of control.

"I don't…usually…have an audience," she gasps.

"Usually?"

"*Ever*. I've never…done…this."

"It's hot as fuck." And I'm gonna come. I'm gonna spill everything right here in my porny kitchen before she gets off. "You're the sexiest fucking woman in the world, and one day, that'll be my dick you're riding. I'm gonna take you so hard we'll both go blind, Kenz. So fucking hard. All night long."

"Oh, god, Brooks, oh, god, *I'm coming*."

Thank sweet fuck.

Her head arches back. She braces a hand on the fridge, and she moans, her fingers buried deep in her pussy, and the sight of her getting herself off pushes me over the edge.

I come in my hand, roaring out my own release at how fucking good it feels to not be alone, to be watching her ride out her orgasm while mine rips through me with the force of a hundred-mile-an-hour pitch splintering a baseball bat.

I can't catch my breath.

I can barely stand.

I have to hit a damn grand slam every time I step up to the plate today if I ever want to get close enough to touch Mackenzie again.

But *fuck*, it's all worth it.

Every bit.

I grab a paper towel and clean myself while she sags against the olive green fridge, panting, eyes squeezed shut.

And that's not a pretty rose making her whole body blush.

It's red blotchiness.

Like her skin itself is telegraphing the regret already sinking in.

I toss the paper towel and step beside her, gripping her chin until she looks up at me. "I'm gonna have the best fucking game of my life today. And when I get back from this road trip, we're doing this again."

She visibly swallows. Her gaze wavers, and fear settles in the deepest pits of my stomach.

"And we still need pancake sandwiches," I add as I release her chin.

It's normal.

It's what we do.

We eat Nutella-bacon pancakes.

And the Fireballs win.

Regardless of how I play.

"I like you," she whispers.

I grin. "Thank god, because I'd hate to see what you do to someone you don't like."

Coco Puff barks, and his collar does its thing. "Fuck you all, motherfuckers!"

"Oh, is someone feeling neglected?" I glance at my dog, realize he's made himself at home right in the middle of Mackenzie's discarded shirt, and suddenly have images of him peeing all over her clothes.

Which would mean she'd have to wear one of my shirts on her way out the door.

Huh. Suddenly can't see the downside.

I grab my pants, because I don't really want to risk going on the injured list for cooking injuries sustained to my junk. I survived getting head-butted in the cup by a goat, but I'm not wearing protective gear right now. "Extra Nutella for luck?"

She blinks at my sweatpants and starts smiling like she knows what I'm thinking, and the entire world rights itself back on its axis. "Only for me. You need everything else to stay the same this morning."

I stagger with a hand to my heart. "Cruel, cruel woman."

Something wavers in her gaze again, and I know we're walking a fine line.

But she doesn't run away.

And an hour later, when she's on her way out the door to get ready for handing out *Fiery Forever* buttons at Duggan Field before the game, she slaps my ass. "Play good today, tiger."

Good.

Fuck that.

I'm giving her my *best*.

25

Mackenzie

I BASICALLY SPEND the entire afternoon holding my breath. Every time a ball bounces Brooks's way at the game, my hands clench into fists, I squeeze my eyes shut but still try to peer through them, and every muscle in my body goes into fight or flight mode. And don't ask how bad it is when he steps up to the plate.

The game isn't even in the second inning before Sarah demands to know what in the hell is wrong with me today.

Politely, I mean.

Sarah's never rude.

"I can't tell you," I whisper to her. "It might curse us more than it already has."

The mascots race through the stands between the third and fourth innings, each carrying a picture of one of the players' faces, and seeing who can get the most people to kiss their favorite player.

Cooper Rock wins by a landslide, naturally.

Brooks isn't even an option, and now I'm wondering if that's good or bad luck for him, because Cooper hit a home run after he won the kissing contest. Maybe the same would work for Brooks?

Or maybe it would be the opposite?

By the fifth inning, I'm wound so tight my neck and jaw are

sore, and Sarah's not having it anymore. She marches me past security—they love her here, but then, people love her everywhere—and up to the owners' suite.

It's decorated in Fireballs colors with all-new lighting, paint, furniture, and flooring, with sliding glass doors opening to enough seating for about fifteen on the deck. Tripp and Lila and their kids are all here, along with Beck, his sister, her husband, and their son.

I dig my heels in before the suite door closes behind us. "Sarah, seriously, I *cannot* talk about this in front of them."

She points to a cozy Fireballs-red leather chair in the corner, which is more orange than red, because Tripp and Lila are changing *everything*. "Sit. Stay. And don't make me regret the birthday present I'm already planning for you."

It's only loyalty to my oldest non-family friend that has me obeying.

She pokes her head out onto the deck, says something to everyone else, and then slides all the glass doors shut. Then she turns and crosses her arms. "Talk. Now."

"Brooks and I masturbated together this morning."

I bury my face in my hands so I can't see the disappointment in her face, because now that I've come down off the proximity orgasm high, I'm truly ashamed of myself. "I let my sexual desires get in the way of what's best for the team."

"Was it good?"

I peek at her from between my fingers, and I realize she's holding in a laugh. *"This isn't funny."*

"Mackenzie. *He got a hit.*"

"Only because St. Louis's short stop fumbled the ball."

She sinks into the chair next to mine and pulls my hands away from my face. "It takes two to mutually masturbate. Did he participate because he's trying to punish you for cock-blocking him and he's taking advantage of your feelings to make you feel bad if he performs poorly on the field today, in which case I'll be calling my parents to come join yours in castrating him, or has he finally realized what an amazing woman you are?"

"He asked me to puppysit Coco Puff."

Her eyes narrow. "Did you masturbate with him to talk him into letting you babysit his puppy?"

"I would *never*."

She's pinching her lips together again like she's fighting a smile. "Do you have any idea how much I love you?"

My shoulders sag. "Yes. And I love you too. And I'm not ashamed of masturbating with a man. Just of how it's going to impact his game. This isn't like last year's superstitions, Sarah. Or even the rest of my life's superstitions. I have contact with him *every day*. I influence how he feels *every day*. I'm one degree of separation from *all* of the players now, and what if I'm in a bad mood one morning and I can't hide it and I pass him my cosmic anger, and he says the wrong thing to Lopez, who flips off Cooper, who tells Darren that the name he and Tanesha picked for the baby is ugly, and then the whole season goes to crap?"

"The very fact that you'd worry about that being a possibility is why it's not going to happen. Your love for the Fireballs is too pure for you to ever impact the team negatively."

"But I masturbated with Brooks when *I know* he can only hit a ball because he's stayed a virgin. Like, did I virtually take his virginity? Is his aura no longer a virgin?"

Tripp knocks at the door, and we both jump.

He points at James, his four-year-old, who's doing the potty dance, then shrugs apologetically.

"What did you tell them?" I whisper.

"That we needed a minute."

"Sarah—"

"Cross my heart, I won't even tell Beck."

"I don't deserve you."

"Mackenzie. *Yes, you do.*" She hustles across the suite to let Tripp and James in, and the little boy dashes to the bathroom.

Tripp smiles at me. "I don't know what you're doing for luck these days, Mackenzie, but keep it up. The team's getting there."

I stare at him, because he did not just tell me to mutually masturbate with Brooks before every game.

I know he didn't.

Sarah makes a strangled noise and turns an unusual purple-red that flags Beck's *Sarah-is-uncomfortable* radar, and he leaps over the back of his chair to charge the room.

Sarah gives him a subtle head-shake that's mostly her eyeballs telegraphing that she's okay while she smiles at Tripp. "Must be Mackenzie's *bring back Fiery* campaign."

Now Tripp's the one turning interesting colors while she

silently dares him to argue. He scrubs a hand over his face when he looks back at me with guilt written all over his face. "Mac..."

"Go on. Tell me it's impossible." I wave a hand. "You know what I have? I have *faith*. You'll do the right thing."

Sarah lifts a brow at me.

I get it.

I hear her.

Have faith that mutually whacking off with Brooks isn't going to blow the Fireballs' season.

I do. I hear her.

But I have a lifetime of superstitions to contend with if I'm ever going to believe it.

26

Brooks

AS EXPECTED, this Fiery thong is uncomfortable as hell.

I can see why Mackenzie's dads call it making peace with the universe.

I'm the last one to leave the locker room to head out to the dugout for warm-ups before our series opener with Minneapolis, where it's colder than my sister's third boyfriend's nipples after my brothers and I iced them until he cried and promised he'd never take nude photos of another woman as blackmail material, especially given how he doctored her photo, which I still can't think about without feeling psychologically scarred.

I was ten or twelve, and it was my initiation into helping my brothers avenge our big sister.

You could say it left an impression.

On me, I mean. I was old enough to know that my sister was awesome, but some fuckwads didn't see it. And with three brothers between us who understood the world even better than I did—even if we were all kids—I got plenty of lessons in respecting people of all sizes, shapes, colors, and personalities.

So yeah, I'm wearing my thong for punishment, because I was a total dick to the universe in fighting against joining the Fireballs.

Still wouldn't have been my first choice if I had to leave New

York, but it's where I am, so it's where I'm going to play my heart out.

Luca's tying a shoe outside the batter's box when I hit the field, and he stops and stares. "What. The. Fuck?"

I turn so he can admire my cape. "Don't be jealous, Rossi. Not everyone can make an eye mask look this good. You're gonna have to settle for being less than Fireball Man."

"Dude, I think you gave Santiago heartburn." Cooper's on the ground stretching, and he's unabashedly grinning at my crotch. "That's some thong."

I grab my crotch. "Fucking right."

"Elliott, what the hell are you doing?" Addie Bloom—our batting coach, who takes zero shit from any of us and who's been trying to get me to change my stance to improve my swing—looks up from monitoring Lopez in batting practice. Even with her sunglasses on, I can feel the *why me?* glare coming off her.

I pick the thong string out of my ass and hope it doesn't leave marks on my uniform. All the cameras are turning to get me at all angles, and I hope Mackenzie's watching, because she was right.

Fiery looks damn cool stretched out over my cup.

I smile at our batting coach. "I'm channeling my inner slugger."

She stops in front of me and looks directly at my crotch. "That cutting off circulation to your legs?"

"Only in the good tingly kind of way."

No reaction. "Great. Get in the box and take a few swings. Let's see if we need you wearing that *under* your uniform for the rest of the season."

Addie's a few years younger than me, with about the same number of older brothers that I have, and it shows in the way she handles all of us.

Basically, she doesn't let any of us get away with anything.

"And if you get your bat caught up on that cape and hurt your shoulders or strangle yourself, you get to explain to management where your head is this morning." She claps her hands. "Lopez, you're done. Let Super Stud here see what his panties can do for him."

"Three more, coach?" Lopez calls from the batter's box.

She jerks her thumb in a *get out* motion.

He steps back from the plate. "So if I wear a cape and mask tomorrow, do I get to finish my swings?"

"You strike out every at-bat today, and we'll get you Fiery on your crotch too."

Santiago's shaking his head, but there's a gleam in his eye. The skipper's been around the league long enough that this is undoubtedly not the weirdest thing he's ever seen.

Makes me want to try harder next time.

"Leave him time to talk to the media before the game, Bloom," he says as she marches me past.

"Understood, Skipper." She lowers her voice. "Smart, not doing it at home. You'd get pulled from the game so you could stand in as the fourth mascot option."

I grab my crotch again. "Fiery forever."

She smirks.

So do all of my teammates.

They know what's going on, and I don't care.

Jacking off while watching Mackenzie work her pussy until she couldn't stand?

I want more of that. A *lot* more. And that means I need to be able to hit a fucking ball today.

So that's what I'm going to do.

Whatever it takes to prove to her that we can kiss.

We can touch.

We can have sex.

I'm done letting my personal life negatively influence my professional life. Superstitions can suck it.

And Brooks Elliott, professional baseball player, kid at heart, is going to win the fuck out of this game today.

2 7

Mackenzie

I HEAD to Brooks's apartment after work on Monday, hoping he's not going to kill me.

He can't today—he's not even there—but this plan is either sheer brilliance, or it's going to completely destroy any chance that he'll ever hit a ball for the Fireballs again.

Possibly on purpose.

When I get to his floor, I can hear the banging and cussing and squealing around the corner, which makes me wonder if the crew is that loud, or if some insulation improvements might be in order.

Queen Bijou swings the door open as I approach, and when I say *Queen Bijou*, I mean *Queen Bijou in a mood*. I can tell she's in a mood because she's in four-inch rhinestone heels under her red velvet pantsuit, with her favorite rhinestone choker on, and her lips are purple.

It's her *I'm in a mood* outfit.

And it's basically my favorite, because Queen Bijou in a mood gets shit done.

She's holding Coco Puff in one hand and the dog's collar in the other. "This is bad for his aura. I'm having it replaced, and whoever gave it to him can suck my balls." She lifts the collar closer to her mouth. "Did you hear that, person listening in through the recording device that might be in here if this is a gift from who I think it is? You can suck my balls."

"QB, he likes it."

"I don't care. You asked us to straighten him out. That's exactly what we're doing, starting with his self-esteem."

Coco Puff yips. The collar gives a long, drawn-out "Ffuuuuu-uuccccckkkk yooooouuuuuu," in a broken mechanical voice, and I eyeball my dad again. "Did you hit that with a hammer?"

"Of course not. I made Chocolate Éclair do it."

Periwinkles' bouncer lifts a crowbar from the kitchen and grunts at me.

The cameraman covering the drag queens making over Brooks's apartment turns the lens on me. "Say hi to your fans, Mackenzie."

"Not until she's in costume, darling."

Papa, in full Lady Lucille attire, which today means a sparkly red jumpsuit and his favorite blond wig, emerges from the hallway to the bedroom and bathroom. "I don't know who hates him enough to have rented this place for him. I hope he knows how lucky he is to have us here. Also, that chandelier is fabulous, and it's staying."

There's olive green tile all over the kitchen floor. The carpet's been ripped up, exposing the subfloor. Someone's taken paint to the ceiling and written *who cares if you have four heads if you're not at least eight inches long?* in pink paint pen around the artistic echidna dick.

"Oh, don't fret, Mackenzie. We're painting the ceiling too," Queen Bijou tells me.

Coco Puff barks.

His collar moans out a pathetically mechanical *mooooot-theeeerrr fuuuuuu…*

Then it dies.

"Can we get this all done before he gets back from this road trip?"

Queen Bijou tosses her hair. "Did I go through your phone and find the phone numbers for all those hockey players who wanted to know what they could do to support the Fireballs?"

"Please tell me the answer to that is no."

"Darling. *Of course* I did. They pull so many pranks, I knew they'd know the best construction crews in the business, since pranks require repairs, and they're pitching in cash if we agree to put their framed photos all over his bedroom."

"Renovation ain't cheap, but the landlords here are," Chocolate Éclair offers.

Lady Lucille hands me a crowbar and orders me to pose under the unicorn chandelier in the bedroom. "I can't believe you're all grown up and dating a baseball player and standing in his bedroom under the world's most wrong chandelier."

"You know that amazing lady billionaire I adore has a chandelier shaped like a dick at her mansion in Miami," Queen Bijou calls.

"When Brooks is a lady billionaire, he can get one too. Until then, he's damn lucky he has friends with taste who give him gifts like this."

"And you two usually have such good taste," I murmur.

Lady Lucille steals my crowbar before I can use it on the chandelier. "We called Sarah too, of course. Her boyfriend's family does all of those fancy eco-friendly renovations, and she asked him to ask them if they could donate some materials to the cause. It's all arriving tomorrow."

Queen Bijou bursts into the room. "*Mackenzie. Look.*"

She shoves her phone at us.

It's open to the baseball app, playing a video of one of the normal pre-game interviews that all of the teams post.

Except this one features the man whose apartment we're in, wearing a mask, a cape, *and the thong.*

He's nodding at the reporter, who asks him the standard *How are you feeling about the game tonight?* question.

"Oh, yeah, I'm feeling really good about the game tonight." He flexes an arm and flashes a grin. "Full superhero mode. I'm gonna knock one so far out of the park, it'll land in Chicago."

Coco Puff goes nuts at hearing Brooks's voice, and I can't deny the impact it's having on me too.

Nipples alert. Peering closer at the phone like that can bring him physically closer to being here in the room with us. Vagina fanning itself at the memory of watching him stroke his erection yesterday morning while he devoured my body with his eyes and ordered me to touch myself.

"He wore the thong." Lady Lucille's touching her lips in utter joy. "Lord have mercy, that man can fill it out, can't he?"

"It was an extra-small. We're lucky it could stretch that far."

Queen Bijou gives me a look. "After all these years, you'd doubt us now?"

I shush them and tune back into the interview. "You're feeling good about the Fireballs organization?" the reporter asks Brooks.

He nods. "They've got great ownership, solid management, an amazing coaching staff—there's nothing not to like here. Add in the fans, and I'm the luckiest guy in the world to be playing ball for Copper Valley."

"And your puppy?"

He smiles, and I swear it's a full-body smile. His entire aura is glowing under that super suit over his uniform. "Coco Puff's the best puppy in the world."

There's a distinct *snap*, and he winces and jumps while the reporter looks down at his crotch, where the elastic strap on the thong has given up on life.

Brooks shifts uncomfortably and looks down too.

It looks like Fiery is trying to desperately cling to his cup, but is losing the battle as the dragon shrinks back to its normal size, which I know for a fact is closer to an inch and a half high, as opposed to how large it looked fully stretched out.

"You, ah…" the reporter starts.

"Gotta finish getting ready for the game," Brooks replies.

The camera pans to Cooper, Luca, and half the rest of the team rolling with laughter, and the reporter's snort comes through the app loud and clear before the video abruptly ends.

"If I were twenty years younger," Queen Bijou starts.

I cut her off with a shushing motion. "Back off. Mine. I mean, not *mine*-mine, but you can't have him, because he needs to hit a ball."

My dads share a look and both giggle.

I sigh. "And Coco Puff needs to go for a walk."

Queen Bijou hands him over. "Don't be too long. We need the meatball to do a walk-through to survey and approve the damage."

Coco Puff barks. His collar whines, which makes him give me sad puppy dog eyes.

"You really like cussing?" I ask him.

He yips and wriggles in my arms until I lift him to my face so he can lick my nose.

"We'll be back," I tell my dads. I hug them both. "And thank you. I really hope this helps the whole team."

"We do too, baby girl. We do too."

Brooks

SUNDAY NIGHT, we land back in Copper Valley, and for the first time in seven years, the Fireballs have won more games than they've lost in the first month of the season.

For the first time in my life, I get a warm glow in my chest as we fly over rural areas, blue-tinged rolling mountains at sunset, and land in a place that isn't New York City but still fits the definition of *home* for me.

I go straight to Mackenzie's place when I get off the plane, riding the high that comes with knowing I made a big fucking difference in these past two series.

She swings open the door and blinks at me like she doesn't know me. "What are you doing here?"

Kissing her.

That's what I'm doing here.

I'm kissing the hell out of the woman who's occupied every waking thought that wasn't distracted by playing a damn good baseball game, because I know I don't get to kiss these lips and thrust my fingers through her hair and press my body against all these curves if I don't deliver on the ball field.

She squeaks, but then melts into me, looping her arms around my waist and kissing me back, and *fuck, yes*, this is what I want to come home to every time.

Coco Puff erupts in excited puppy barks and charges from wherever he was hiding. "You're here! I love you! You're the biggest winner!" his collar crows, which startles me enough that I pull out of kissing Mackenzie to stare at my puppy.

Swear he's doubled in size since I left. And when he leaps at my legs, he can reach the bottom of my knees now.

He's still barking, and his collar's still translating. "You give the best hugs! The world needs your smile! I love you!"

Mackenzie smooths her hair and steps back while I pick up my puppy. He licks my face as I hold his wriggling body at eye-level for inspection. "Who's the best boy in the world?"

He barks. "You make me happy!"

"Did Aunt Eloise remotely fix your collar? Did she get mad that I wasn't mad that you had a potty mouth?"

"Um, that's my fault." Mackenzie rubs him behind his ears. "We thought some positive reinforcement might be better for your overall happiness."

"We?"

She's turning bright pink, and I want to kiss her again, but she's angling away like she knows it and doesn't want to risk what it might do to my game. "Coco Puff and me."

That's her *I'm lying* voice. "Your dads did this, didn't they?"

"No."

I lift a brow.

"*Fine*. Yes. It was my dad. But he's not wrong. Spreading happiness is always better than spreading name-calling. For both you *and* Coco Puff. But don't worry. We got all the video we needed of Meaty walking your foul-mouthed dog through Reynolds Park and horrifying half the residents of Copper Valley *before* the, um, incident that required the collar to be upgraded."

I can't decide which part of her story is making me smile bigger. "Video for after you lead Meaty to victory? To prove he was a lying, cheating, profane bastard of a mascot who can't be allowed to continue?"

"I don't know what you're talking about."

"I talked Lila into ordering Fireballs pajamas for the whole team to wear on the plane ride for our next away series. With Fiery on them."

"Oh my god, stop talking or I'm going to strip out of my clothes and seduce you right back."

I follow her deeper into her apartment. It's not like we have far to go—the place isn't big. "I hit a *triple* yesterday."

She licks her lips and her gaze dips to my mouth. "I saw."

"And a double today."

"*Two* doubles."

"Plus that diving grab at third in the fifth that robbed Atlanta of two runs…"

Coco Puff barks. "You're the bestest human in the history of humans!"

"Don't forget his ego, Coco Puff." Mackenzie's still backpedaling, but she's smiling, and I'm having visions of stripping her out of that *Fiery Forever* T-shirt. "It's huge too."

"I earned this ego."

"Have you?"

"You know I have. And doesn't good play deserve a reward?"

She stumbles against the edge of her couch, which is lined with Fireballs throw pillows and a plush Fiery the Dragon. "I was going to meet you at your place so you didn't have to come all the way over here."

"I like it here better."

Her eyes crinkle weird, but she quickly straightens and dodges the couch while Coco Puff and I trail her. "Here's awful. The neighbors upstairs like to dance Irish jigs. And it makes my bobbleheads all click together. I'll get my keys, and then I can follow you to make sure you get home okay. We can't risk doing anything else that'll mess with your hitting streak."

My dick gives a long-suffering sigh, but the rest of me—the rest of me likes the thrill of the chase.

And then there's the part of me ready to fully acknowledge that it could be sexual frustration fueling the power I put behind my bat, and she could be doing the best thing possible for my career.

I've started getting addicted to the idea of being a leader on a team that goes from zero to hero within a year.

I've also discovered that all of my favorite pranks that no longer worked in New York are fresh and new here. It's like being given a second chance at life after forgetting all of the things you used to love.

"I like Irish jigs," I tell Mackenzie.

Coco Puff barks in agreement, and his collar does its job, this time belting out a song lyric about sunshine and cloudy days.

The smile Mackenzie aims at my puppy is so sweet and pure, I can't help laughing for the sheer pleasure of being happy.

Her eyes fly to mine. "Your sister-in-law won't retaliate by sending you even worse puppy toys, will she?"

"Nah. I can handle her."

There are roughly two dozen dog toys scattered around the room—mostly because Coco Puff is lunging out of my arms to get to them—and as I set my puppy down, something she said a long time ago comes back to me. "Why don't you foster dogs anymore?"

"You really want to push my buttons tonight, don't you?"

No, but now I want to take her out for a Nutella bacon milk shake, because watching her go from happy to sad and knowing it's my fault is making me feel like an ass. "That painful?"

She stops with her bobblehead collection framed behind her, and she fingers the fringe on the woven Fireballs blanket on the back of her chair. "No. I mean, *yes*, it was painful, but also…well, stupid. I don't always know my limits. And sometimes I ignore other limits. Like how many dogs I'm allowed in my apartment…and how many I can handle on a leash at once…"

I was waiting for her to tell me she had to say goodbye to a favorite, or too many of her favorites got adopted. But no—this is a pure Mackenzie answer.

The woman is incapable of half-assing anything.

She scowls at me. "It's not funny."

"I'm not smiling."

"Yes, you are."

"Took a ball to the head in warm-ups. My face keeps twitching. I can't help it."

"Liar."

"You're fucking adorable."

Those big blue eyes blink slowly at me, like she's trying to decide if I'm serious or not. "I shouldn't be your new good luck charm. It's a bad idea."

"I'm not here because of *luck*, Mackenzie. I'm here because I like you."

"That makes me really worried about your mental state."

She says it like she's trying to make a joke, but the way she's holding her shoulders and clutching the fringe on that blanket tells me she honestly doesn't think it's possible for a sane person to like her.

"Who hurt you?"

She jerks her attention to me at the question, and then we both glance at her hand.

As if that's what I meant.

She's not wearing bandages anymore, but she clenches it like she doesn't want me to see. "No one hurt me. I just haven't found anyone who appreciates my unique outlook on life."

"Seeing the world as a happy place and having hope and belief in something makes you unique?"

"I'm obsessive, I'm overprotective of my dads, and Sarah is literally the only friend I have outside of Periwinkles who's stuck with me for more than two years."

"You know you're the Fireballs' favorite fan."

"And I couldn't even talk to any of you until spring training. *That's not normal.*"

"I share genetics with people who do things like marry guys named Randy Pickle and decorate like they're seventies porn stars. Normal and I haven't ever shared a glance. We might've passed on the street once, but we pretended like we didn't see each other. It was awkward. For everyone."

She stops playing with the fringe. "Randy Pickle?"

"Repeat that to Parker, and my brothers and I will have to carry you up the side of a building to burn your eyebrows off one hair at a time while we make you repeat good things about her." *Dammit.* There I go again. I swipe a hand over my mouth. "Kidding."

Her eyes narrow. "No, you're not. I know about some of the things you guys did to Knox."

"You've never defended your dads?"

"Not with—" She stops and turns that adorable pink. "You need to go home. Get your slugger sleep. Out. Go."

"Mackenzie."

"I'm serious. Coco Puff needs you to spoil him rotten, and you need to take advantage of every minute you have to rest up before the game on Tuesday. And meditate. You should meditate.

Actively picture yourself hitting a home run thirty minutes a day."

"What did you do to defend your dads?"

"What wouldn't you do to defend Parker?"

"Nothing." Not that she needs me to anymore—she has Knox, and he's a good dude, especially with how tolerant he's been of all the tests my brothers and I have put him through.

But who does Mackenzie have to help her?

No one like my brothers, that's for sure.

"That's the same as I'd do for *any* of my family at Periwinkles." She points to the door. "Now go. I'm serious. You need your rest, and you could tell me that you got a full-body tattoo of Fiery, and I'd still kick you out even if I wanted to lick it all over."

"You'd lick me all over if I got a full-body Fiery tattoo?"

A blue flame glows in her eyes, but she quickly squeezes them shut and points. "Out."

"You're pointing to the kitchen. Do you want me to make you a sandwich, or do you want me to leave? Or I could paint Fiery on you with Nutella."

I need to shut up, because watching her skin flush is making me want to kiss her again.

Could I talk her into it?

Damn right.

Would I feel like an ass afterward, because I know how hard she's trying to resist in the name of the game?

Yep.

"Thanks for watching Coco Puff. He likes it here."

She pries one eye open and watches me while I pick up my puppy and the monster dragon squeaky toy that he won't release.

She points again, this time to the door. "His bag's there."

"I see it."

Now she's watching with both eyes, and she's biting her lip again. "Are you mad at me?"

I grin. "Not a fucking chance. I love a good chase. And you can't stop me from stepping up to the plate with the memory of you with your fingers up your pussy, so I'll hold onto that for as long as it takes for you to realize you're my *good luck* charm."

I blow her a kiss on my way out the door.

She's standing there, her pink lips round, her eyes dark, her cheeks that perfect rosy blush.

Yeah.

That's one for the memories too.

Mackenzie

BROOKS DOESN'T CALL when he gets home.

He doesn't text.

I have *zero* idea what he thinks of what we did to his apartment, and the silence is making me nervous.

Did we mis-read him? Does he truly *like* browns and yellows? Did we ruin everything? Does he hate me now?

I sleep like crap, partly because I'm now obsessing about potentially destroying his season by destroying his apartment, and partly because giving myself an orgasm while playing his words over and over in my head basically only makes me hornier.

He didn't really mean it when he said he thought about me and us and what we did when he steps up to the plate...did he?

Work Monday morning is full of status meetings that give me a headache, and wrong calls on my office line, and a stack of new EPA regulations that I need to review for compliance.

I *know* my job is important for the environment, and usually that gives me a similar kind of high to how I feel when the Fireballs win, but I'm on the struggle bus today with being excited to be here.

Why hasn't Brooks called?

It's not like he'd suspect someone *else* gutted and renovated his apartment last week.

Would he?

I actually gasp out loud in the middle of a meeting as it strikes me that he could have other friends that I don't know about that he'd suspect of ruining his seventies porn haven.

I cover the gasp with a yawn and apologize for not going to bed earlier last night, which is totally lame and awkward, because *who cares* what time your coworkers went to bed?

By eleven, I'm debating if I can take the afternoon off and make up the rest of my hours later this week.

Brooks is off today. And I know from listening to the guys talk the last couple years that they love their days off during the season. What's he doing? Is he running errands? Is he washing his car? Did he check himself into the hospital thinking he was hallucinating when he got to his apartment with no warning that when the seventies called, we sent his décor back?

No, that's something I would do. Brooks has his head much more firmly in reality, plus, Meaty left him a note.

So maybe he feels violated now, and he doesn't know what to say, and I've completely ruined his life.

I thunk my head against my desk three times before sitting straight and getting back to work. *Happy thoughts, Mackenzie. Happy thoughts.*

Maybe he and Coco Puff took his motorcycle out for a ride in the mountains, because *it's a flipping day off.*

Now I'm picturing Coco Puff in a sidecar, his silly little tongue hanging out, Brooks all in leather, meandering through the Blue Ridge Mountains, and I want to be behind him with my arms wrapped around his waist and the crisp spring air blowing through my hair.

Except this fantasy only works if he's a normal guy whose state of mind—or virginity—doesn't influence how the Fireballs play on any given day.

My phone rings, and I drop the coffee cup I forgot I was holding.

Hot mess, level eleven today.

"Hello?"

"Mackenzie? This is Mona at reception. You have a visitor."

She lowers her voice. "And if I were you, I would definitely *not* come back after lunch."

I cringe, because that probably means my dads showed up in drag.

For the most part, people here are cool about them. But there are a few who'll stop by my desk and want to ask inappropriate questions like if their boobs are disposable or reusable, and how tuck panties work.

Because clearly, that's what defines my dads as people. Massive. Eye. Roll.

I grab my purse and head through cubicle land to the elevators.

When I step off at the ground level, the first thing I hear is a bark, followed by a happy mechanical voice. "When you smile, the world smiles with you!"

Awesome.

My dads are here trying to sell those collars to my co-workers. And while the collar is definitely something that needs to go mainstream, *time and place.*

My workplace is not the time and place.

Except—that is *not* either of my dads' voices talking and making Mona do her high-pitched *oh my god, you're so funny* giggle.

I turn the corner and freeze.

There's Brooks, in black athletic shorts, an orange Fireballs hoodie, and sneakers, teasing Coco Puff with a dog treat to make him bark so that the puppy's collar spews happiness and sunshine throughout the lobby.

The poor man has no idea what he's training that dog for. Someone needs to help him out.

Probably me.

Mostly because there's no way I could resist him, which makes getting closer to him basically the worst thing I could do.

Also, I'm more than a little concerned that he's had absolutely no reaction at all to his apartment, unless showing up here at my workplace *is* his reaction.

At least he's not mad.

Or is he?

He lifts the puppy to his face while he whips out his phone. "Coco Puff want his picture taken?"

Coco Puff licks his nose while he snaps a selfie, and I. Am. In. So. Much. Trouble.

Pretty sure I've fallen the rest of the way in love with the man.

"Oh, hey, Mackenzie. You wanna grab some lunch?" He grins at me like he knows there's no way I can turn him down while more and more of the Copper Valley sanitation department employees gather around, peering curiously at me, but more so at him.

"She knows him? For real?" someone whispers.

"Man, if I'd known this could happen, I would've started that *Save Fiery* campaign myself."

"Do you think he'd sign my pocket protector?"

"No, Jerry, but I think he'd sign a baseball. I hope he can keep the team winning. Hasn't looked so good so far, has he? Not that many millions of dollars worth of good."

"Shut up, Steve. You couldn't even hit a stationary yoga ball with a two-by-four."

Yeah, that last one was me, and Steve glares at me for pointing out the truth.

I glare right back. I have zero tolerance for fair-weather fans who can't even give my team a basic level of belief.

"I missed a stationary watermelon with a croquet mallet at a picnic once," Brooks offers. "'Course, I was swinging from a hotel in Toronto while my family was with the watermelon at the picnic in the Bronx, but they said they felt the breeze."

Oh my god.

I do. I love him.

I love his sense of humor. I love that he keeps coming back. I love that he lets me puppysit. I love that he's not mad that we fixed his apartment, even if he hasn't said so in so many words.

He wiggles his brows at me. "Lunch?"

"Pancakes?"

"Nah, I have something better in mind."

Yep.

I'm in for *better*.

I mean, not *sex* better. I still need him to hit a ball. But *gah*, am I tempted, because he *did* hit the ball after we masturbated together.

So tempted.

He takes my hand as we head to the door, and my whole body flushes.

Brooks Elliott just told my entire office building that we're dating.

Not with words, but when he inclines his head to mine and whispers, "Coco Puff misses you," then follows it with nudging his dog to lick my cheek, it's like a flashing neon sign.

These two people are intimately acquainted, and now they're going on a lunch date.

He's parked his Land Rover in the fire lane, and I give him a look.

A very specific look that my dads have aimed at me more than once, usually when I blew off homework or wore intentionally clashing colors during my rebellious years.

But once again, I get a lopsided smile. "Needed to be ready for a fast getaway. Trust me. It's better this way."

"Brooks! Brooks, wait!" some guy I recognize from the accounting department calls.

Brooks lifts a brow at me—*see? Fast getaways are important*—while the guy thrusts a crumpled paper bag at him. "That's my good luck cheesus butter sandwich. I want you to have it. For the Fireballs."

Cheesus butter sandwich?

And I thought I had bad superstitions.

I get another hazel eye of *I told you so* aimed at me briefly before Brooks turns his smile on…what's his name? I have no idea. "Hey, thanks, man. How about I sign the bag instead? Then we get to share the luck."

Accounting guy—who'd be a fairly normal dad-type if it wasn't for the cheesus butter sandwich—reaches for the bag, drops his hands, and pats his pockets. "Oh, yeah, that would be —wow. That would be awesome. But I don't have a pen."

Brooks hands me Coco Puff, who tries to lick my chin off, then pulls a Sharpie out of his back pocket, mutters something that sounds like, "Thanks for the tip, Zeus," which makes sense if you know the hockey players that Brooks knows.

He makes quick work of sending Accounting Guy back on his way, then hustles me into his Land Rover. "Tacos?"

I mock gasp. "And again, stop talking dirty to me."

That earns me a peck on the cheek and the honor of holding onto his puppy while he dashes around to the driver's seat.

"I poked around, asking about Robinson's foundation." He glances at me as he steers out of the parking lot. "He knows what he wants to do, but he's too young and doesn't have the name or the connections to pull it off. We're hooking him up."

I lift Coco Puff as a shield. "I know what you're trying to do, and you should know that you're going to have to do something harder than the easy stuff if it's going to work."

He laughs. "What am I trying to do?"

"Buy your way back into the baseball gods' good graces. You want the good karma, you have to figure out something that the average Fireballs fan couldn't tell you."

"The average Fireballs fan couldn't have told me that. Or that Darren hums 'Twinkle, Twinkle, Little Star' to himself before he goes up to bat every time."

"No!"

"He does. I got the rest of the team to hum it with him too, fourth inning Saturday."

"Is *that* why he was smiling when he stepped up to the plate?"

"Yeah. Pitcher should've known not to try to sneak a fastball past that smile. Best home run of the season."

"That's exactly what I said!"

He squeezes my thigh, and my vagina winds up for a home run.

It's not like we didn't talk while he was out of town. We texted a ton. I sent him regular picture updates of Coco Puff, and a few of them made it onto the puppy's Instagram page.

Like the one of Coco Puff staring longingly out the window of the Fireballs Mobile, and the one of him sleeping on his back, legs akimbo, with his tongue hanging out while he snored softly.

But while he was out of town, I could tell myself he was checking up on his dog, and pretend that the inquiries about everything from *how was work today?* to *what are you wearing right now?* were things he'd ask anyone who was petsitting for him.

I mean, my dads ask what I'm wearing all the time. That's a normal, not-hitting-on-you question.

And yes, I totally know I'm lying to myself.

Also, he *still* hasn't said a thing about his apartment.

So I don't either.

He parks illegally outside a popular taco restaurant downtown, and then sits there.

My blood pressure starts to rise. "Tell me you know you're breaking traffic laws."

"Yes, meatball thief."

"Hey!"

Coco Puff barks, and some song about everyone in a big family loving each other plays on his collar.

Brooks blinks. "Is that the *Barney* theme song?"

"You like the big purple dinosaur?"

"Parker used to use it as my babysitter."

There's a knock at my window. A college student in a bright yellow uniform lifts a bag and pretends like she's not gaping at Brooks. "I got your order, Mr. Elliott."

"Thanks, Tina." He reaches across me, trades two hundred-dollar bills for the bag of tacos, and winks at her. "Call me Brooks, okay? Mr. Elliott's my oldest brother. He's a pain in the ass."

She faints dead away. So do the pigeons within line of sight of that wink.

Okay, not really. But she does make a muffled squeak when he hits the button to roll my window back up, and there's a solid chance that the barking chihuahua walking past is going to try to steal her tip and get away with it.

He looks like the miserly type who'd bury it in a hole somewhere.

Coco Puff thinks so too, because he starts barking right back, with his collar desperately trying to translate quickly.

"I love you!"

"Smiling cures everything!"

"You're a winner to me!"

"Are you tired? Because you've been running through my mind all day!"

We both crack up while Brooks pulls away from the curb and swings around the corner to—oh, boy—his apartment complex.

"There's a park down the street, but I need to drop off my laundry before the maids get here," he says. "It'll barely take a minute."

He mistakes my gawking for—well, for I don't know what,

and adds quickly, "Or you can come up. If you want. I thought—I mean, it's a nice day, and I didn't want to imply—"

"You haven't been home?"

"I know. It's a sign. I need to look for a new place. Lopez invited a bunch of us over for a party after I left your place, and Jarvis brought his dog, so I had to prove my dog's better, and we all passed out before we could agree. I need to—ah, there he is. Two seconds."

He hops out of the car and grabs two bags, which he hands over to the doorman, like it's normal for a guy's doorman to deliver his laundry to the cleaning service.

But more importantly—

He hasn't been home.

All morning—all night—I've been fretting, and *he hasn't even seen it.*

I really need to learn to not be so neurotic.

Maybe next week.

3 0

Brooks

MACKENZIE KEEPS GIVING me weird looks as I drive us to Reynolds Park. It's not far, though finding parking isn't easy. I end up backing into a questionable spot at the end of a row beneath some kind of blooming tree.

We find a picnic table not far away, and I make her tell me everything she does at her job while we eat tacos and while I text pictures to Parker to make her jealous.

Wouldn't be doing my job as her baby brother if I didn't.

I also wouldn't be doing my job as a good puppy daddy if I didn't snap pictures of Coco Puff playing with a squeaky taco.

Mackenzie balls her wrapper and makes a face at it like she's realized we've spent the last thirty minutes discussing how there's too much trash in the world, and here we are, making more.

Mental note: Take my own to-go containers next time.

"Why all the questions?" she asks.

"You know about my job, but I don't know about yours."

"But your job is awesome."

"Yours is saving the planet. You win."

She goes pink in the cheeks again, and I pretend I don't know she's thrilled when Coco Puff jumps at her knees, squeaking the toy and making his collar go off. "There's no such thing as too much love!"

"You're such a smart boy." She ruffles his ears, then tosses the taco a few feet. Not too far, or he won't be able to reach. He's on a pretty short leash.

He leaps on it, and it squeaks so loud he startles himself and dashes back under the table to bark at the toy.

"You're my best friend! I want to love you forever! You can do anything you set your mind to!"

I reach down and rescue him. "You're my best friend too, Coco Puff. And I promise to love you forever."

He licks my nose.

I nod. "Agreed. Time for Mackenzie's surprise."

She blinks at us both. "Good surprise, or bad surprise?"

"Still don't trust me, hm?"

I stand and offer her my hand, and she only hesitates long enough to give me the flirty kind of suspicious glare.

It's impossible to not smile at that, because if there's one thing I love more than making her blush, it's teasing a reaction out of her.

One day.

One day, she's going to join me in this belief that I can will myself to be bigger than any superstition, and the day she does, I'm going to rock her whole fucking world.

Or possibly she'll rock mine, and give me another few chances to figure out how to rock hers.

It's not like I haven't read up on how to be a good lover. But book smarts and practical application aren't always the same.

For now, I'll take her holding my hand and giving me that weird look again. "You really haven't been back to your apartment?"

I stretch my neck, which, yes, is an excuse to avoid eye contact. "Luca got me the number of his real estate agent. I'm gonna start looking for a new place soon. Stupid to get paid what I get paid and live in an apartment where I have to jiggle the key to get in."

I risk a glance at her and am rewarded with the sight of her eye twitching.

And by *rewarded*, I mean I get to feel like an idiot.

"Yeah, I know." I shrug. "My bad for asking Rhett and Eloise to do my house-hunting for me. I should've known. It's some-where they'd actually like."

"That's...unexpectedly believable."

"Eloise has other issues too."

Mackenzie sucks her lips into her mouth like she doesn't want to say anything bad. Her cheeks are flushing again.

I want to make her whole body flush again.

I clear my throat while we approach my SUV. "She pissed off this internet troll a few months back, realized he could hack her electronic toilet, and she's been on this *back to simple times* kick."

"Electronic toilet?"

"Yeah, it had this control panel and sensors, and it was Wi-Fi-enabled, so like, you could tell it when you got home, and it would heat the seat. The lid lifts automatically when you—"

I'm talking to a woman I'd like to sleep with about *toilets*.

This really does explain so much about my virginity.

"It's cool for a toilet," I finish in a mutter. "And she has trust issues now."

Mackenzie's hand is shaking in mine. I glance at her again, and her whole face is contorted in suppressed laughter.

She coughs twice, giggles once, and coughs once more. "You love your family."

"Well, yeah. They make me look normal, plus, growing up wasn't dull. Neither are holidays. And it gets better every year." I click the fob to unlock my SUV. "And speaking of better, I have a surprise for you."

"If it's a big black plastic bag that you're going to use to stuff my body in because you're finally done with me, can you at least give me a head start on running away?"

I momentarily freeze, because there *is* a big black plastic bag in my back end.

And it *does* look big enough to hold a body.

She freezes too.

We both look at the back of my Land Rover.

She reaches for the handle.

I block her.

"Brooks..."

"It's not what it looks like."

Coco Puff barks. "Never apologize for cutting toxic people out of your life!"

Mackenzie's eyes dart between me and my dog like she's trying to decide if she should run, or if she should grab Coco Puff and save him too.

"It's Meaty," I blurt. "But it looks…like a body in a bag."

"You went to see my dads?"

"No. Tripp and Lila had a new version made. I…stole it for you."

Her eyes go wide and her mouth flaps like a dying fish, which is pretty much my favorite expression on her face ever, because it's so fucking real.

"You didn't," she whispers.

I pop the rear hatch, wince as I realize anyone walking past might think I'm showing her a dead body in my back end, and gesture for her to lean in.

Coco Puff starts barking, so I lift him up and put him in the back too.

"Shh," I tell him.

"If you're happy and you know it, shake that sweet ass!" his collar replies.

Mackenzie pries open the trash bag like she's done this a time or two, and considering she has her own Meaty costume stashed apparently at her dads' house, she makes quick work of confirming what's in the body bag.

"Oh my god, you did," she breathes.

I cross a finger over my chest. "I would never lie to you about Meatball theft."

"I love you."

The words barely register before she leaps on me, wrapping her legs around my waist and sealing her lips over mine.

I stumble—not because I'm a weakling, but because I'm startled—but I recover faster than it takes me to knock a fastball out of the ballpark.

Mostly.

I trip on the curb trying to get my footing, and Mackenzie slides off me.

But then she grabs me by the strings on my hoodie, yanks, and we both tumble into the back end.

I lift Coco Puff over the seat to deposit him in the middle of the SUV.

Mackenzie hefts the bag of Meaty to one side.

And as soon as I hit the button to lower the tailgate and shut us in here, cramped as it is, she attacks me again.

The good kind of attack, I mean.

The kind that involves hot kisses and shoving me against a costume in a plastic bag and straddling my hips while I try to figure out how to bend my legs to fit in here.

"You are so hot to me right now," she gasps against my mouth.

Fuck, yeah. "Steal a mascot…every day…for you."

She grips my shirt harder and kisses me like I'm oxygen until she needs actual oxygen, and she breaks away with a groan. "I'm so tired of fighting this, Brooks."

"So stop."

"I don't know if I can."

"Mackenzie, angel, I swear to you, short of actually killing me, there's not a damn thing you can do to stop me from smacking the shit out of that baseball tomorrow night, and the next night, and the night after that, because I'm damn well gonna have my cake and eat it too. And in case you're wondering, you're my cake. You will *always* be my cake."

She makes a throaty whimper, and then she's mauling me again.

I would happily die being mauled by this woman.

Especially since she's rubbing the flat of her hand against the bulge of my dick and making me go cross-eyed.

I'm gonna need some more of that. Preferably skin-on-skin.

"Want…you…so…bad," she moans.

Coco Puff barks. "If you can dream it, you can do it!"

Fuck right.

I slide my hands under her simple white satiny blouse, find her nipples poking at her lace bra, and I brush my thumbs over them.

She moans again, pulls her hand away from my hard-on, and rocks her pelvis against it instead. "I can't wear these pants back to the office this afternoon."

The scent of her arousal hits my nose, and *fuck*. Just *fuck*. "Take them off."

Those pretty baby blues flare wide as she meets my gaze again. There's a clear debate going on in her head, and I don't think it's a battle of good versus evil.

Pretty sure it's a battle of loyalty versus belief.

I know without a fraction of a doubt what she's thinking.

If she does this, and I don't hit another ball for the rest of my life, she'll blame herself.

But if she does this, and I *do* hit the ever-loving fuck out of the ball the rest of the week, then what do we both gain?

Sex.

All the time.

With each other.

That's what we gain.

"I'm gonna fucking kill that ball," I growl. "And not a single damn thing that we do right here, right now, will change it. Except for the part where when I send it flying to the moon, you'll know exactly who I'm hitting it for."

She fans her cheeks. Blows out a short breath.

And then she does the last thing I expect, and she reaches for the button on her work pants.

Halle-fucking-lujah.

My dick's so hard, it's turned into petrified lava.

And that's before she shimmies out of her pants, panties and all, giving me an unobstructed view of her sweet, wet pussy.

I swallow hard.

Possibly gulp.

Say a prayer to the baseball gods that my dick and I can nail this on the first try, because I am *not* blowing my load early.

I have too much to prove right now.

"Touch me," she breathes.

It's my moment of truth.

Can I touch a woman today and still hit a ball tomorrow?

Fuck, yes, I can.

All I need to do is believe.

And I believe I'm scrunched in the back of a car like a sixteen-year-old, instead of a thirty-year-old, sliding my fingers into a woman's slick folds for the first time in my life, watching those bright blue eyes watch me, and then cross as my thumb connects with a tight little nub at the top of her slit.

"Oh, god, Brooks, *more*."

My dick whimpers.

It wants to be my fingers.

It can slow down and learn a thing or two, because I'm not

gonna be some two-thrust Chuck who doesn't give the lady her own orgasm first while I get the joy of touching that warm, wet skin that I've dreamed about touching for decades.

Not that there's anything smooth about me trying to shift in the back end here, half-lying on a meatball costume in a black plastic bag that squeaks like a fart every time I move wrong while my dog and his collar cheer me on with enthusiastic phrases like *Get 'em, Tiger!* and *You're everything that's right in the world!*

I swallow again, because the sight of her watching as I slide a finger inside her slick, hot channel is making me lose my mind. "You feel so damn good."

Translation: *I'm gonna die a happy man right here.*

She grabs my hand, presses my thumb to her clit, and rides my fingers as her eyes slide shut. "You're going to hit the ball out of the park tomorrow."

"All the way out of the city and up to the moon."

"You talk so dirty."

"You're fucking gorgeous when you're turned on. I pictured you naked and touching yourself every time I stepped up to bat the last week."

"*Aaaahhhh!*"

Her tight inner muscles clench around my finger, and *fuck me*, that feels so good.

So. Fucking. Good.

And with her head thrown back, all that hair tumbling down around her bare shoulders, her chest heaving inside that bra, I am not going to last another second before I lose all control.

Think about Knox's nana. Think about Knox's nana.

I start breathing again as my dick softens a millimeter, moving away from imminent eruption danger as I force myself to picture the elderly woman who terrorizes all of us with tales about her really bad erotic alien romances.

Mackenzie strokes my chest, down to my waistband, and teases my hips right above the fabric. "Your turn."

And with two simple words, she puts me back in the danger zone.

Her eyes waver. "Unless you don't want—"

I don't let her finish before I'm kissing her again. "I want," I gasp against her lips. "I've wanted you from the minute I first saw you, and I want you more and more every single day."

The windows are steaming up. My shocks are getting a different kind of workout. And all I care about is helping Mackenzie strip me out of my shorts in this confined space without either of us getting a concussion.

We manage, and she sits back on my thighs and grips my hard-on with both hands, licking her lips and making me wish I was a real superhero, because god almighty, those hot palms squeezing my bare cock are the closest thing to heaven I've ever experienced, and I don't want this to end.

Not badly. Or prematurely. Or basically ever.

"Are you sure?" She glances around like it's suddenly occurred to her that we're in the back end of a car, and swear on my overenthusiastic puppy whose collar is still barking out encouragement, I've gone and fallen in love.

I grip her hips and tug while I start grinning, because why the hell shouldn't I do this like I would've as a kid? "Ride me, Kenz. I want *you*. And I want you *now*."

She blows out a short breath and fans herself again. "Oh, god, I think I just came again."

Yeah.

In. Love.

And because I've been waiting for this forever, I know exactly where I have a condom stashed in my car, and because apparently we both like it when Mackenzie's stroking me, she does the honors of suiting me up.

"You know you're big?" she whispers.

"Fuck, yeah. And it's all for you."

She giggles. "Brooks. We're *in the back of your car*."

"You're making my first dreams come true."

I grab her hips and pull her over me, watching my over-eager cock straining for her pussy. Her body brushes my tip, and yeah, *we're doing this*.

"You really could've picked someone more normal than me," she whispers while she leans in to kiss me.

"I wouldn't want anymore more normal than you."

If you'd told me fifteen years ago that I'd be sliding my cock into a woman for the first time while we were both laughing about what weirdos we are, after I basically hated her the first time I realized who she really was, I probably would've said a few things that would've gotten my mouth washed out. But thrusting up to meet Mackenzie, burying myself deep inside her tight sleeve while we both chuckle at the unexptectedness of life throwing the two of us together—both of us definitely oddballs in our own way—is so damn perfect.

Better than perfect.

My laugh dies in my throat as the sensation of her body wrapped around my entire dick takes hold. She squeezes me with her inner muscles, and my head drops back against the plastic Meaty bag while the sensation of heaven expands from my hard-on to my stomach and legs and spreads everywhere. "Fuck, Kenz…"

She lifts her hips, pulling off me, stroking me with her body, and instinct takes over.

I angle back, then thrust as she lowers herself again, igniting nerve endings in the end of my cock and my tight balls and everywhere from the top of my head to the tips of my toes, and fuck baseball.

Making love to Mackenzie is what I was born to do.

Once won't be enough.

She rolls her hips while I pump into her, everything tightening in the pit of my stomach in a familiar, but brand new feeling. *This* feeling goes with locking eyes with those gorgeous, glittering baby blues, watching her panting out of her parted pink lips while her fingers skim my pecs and I make love to her.

Not screw. Not bang. Not have sex with.

Make love.

I thread my fingers through her hair while my dick warns me we're about done. "You're so fucking gorgeous."

"You're *everything.*"

And I'm done.

Again.

"Mackenzie—"

"God, *so good,*" she cries, tightening hard around me. "Love… you feel…inside me."

My hips buck uncontrollably, and then I'm coming too, there, inside her, with her body clenching around my cock and coaxing my release harder than I've ever felt it.

I can't catch my breath.

I've gone cross-eyed.

All I know is that I'm hanging on to Mackenzie with everything I have, and she's crying out even as she's peppering my mouth with kisses again.

Mind.

Blown.

Life.

Changed.

And I don't want this to end.

Ever.

She collapses on top of me while I'm still straining with the last bits of my release, and I wrap her tight in my arms.

"I'm gonna hit a fucking grand slam," I say as soon as I can talk again.

She kisses my shoulder. "I know."

My legs are bent weird. My neck's twisted funny on this costume bag. Coco Puff's staring at us from over the seat like he's traumatized for life.

And I could still fall asleep. Right here. Wrapped in Mackenzie.

I stifle a yawn. "And we're doing this again."

"*Yes.*"

Coco Puff whimpers.

We both crack up.

And then the banging starts. "Hey! Out of the car. You're under arrest."

Mackenzie

"OH, god. Oh, god. Where are my panties?" I'm twisting around the trunk of the Land Rover, because _getting arrested is not a good sign._

Especially getting arrested without pants.

Brooks grunts, and I squeak as I turn horrified eyes on him. "Oh, god, did I knee you in the nuts? Tell me I didn't knee you in the nuts."

"Just the gut." He's pulling his legs away and twisting too while the banging continues on the window.

The windows are tinted. And—whoa.

And super steamed up.

There's no way the cops can see in, but I guess the shaking car was a pretty good indication.

My dads are never going to let me live this down. Neither will Sarah.

I can see the police blotter now.

The Fireballs most rabid fan arrested for public indecency and for deflowering the team's newest power slugger. Charges pending for ruining the season.

I thought I was okay. I thought I could do this.

But _I'm getting Brooks arrested because I jumped his bones._

This cannot be good for his game.

"Mackenzie. Breathe. It's okay."

"I said *get out*," the voice says outside.

Brooks hands me my panties as the cops bang on the window again, and I shimmy into them faster than a cheetah leaping on a hunk of fresh meat.

Which is basically also what I did to Brooks.

I jumped him like a hunk of fresh meat because he stole me a meatball costume.

He's pulling his T-shirt back on as I scramble into my pants. Coco Puff's whimpering, which his collar translates to mean *Life is a bowl of cherries!*

Cherries.

Oh my god.

I took Brooks's cherry.

"Mackenzie." He cups my cheeks and makes me look him in the eye. And then he starts grinning.

Then he grins bigger.

And suddenly he's laughing.

"*What?* Oh, no, my makeup. Is it running? Do I have lipstick smeared everywhere? You have—"

I reach out and try to scrub the pink marks off his sand-paper cheeks, but before I can finish the job, he's kissing me again.

And okay, yes, it's a little hard to panic when the man I'm worried I destroyed is so damn happy, and so remarkably adept at figuring out how I like to be kissed, and also smells like a very good roll in the hay, if you substitute black plastic body bags of meatballs for hay.

This kiss though—I mean, if I'm going to get arrested, maybe I should *really* get arrested?

Brooks pulls back like he knows what I'm thinking while the banging comes yet again.

And not the good kind of banging.

"You dressed?"

I nod.

He hits a button, and the tailgate lifts.

My heart's basically in my throat, but dammit, I'm going to own this.

My mistake.

Mine to make up for.

I lift my head, prepared to face the consequences like the kick-ass, mascot-saving woman that I am, and— *"You're not the police!"*

Luca Rossi, Darren Greene, Francisco Lopez, Robinson Simmons, and Trevor Stafford are all watching us climb out of the back of the Land Rover with varying degrees of amusement to horror.

And that's not all.

They've brought friends.

My friends.

Sarah's eyes are as round as I've ever seen them. Beck's face is an entire production of *I don't know what sort of face I'm supposed to be making right now.*

Rossi does one of those man-punch things to Brooks's bicep. "Nice, dude. Next time, tell us to get here twenty minutes later though."

I cover my eyes with my hands, suck in a deep breath of spring air, and pretend I'm in my happy place, which is usually Sarah's house, with my Fireballs banner hanging from her curtain rod, and pumpkin spice candles burning everywhere, but for some strange reason, that's not helping right now.

"Is the, ah, costume defiled?" Trevor asks.

"Oh, for the love of baseball, quit being such idiots." Sarah marches around all of them, pats my hair down, and links her arm in mine. "Beck, the costume's back here. Luca, give me the camera. If you all lose the baseball diamond because you're standing here making a big deal out of what's clearly *none of your business*, then Brooks basically stole this thing for no good reason."

She tugs me toward the path that leads to the ball diamonds, and I whisper a quick, "Thank you," before glancing behind us to see the baseball players falling in line.

Including Brooks, who meets my gaze after he sets a leashed Coco Puff on the ground, then breaks out in another smile that's impossible to not smile back at.

Sarah leans into me. "You okay?"

"On the verge of hyperventilating in fear that I've done something I really can't ever take back with lasting repercussions for the Fireballs, but otherwise, I'm pretty damn fantastic."

"Ride the fantastic high, and trust the universe. Whatever Brooks did to be a big enough dick to get himself cursed with having to stay a virgin to hit a ball, I'm sure he's making up for with putting that goofy grin on your face."

I touch my lips and discover I am, in fact, grinning.

I might even be glowing.

"He hasn't been home," I whisper.

"No!"

"I'm serious."

"So that wasn't a *thank you*?"

I shake my head. "He...he stole the meatball for me. And I..."

She bursts out laughing, because I don't have to finish that sentence. She knows.

We wind around the path and arrive at the ball fields to find Rocky Jarvis—the Fireballs' catcher—signing autographs and chasing away anyone who tries to steal the field.

Actually—nearly the whole team's here. Plus Darren's pregnant wife, who was super sweet and kind and welcoming while I was at spring training, even though I'm a total dork, and Jarvis's girlfriend and their dog, and— "Is that one of the ushers from Duggan Field?"

"Cooper texted Beck that Brooks was planning something, and they were gathering all the troops."

She's not kidding about *all the troops*.

Santiago's out there too. Rubbing a ball on the mound.

Our head coach is in on the meatball theft.

He points to me. "Montana. Get your uniform on and get out here."

I gasp.

Brooks stops beside Sarah and me, and he hands her the dog's leash. "You mind?"

"That's what I'm here for. Don't hurt Beck. He has to look pretty in Milan next week."

"I'm indestructible, babe," Meaty says.

He slaps her on the ass with his big foam hands, and Coco Puff growls.

"It's never too late to turn over a new leaf!" his collar announces.

Brooks grabs my hand. "C'mon."

"What *is* this?"

"Mascot ball."

"Mackenzie, I've got your shirt." Tanesha Greene waves a *Fiery Forever* T-shirt at me.

Max Cole brushes past and slides a sly grin at Brooks. "Not as good as all of us in thongs."

"Dude, shut up."

"Afraid my Fiery crotch is gonna make yours look like a toddler Fiery crotch?"

"That's really not possible," I interject.

And then my brain catches up. "Are you—"

Brooks clamps a hand over my mouth. "Shh. Santiago's birthday is next week. It's a surprise."

I stare at him for a minute, and then once again, I'm attacking him like I need a twelve-step program to break my addiction to him.

He's bringing the team together.

He's stepping up.

He's having fun.

And *that's* what the Fireballs have been missing.

"Elliott, if you don't keep your mouth to yourself on this field, you're benched," Santiago yells.

I make myself pull back from kissing him, and then I make myself put seventeen feet of distance between us.

At least.

"Can you hit?" he calls while I take my T-shirt from Tanesha.

"Not at all," I call back.

"Great. You can be on the mascots' team."

That smile.

That smile, and the mischief in those eyes, and the underlying promise that everything's going to be fine—*better* than fine.

"Of course I'm on the mascots' team," I call back. "I'm representing Fiery, but I'm more like the distant, chess-playing cousin standing in in his place. Because Fiery would kill it in this game, and I'm pretty sure I won't."

"Yes, you will."

I need to call in and let my boss know I'm not coming back today. And then I need to call my dads and tell them to get out here to watch me play baseball for the first time in my life.

And then I need to figure out how to talk Brooks into going up to his apartment, because he really should see what we've done with it.

Santiago heaves a long-suffering sigh that's completely at odds with the twinkle in his dark eyes when he agrees to leave the Fireballs in Stafford's hands, and volunteers to take over coaching duties for the mascots instead.

And sure enough, there are the other three teammates for my team jogging over.

With a scowling Tripp Wilson coming along behind them.

"Uh-oh," I whisper as Tripp points at Brooks, who's donning a *Fiery Forever* T-shirt in red, instead of white like mine.

Brooks looks behind himself, like he's trying to figure out who Tripp's pointing to, then makes the universal sign for *you talking to me?*, pointing to himself and acting so innocent that I have to turn around before I crack up.

He is such a youngest child.

"You getting my third baseman in trouble?" Santiago asks me.

If baseball players are gods, their team manager is like the head of the gods. But I meet his gaze head-on and shake my head. "I'm helping him find all the reasons he needs to love us."

And me.

Whoa.

I mean, *whoa*, but also, *yeah*.

It's not about falling for a baseball player.

It's about falling for a guy who's real. Who turns a little ruddy in the cheeks when he catches himself talking about toilets on a date. Who doesn't quite fit the way he pretends he does. Who happens to share my passion for Nutella and bacon, and also baseball.

And who's going to hit a home run for me in the game tomorrow.

That part really doesn't hurt.

And the doubt rearing its ugly head deep in the recesses of my overly-superstitious head can bite me.

"Mr. Elliott," Tripp says.

I roll my eyes. "'Scuse me, Skipper. I need to go talk a man off a ledge."

I get a rare smile out of the team's manager, and I turn and march my little butt right up to Tripp Wilson, who's so intent on watching Brooks grin as he makes his own slow march over here, the team's owner doesn't see me coming.

"Excuse me, Mr. Wilson, we need a word."

"Pretty sure *this* mascot theft wasn't your doing, Mackenzie."

"And I'm pretty sure the only way to win the loyal support of your team is for you to put on one of those Fiery Forever T-shirts that I *know* you want to wear anyway, and come play for the mascots."

He doesn't move, but his blue eyes slide sideways to study me for a brief moment.

"You've seen all the movies. You know how this works. The team has to unite against the enemy. You don't want to be that enemy. You know you don't."

He scrubs a hand over his face. "I'm losing all semblance of control here, aren't I?"

"I mean, you're a dad. Losing control is where you shine, right?"

"I'm going to fire you later."

"I don't work for people who let their fiancées fire Fiery."

Brooks stops in front of us, still grinning, and I can totally see the youngest-child thing coming out in him. "Hey, boss. How's it hangin'?"

Tripp looks at him.

Then at me.

Then at my hair.

Then back at Brooks.

He does another one of those sigh-and-try-to-scrub-the-day-off-my-face things, then throws his hands up. "Yep. I'm on the mascots' team. Anyone gets hurt here, you're benched." He takes my elbow and glares at Brooks. "And no fraternizing with the other team."

"That won't be a problem," I assure Tripp. "I can't hit a ball for anything."

"Loser buys dinner, Kenz," Brooks calls.

Tripp lifts another brow at me.

And I almost manage to keep my pulse steady while I smile back at him. "New year, new superstitions. Trust me. Would I do anything to hurt the team?"

He shakes his head. No question, no hesitation. "No. Not you."

I really, really hope we're both right, and that neither of us has misplaced our trust.

Brooks

MY TEAMMATES GIVE me shit through the whole pick-up game against the mascots, Mackenzie, Tripp, and random fans who happen to be in the park at the right place and right time. We're playing modified back yard rules, which means the pros get three at-bats at the top of the inning, then we let the mascots bat in the bottom of the inning until they score.

And I love every damn minute of it.

Especially since Max took the mound, lobbed a soft one to Meaty that hit the meatball right in the flames—automatic walk right there—and then kept pitching to Mackenzie until she got a dribbler down the third-base line that I fumbled so bad, she got a double off my mis-throw to first.

Totally worth it to watch her pump a fist as she jumped on the bag, then stare at me in horror, like she thought I truly fumbled the ball.

Had to stop play for five minutes while I tried to pick myself up off the ground and failed from laughing so hard.

"You still know how to hit a ball?" Rossi asks before I step up to the plate at the top of the third inning.

I flex my grip on the bat and take an easy practice swing. "Nope. Muscle memory's gone. Forgot what the ball looks like, so I can't keep my eye on it. Pitcher's unpredictable. Maybe I'll stand there and hope I get a walk."

Cooper snorts. He was late because he stayed out in Shipwreck last night, so he's playing coach for us. "Go hit the ball, dumbass. Two points if you nail that duck between the eyes."

I head to the plate, and Tripp straightens from his spot playing second. "Hold up. Pitcher change." He points to the third center fielder. "Mackenzie. Get up here."

Yes, third center fielder.

The mascots have nineteen people on the field instead of the usual nine.

"Not fair to put her in without a warm-up, coach," I call.

There's a snort from Spike the Echidna, who's playing catcher, which really means he's letting the ball bounce off him and then turns in circles trying to find it while one of the security guards from Duggan Field who came with them jogs over to toss the ball back.

The cameras love it.

"Problem, Spike?"

"Pretty sure you warmed her up plenty, Elliott." His voice is decidedly feminine, and it sounds like the big boss lady. "Hit her with a line drive, and that's all on you."

Oh, shit.

I look back at the infield.

Mackenzie's arguing with Tripp and the current pitcher, a walk-on fan who played softball through college and brings the heat, and it's very clear that neither woman wants to switch up.

I swing my bat up onto my shoulders and loop my arms over it, getting in a good back stretch while I twist back and forth. "C'mon, Kenz. Make him regret it."

She glares at me. "I'm going to hit you with a ball because *I can't throw*."

"Then it won't hurt."

Her *you shut your mouth right now* glare is adorable, and I duck my head, but I know she can still see me laughing, so I step back from the plate. "Take a warm-up throw. And don't worry. I have good reflexes."

Tripp says something else to the two women, and the pitcher nods and hands Mackenzie the baseball.

I know it's not the first time she's touched a baseball.

And she's wrong. She can throw.

Maybe not pitch, but she can throw. She manages to get Spike right in the gut.

"You okay?" I ask Lila, who *oofed* inside the costume.

"Quit smiling, Elliott."

"That looked like it hurt. Like maybe you should've let Fiery catch today."

"I'd fire you if this game hadn't been your idea."

"Your fiancé's the one who put Mackenzie on the mound. Take it up with him."

"Ready," Mackenzie calls. "Batter up! And if you don't hit this ball…"

I square up to the plate and dig in, which isn't as easy without cleats on, but I'm not going to hit this ball.

Not hard, anyway.

She winds up in an impressive imitation of Max's pitching stance, and when that ball leaves her hands, it's on a straight trajectory to somewhere at least six feet outside the batter's box on the other side of home plate.

"*Strike one!*" Cooper yells.

I look at him. "Dude. Same team."

"She's prettier."

I'd flip him off, but there are three camera crews capturing the game, and also, yeah, we can totally call that a strike.

"Go easier on the next one," I call to her.

Her nose crinkles.

Ah, that nose. I want to kiss her nose. Her cheeks. The corners of her eyes. That little mole in front of her left ear.

Her left ear.

Her right ear.

Shit, I'm not wearing a cup.

Think about Knox's nana. Think about Knox's nana.

Picturing the ancient old bird chatting about alien penises shaped like evergreen trees—complete with pinecones—and vaginas with teeth definitely helps.

Mackenzie misses the ball when the security guy throws it back to her.

The main pitcher retrieves it for her and slaps her on the butt. "You got this, kid. Aim for his head."

"I don't want to hit his head."

"Trust me."

Mackenzie locks eyes with me.

I tap my noggin, then square up in my batter's stance.

She squeezes her eyes shut and lets the ball fly.

"Strike two!" Cooper yells.

Lopez mutters something in Spanish that roughly translates to, "It went into the dugout, idiot."

But a little more colorful.

Cooper shrugs. "No take-backs."

Mackenzie jogs over to her own dugout and fishes out the ball herself, then trots back to the mound.

She's in stilettos.

She's playing baseball in work pants, a white blouse that's dusted brown from the dirt kicking up all over the field, and stilettos.

I'm going to marry this woman.

"I'm going to roll this one," she calls to me.

"Let it fly, baby."

"Don't call the opposing team *baby*. It's bad luck," Max yells from our bench.

Cooper points at him. "Hey, hey, there's no superstitions in park ball. You're grounded. Jarvis, think you can pitch? Stafford, you're at third. Elliott, right field."

We all stare at him.

"Go! Go!" He flaps his arms at us. "Inning's over. Mackenzie struck everyone out."

"She's thrown two pitches, and Elliott's our first batter."

"Yeah, and you saw those pitches. She's gonna strike all of you losers out. You want me to forfeit the game, or you want to try to make up some runs from the outfield?"

"I'm not done!"

We all look back at the mound, where Mackenzie stomped her foot so hard, her stiletto got stuck in the ground, and she's struggling to pull it out of the dirt.

Cooper holds his hands up in surrender. "Okay, okay. You can embarrass us. Simmons. Get out there and help the lady before she falls."

Too late. I'm already on my way.

"Quit laughing," she says as I make her lean on me while I pluck her shoe—foot and all—out of the dirt.

"You're magnificent. And I can't remember the last time I had this much fun." I tilt my head as I straighten, making sure she's back on solid footing. "Maybe that time I helped Rhett take down a few commandos when Eloise was in trouble, but in a different kind of way."

She blinks like she's trying to decide if I'm serious or not.

I decide she probably doesn't want to know, and instead, distract her with something else. "Lila's in the Spike costume. This is your only chance to show her how you really feel about this mascot contest. I know you can throw a real strike."

"I *will not* strike you out."

"It's for fun, Kenz. You have to. And then tomorrow, I'm gonna whoop some San Francisco ass."

"I also can't actually throw a ball at Lila. That's mean."

"Yeah, and killing Fiery wasn't mean at all."

Irritation lights her eyes.

"Elliott! Get your hands off the pitcher. This isn't flirt ball. It's baseball!"

We both look at Cooper, and we're not the only two people on this field silently calling him two-faced.

In the friendly way, of course.

The mascot team's real pitcher smacks her fist in her glove. "Get back to the plate, Elliott. We need to finish you off."

I step away from Mackenzie and nod to the other woman. "You got it, boss."

"And can you sign a ball for me before you go?"

"Absolutely."

"Ohmygod, thank you so much. My grandma is like your biggest fan. She's gonna sleep with it."

"So you know," Spike-Lila says as I square up at the plate for my third pitch, "if you hurt Mackenzie, they won't ever find your body."

Considering what I know about Lila's connections, I believe that.

Mackenzie lifts her glove and peers over it, and for the love of all that's holy, the sight of her in those stilettos, holding a baseball glove and peering at me with raw determination flashing in her baby blues, is going to fuel every last one of my spank bank fantasies for the rest of my life.

Her eyes shift from me to Spike, and I see the exact moment she makes up her mind.

She drops her glove, winds up, and lets that ball fly.

It hits the dirt three feet in front of her and rolls slowly the rest of the way to the plate while we all watch.

"Strike three!" Cooper crows. "Elliott, get your butt back here for remedial batting practice."

"Nice pitching, Ms. Cy Young," I call as I head back to the dugout, kicking the dirt for extra effect.

"I expect my trophy delivered by tomorrow," she calls back.

Everyone in a six-block radius cracks up, and she curtsies before handing the ball back to the pitcher.

Cooper slaps me on the shoulder as I make my way past. "Hurt her and die, dude."

Luca shakes his head. "Dying's too good for him. Plucking his toenails out and permanently tattooing hearts on his face first."

"Doesn't anybody care that they're both smiling for the first time in forever?" Robinson asks.

I fist-bump him.

"Ah, to be young and idealistic," Cooper sighs.

Fuck, I love these guys. "Don't you have a goat to torture?"

"No, the goat and I are planning a bachelor party. Big difference. Get your glove. Darren and Francisco are about to strike out too. And I meant it. Right field for you. You can pitch in the fifth."

An hour later, the mascots have whomped us seventeen to nine, and my face hurts from laughing so much. We all sign autographs—including Mackenzie and the pitcher—until Tripp and Lila and security order us all to get out of the park.

The local news picked up the story, and the crowds are getting a little too big.

I snag Mackenzie and drag her and Coco Puff back to my SUV. "You need to go back to work?"

She frowns at me. "I struck you out."

"That was rigged. My game is *fine*. Better than fine. The best." I kiss her nose, because I can. "Keep the belief, Kenz. Keep the belief."

33

Mackenzie

I BELIEVE.

I believe.

I believe.

And I believe that if Brooks doesn't take his ass back to his apartment to see what we've done to it in the next five minutes, I'm going to break and tell him everything.

He pulls out of the parking lot with a few disappointed fans dashing behind the Land Rover, which I swear smells like our naked bodies, and which I would like so much more if he'd gotten a hit in our pick-up baseball game today.

I shift in my seat to look at him, and I can't resist settling a hand on his thigh, because first of all, it's a very nice thigh, and second of all, I need to touch it while I still can. "Can we go to your place?"

He starts to wince, and I blurt, "It's closer," and tug my shirt low while I push my breasts up.

The Land Rover swerves, and his shorts tent. "Yes."

I don't remember getting to his parking garage. Or getting in the elevator.

But now that we're here, I'm very much enjoying having his hands up my shirt while he backs me against the mirror and kisses me like nothing in the world exists except the two of us.

We might accidentally ride the elevator all the way to the top of the building, which is several floors above Brooks's apartment, and where an old lady joins us.

"Give her breathing room, sonny," she snaps.

We leap apart.

She punches the button for the ground floor.

Brooks rubs the back of his neck and angles his body away from her—presumably so she doesn't see the pole in his shorts—while I push the button for his floor.

She *harumphs* at both of us, and I get the feeling she'll bop us both with her cane if we try anything in the meantime.

I meet Brooks's eye.

He coughs, lips twitching, and I struggle so hard to suppress a giggle that I end up hiccupping.

Coco Puff barks.

"The world is better because you're in it!" his collar announces.

And even the old lady giving us the stink-eye smiles at the puppy.

We tumble out of the elevator on Brooks's floor after what feels like seventy-five million years trapped with the old lady, who's starting to smell like roses and microwaved fish. Even Coco Puff snorts out a sneeze of relief when we get to fresher air.

Brooks fumbles with his keys, then fumbles with jiggling the right key in the lock, his ears turning brighter and brighter red the whole time. When it finally clicks open, he turns to block my view without a single glance inside. "I told Rhett to find me a shithole."

My brows shoot up, and he keeps talking. "I knew, without a doubt, that I wasn't really coming here to stay, that New York would want me back once I was gone, and that this would be temporary. I knew they wouldn't betray me like that."

"Brooks," I whisper, because my heart hurts like someone's taken the Fireballs from me.

I don't know how that would feel. I don't *want* to know.

But he knows.

He knows, because he's lived it.

He shakes his head. "You were right. I forgot what it meant to be a baseball player. I forgot what it meant to be someone that little kids all over the country look up to. I forgot why I visit children's hospitals. I forgot why I donate to everyone else's foundations. And I forgot why I ever wanted to wear a uniform in the first place. And I didn't forget in spring training. I didn't forget when I got here to Copper Valley. I forgot sometime between the time I made it to the big leagues and the end of last year. New York knew it. I wasn't a leader in the dugout anymore. I was playing for the paycheck. I was *relieved* when we didn't make it to the post-season."

I swallow hard. "Burnout happens. You've been playing for a long time—"

"Being here—having you holding me accountable, believing in the team, pushing me to be better again—I get it. I remember. I *want* to be the guy the rookies come to when they need to figure out how to navigate the big leagues, how to know when their agent isn't looking out for them, and which veterans they can prank without waking up with a taxidermied snake in their freezer. I want to be the player that kids pretend to be while they're catching balls. I want to remember how it feels to make a difference. I want to be the hero you thought all baseball players were, until I fucked that all up for you."

Oh, my heart.

This *isn't* about him having sex or staying a virgin. It's not about where he lives.

It's about who he is. Who he was. And who he wants to be.

"Gods," I whisper.

"What?"

"I thought baseball players were gods."

"Fuck, Mackenzie, I can't fix that."

I shake my head. "But you did. I *shouldn't* have thought baseball players were gods. You're not. You're human, and I expected too much. You get to have off-days, Brooks. You get to make mistakes."

"Not at this level."

"At *every* level. You get to be a real person with flaws. And you *should* enjoy your job."

"You're helping me remember why I loved it in the first place."

He pulls my fingers to his lips and presses a soft kiss to my knuckles, and I melt into a happy puddle of *I am so in love with this man*.

"I hate this apartment. Let me grab a bag, and we'll go to your place. Or another park. Or bowling. Or somewhere. *Anywhere*. So long as I go with you."

"I like being with you."

He's smiling an eye-crinkling smile as he turns inside and freezes.

Glances back at the door like he's checking the apartment number, then looks at me.

I suck my lips into my mouth and try to look innocent, which I'm sure does the exact opposite.

But that bewilderment making his hazel eyes flare wide and his lips part—yeah, that was worth the wait.

So long as the end result is that he doesn't hate his apartment anymore.

Or, hell, I don't care if he still hates it. He can think it's even uglier. He can miss the echidna penises drawn on the ceiling. He can want his lava lamps back.

I just want him to *stay*. I want him to *want* to stay.

And I want him to be happy, no matter how he finds his happiness.

"Did you—"

He cuts himself off with a shake of his head, then drifts deeper into the apartment, checking out the clean gray slate tile in the entryway, the white walls decorated with blown-up prints of New York City landmarks—everything from the baseball stadium to the Brooklyn Bridge—and even glancing up at the ceiling.

At the end of the short entrance, there's a soft red glow over the fresh gray carpet and new white leather couches in the living room.

He walks haltingly deeper inside, as if he's afraid he'll step wrong and hit a button that'll reset the apartment back to what it was before, and when he glances back at me again, my heart squeezes at the astonishment and the husky tone in his voice. "What's this?"

I let the door close with a soft click. "You needed a home. I needed to say sorry for cock-blocking you."

"But how? And in a *week*?"

"Don't ever doubt a woman with connections and taste. Wait. I should probably ask if you like it before I claim we have taste."

He doesn't answer right away. I follow him into the living room, where there's a blown-glass chandelier with color-changing LED lights that are shifting from red to blue, and which I know will cycle to purple before going back to red, but can be set on any color, right down to a simple white. Gray textured pillows and blankets clutter the new white furniture. There's a small stone statue of Fortuna, the goddess of luck, on the simple coffee table, and decorative lamps on the end tables.

He turns in a slow circle, pausing when his gaze lands on the ficus in the corner. "I have plants?"

"And a watering service if you want it."

Coco Puff races across the rug and leaps into a basket filled with squeaky toys and those dildo-looking dog toys. He barks.

"I'm the luckiest dog in the world!" his collar crows.

I gnaw on my lip and lean in the doorway to the kitchen while Brooks looks at me again. I can't read him, partly because I don't have enough practice, and partly because I'm afraid to believe that all that affection overflowing his warm hazel eyes is real.

"Meaty helped." I grab the card we left for him when we thought he'd come here last night, and hold it out to him.

He glances at the meatball's face on the cover, and his grin is so broad and sudden, it's like someone threw back the drapes and let in all the sunshine. "I wouldn't have expected anything less."

"The other mascots didn't know. Meaty doesn't like them. He's an asshole in person."

"Mackenzie."

"What?"

He takes the card and tosses it over his shoulder, then cups my cheek. "Thank you."

"We did it for the whole team," I whisper while my eyelids drift closed.

"This was all for the team?"

"No. It's for you."

"I'm going to kiss you."

"Thank god."

He tucks a strand of hair behind my ear, his fingers lingering on the outer rim, and then his lips brush mine, and *yes*.

This is the kiss I've waited for my entire life.

The *you get me* kiss.

The *you are my everything* kiss.

The *you're my kind of crazy* kiss.

He's not a baseball player.

I'm not an obsessive nutcase.

We're two people who can't keep our hands and bodies to ourselves, learning all there is to know about each other.

And I'm still learning to trust that this can be real. "Why me?" I ask between soft kisses.

"Because you're the sunshine my life has been missing. And I want to be yours."

"I'm not sunshine. I'm crazy."

"You're Nutella-covered bacon in a baked chicken breast world."

Oh, god, this man. "You're a little crazy too, aren't you?"

"You have no idea."

I'm laughing as I lean in to kiss him again, because I can't contain all of my happiness.

Not when everything in the world is this *right*.

"I want to taste you," he says.

And that's all the warning I get before his lips move to my jaw. Then my neck. Down between my breasts. Over my belly, leaving a trail of kisses down my shirt.

I drop my head back against the wall as his hands and mouth reach my waist, and he deftly unbuttons my top button, whispering all the dirty things he wants to do to me, all the places he wants to strip me bare, how many different ways he wants to take me, and I'm helpless to resist.

I want him.

I want him when he's happy. When he's seducing me. When he's frustrated. When he's agitated with me. When he's playing with Coco Puff.

I gasp.

I definitely want him when he's licking my clit. "*Brooks.*"

"Fuck, you taste good."

I clutch my fingers through his hair while he very effectively demonstrates that while he might not have years of experience, he has something better—sheer determination to always be the best.

And *oh my god*, this man.

He is the *absolute* best.

I don't know what I did to deserve him, but heaven help me, no matter what happens to my team tomorrow, I will do everything in my power to keep him.

No. Matter. What.

34

Brooks

I DO Mackenzie on the floor.

In the shower, the kitchen, the hallway, the living room, and against the door.

On my new bed, beneath my unicorn chandelier because apparently free renovations only go so far, and under the watchful eyes of pictures of the entire Thrusters' hockey team, which is a little weird, but then, what isn't weird?

We do it missionary-style. Doggy-style. Twisted pretzel. Trapeze artist-style.

That last one didn't go so well, but at least we didn't get hurt. Also, her breasts are gorgeous when they're jiggling as she laughs until she can't breathe.

I should have every Monday off. And so should she.

Tuesday morning, I'm a mass of satisfied nerve endings serving my beautiful date fresh bacon-Nutella pancake sandwiches too early in the morning, but she has to get to work early to make up yesterday's hours so she can get to the game tonight.

After delaying her longer than I should to kiss her simply because I can, I go back to sleep for a few hours after she's gone, with Coco Puff snoozing next to me, basking in the scent of Mackenzie all over my sheets.

Crazy woman.

And I say that in the good way, for the record.

She's the one.

She's *my* one.

My game won't suffer for falling for her. I won't let it. I refuse to continue to be that guy letting superstitions rule my life.

Not when I can have Mackenzie in my life.

She's choosing me over her team. Over her own superstitions. Over her own beliefs.

She's choosing me.

And so I'm going to put both our superstitions to rest tonight. Once and for all.

My puppysitter arrives on time, and I get to the ballpark around two. Do my normal stretches and warm-ups with Luca and Cooper. Trade insults about who does the worst Robert DeNiro impersonation, because it's fun.

Talk Torres off a ledge when he hears Santiago's not putting him in the starting rotation tonight.

Have a few interviews with the media, who want to talk about yesterday's pick-up game in the park, what pranks are going on in the locker room, and how I'm feeling about heading back to New York later this week for my first time in the stadium up there wearing another team's uniform.

"Good," I answer. "Gonna feel even better when I hit a home run for the Fireballs."

"How's your family feel about that?"

"Dunno. You'd have to ask Sammy Rogers. Ma's calling him Sammy Rogers-Elliott now. Had him over for dinner last week to interview him for the open position of youngest son."

The roomful of reporters gapes at me.

I snicker, because there's no way my family's adopting the guy the Fireballs traded me for just because he took my spot on New York's roster, and then they all start laughing with me.

"Cooper Rock know his position as funniest guy on the team's in danger?" one of them calls.

"There's never too much funny in a team family."

We have a team meeting where Lila hands out our new Fireballs pajamas and orders us to make sure they fit right before we wear them on the plane to New York Friday morning.

They're fucking awesome.

Footies and all.

But the best part?

The best part is the shock that turns to laughter that turns to trash-talking who's gonna look best sporting Fireballs mascot pajamas when we saunter out of Duggan Field to board the bus to the airport Friday morning.

"This is gonna get me laid!" Robinson crows while he models his pajamas over his warm-up gear.

"It's gonna get Elliott cock-blocked," Stafford calls back.

Nah.

We're done with that.

Even if I show up at Mackenzie's place with a giant Meaty on my crotch, which is, appropriately, exactly where the Meaty mascot landed on my pajamas.

I watch videos of San Francisco's starters and talk with Addie about what sort of pitches I'm likely to see today. I take batting practice and hit the ever-loving fuck out of the ball, including one memorable shot into center field that nearly wipes out Glow the Firefly.

He shakes his big round butt at me.

I line up and hit the next practice pitch at him again, and Santiago yanks me out of batting practice. "Think you got this, Elliott, and I'm not losing a player to an interrogation over a mascot death."

I check my phone. Send Mackenzie a few texts.

Send my family a few texts, because Parker's phone is a thing of beauty and even when I'm in a good mood, it makes me happier.

I corner Tripp and Lila and tell them they owe it to Mackenzie to get her in here to toss out the first pitch one of these days, because she's single-handedly brought half of Copper Valley back to baseball with her *Fiery Forever* campaign.

They give me a lecture about the fact that there are thousands of *Fiery Forever* T-shirts being handed out on the corners like they're official Fireballs giveaways.

I pretend innocence.

They don't believe me, but they also don't fire me.

We all know they're only lecturing because it could've been a safety hazard. Like I didn't call Rhett first to get some of his SEAL buddies mulling around in plain clothes to make sure nothing got out of hand.

The crowd starts arriving. I catch sight of Mackenzie in her regular seat with Sarah by her side right before the national anthem, and when we lock eyes, she smiles and blows me a kiss.

Home. Fucking. Run.

The game starts.

Second batter steps up for San Francisco and smacks a grounder. I can't turn around the ball I snag deep in the pocket between shortstop and third fast enough, and a runner gets on base, but we take him down with a double play and don't let anyone score.

We head into the dugout for the bottom of the first. Darren leads off with a single. Luca follows him with a walk.

I step up to bat.

And that's when everything goes to shit.

35

Mackenzie

THAT DID NOT JUST HAPPEN.

I grope for Sarah's hand in the darkness. "Tell me the lights didn't go out the minute Brooks stepped up to the plate. Tell me I went spontaneously blind, and everything in the game is *completely and totally fine.*"

"It's probably a prank." She squeezes my hand back, but she's moving strangely, and a second later, the flashlight lights up on her phone.

The ambient light from the rest of the city makes the whole field gray, not black, and I can make out Brooks's outline at the plate, stepping back while the umpires all rush to home to discuss the situation.

Santiago's heading out too, and so is San Francisco's manager.

Phone flashlights pop on all over the stadium, but the lights don't come back on.

"Is Beck up in the owners' suite?"

"Yes, but I doubt they have any more of a clue what's going on than we do," she replies.

The video screen is black. There's no announcer coming over the speakers to ask everyone to stay calm, so ushers are making their way down the stairs asking people to hold tight for a minute, please.

"Mackenzie."

I look at Sarah.

I don't have to see her to know what she's thinking.

Do not let this go to your head.

My phone buzzes with a text message from Papa.

Mackenzie Renee Montana, DO NOT LET THIS GO TO YOUR HEAD.

It's like he and Sarah are sharing a single mind.

She grips my hand harder. "You know this field needs lots of work still. A mouse probably chewed through the wrong wire. Or the plumbing leaked into the main circuit breaker."

"Sarah."

"*Coincidence.* Do *not* make me beat you with this *Fiery Forever* T-shirt that we both know that man out there at the plate arranged to have given away today *for you.* Do you know how many people in this entire world would do something like that?"

"Six?"

The lights flicker back on at half-strength as Sarah's glaring at me like she's considering strangling me with the shirt, which is probably fair, since there's actually only one person in the world who would order forty thousand Fiery Forever T-shirts so everyone in attendance at Duggan Field today could get one.

I whip my head around to look at the field to check on him, and there he is, whipping his head around to look straight at me.

Like Brooks, too, knows what I'm thinking.

Of course he does.

He knows *me.* So he knows what I'm thinking.

So I will myself to think something different.

Don't be crazy, Mackenzie. Don't be crazy. Don't be crazy.

I give him a little finger wave, then lift the shirt and mouth *thank you.*

Even from halfway across the baseball field, I can see the worry fade from his eyes. His shoulders relax, and he grins before turning back to talking to the guys who've come out of the dugout with him.

He's fine.

He's happy.

He's in his element.

So the lights went out? So what? They came back on, and they're getting brighter by the minute.

Sarah's phone buzzes, and we both look down at the message from Beck.

Backup generators running. Game'll be back in a few. You two okay?

She texts him back that we're fine while the umpires talk to the managers on the field, and people flip their phone lights off.

And three minutes later, Brooks steps back to the plate.

I cover my eyes.

My heart's about to pound out of my chest.

He has to hit the ball.

He has to.

"Mackenzie. He's going to hit the ball." Sarah squeezes me. "Do you want me to stay here, or do you want me to go to the bathroom?"

"Bathroom! Go to the bathroom!"

The crack of a bat rings out, and I wrench my hands away from my eyes in time to see a long line drive drop into foul territory not thirty feet from my seat.

"Go." I flap my hands at Sarah. "*Go!*"

She's sitting on the aisle for just such an emergency—you know, the superstitious kind of emergency—so she leaps up and dashes up the stairs.

Meaty and Glow poke their heads up over the visitors' dugout while Brooks squats in his batting position again.

Meaty.

Meaty's back.

The pitcher winds up.

I hold my breath.

Brooks tips the pitch. Another foul ball. Two strikes.

Now I'm crossing my fingers. And holding my breath. And going a little light-headed.

"You'd think he'd hit better with what they're paying him," someone grouses behind me.

I turn and glare at him and the popcorn dribbled all over his lap.

The umpire makes that noise that sounds like he took a fist to the gut, which means Brooks isn't out yet—that pitch was ball one, so he still has a chance.

Thank Babe Ruth.

All is not lost.

Seven pitches later, I really am on the verge of hyperventilating. He's hit *nine foul balls.*

Nine.

I mean, good on him for wearing the pitcher down this early in the game, but *why can't he hit the ball straight?*

I broke him.

I did.

"Sweetie, you okay?" a very kind gentleman to my right asks.

"None of us are okay with what we're paying for this dingbat who can't hit," the jerk behind me mutters.

I spin around. "Do. Not. Talk. Shit. About. My. Boyfriend."

Holy crap.

My boyfriend.

Brooks is *my boyfriend.*

The fair-weather asshole behind me smirks. "Right. *Your boyfriend.* At least pick someone who can hit a ball if you're going to play pretend."

I see red.

But it's worse than seeing red.

It's seeing red accompanied by the loud, *"EE-RIGHT!"* from down the third base line that means the ump called a strike, which means Brooks is out.

He stands at the plate and gives the ump the *are you shitting me?* look that I've seen on a thousand Fireballs players before, and I don't have to look at the video screen to know what's being replayed.

Fastball. Barely inside the strike zone.

He didn't swing, but he's still out.

Shit.

My phone dings sixteen times in rapid succession, and I don't have to look at those either.

It'll be everyone who loves me, plus all the people who love them, texting me to remind me that one strike-out after *he hit the ball nine times* does not mean he's in a slump.

Sarah comes jogging back down the steps. "That was such a bullshit call. It was below his knees and *not* over the plate at all."

The guy next to me is still studying me. "You're the *Fiery Forever* lady."

"Yeah."

"You really dating Elliott?"

"Yes, she is," Sarah answers for me before I can fumble it myself.

"Tell him I said that was a bullshit call too. Still watching that dive he made to snag that screamer against Atlanta on Sunday on replay all week. Really liking what the new management's doing for the team this year. Nice to see some hope back in the ballpark."

I fist-bump him.

He's right. The bigger point is that the whole team has hope.

Not that Brooks struck out once.

Baseball players strike out all the time. It's part of the game.

This doesn't mean anything at all.

I hope.

3 6

Brooks

I DON'T BOTHER TEXTING Mackenzie after the game. I dash home, grab Coco Puff, and head through downtown to get to her apartment.

She's probably flipping out. I need Sarah's number. Her dads' numbers. Hell, I'll take her boss's number too.

I bang on the door, and it opens within four seconds, and there she is.

My girl.

With big, worried blue eyes, her white *Fiery Forever* T-shirt— huh, it's kinda see-through—and a bag slung over one shoulder.

She opens the door wider. "I was coming to see you. To make sure you're okay."

That stops me short.

For all the shit I've put her through with being an idiot this season, *she's* worried how *I* feel.

This passionate, optimistic ray of sunshine is worried about *me* when I've gone and done the one thing I thought she'd hate me for, and broke my bat to sleep with a woman.

And the weirdest part is, we've become such good friends under all the attraction, I honestly think she'd ask the same if it had been another woman.

Which it won't be.

Ever.

I study her worried eyes, and I nod. "I—yeah. I'm okay. Are *you* okay?"

Was it fun going oh-for-four tonight at bat? No. Especially when the ump called me out *twice* on questionable strikes.

But there's more to baseball than batting, and I was a fucking rock star in the field, plus I helped give Jarvis some excellent relationship advice.

Don't mistake me being a virgin for so long for me being a clueless idiot, and dude was headed to idiot-land.

She threads her fingers through mine. "I'm okay if you're okay. I was worried you'd think—you know."

Yeah. I know. I step into her apartment and pull her into my body. "I'm awesome. Hazard of being me."

Coco Puff barks. "You're a rock star! It's your birthday! Happy birthday! You're a rock star!"

That'd be a lot funnier if she wasn't wrapping her arms around me and squeezing like she's afraid I'm going to bolt. "My dads dropped off my old umpire voodoo doll. We can put pins in his back and knees."

Coco Puff growls.

I start snickering, and soon we're both laughing while my puppy watches us like we're insane.

She tugs us farther into her apartment. "What the *hell* was up with the lights? Tripp and Lila won't answer my texts and Beck swears he didn't get any answers out of them either."

"Cooper says the stadium's too old."

"Ugh. Sarah said the same. Why did Lopez get caught on camera spitting out his drink the fourth inning?"

"Dunno."

She shoves me on the couch and straddles me. "You were standing *right there* with *that look.*"

"What look?" Better question, who cares? I have a lady who smells like Cracker Jacks stroking my chest with one hand and petting my puppy with the other.

"*That* look. You said something funny to him and made him choke on his Gatorade."

"What happens in the dugout stays in the dugout."

"Are you serious right now?"

"I have a very sensitive heart, and I need to know you'd still like me even if I didn't have all the inside dugout scoop."

Truth? I'll tell her anything she wants to know. Even filed away about a dozen stories about my day that I'm dying to share, because I know they'll make her laugh.

She grimaces. "This would be so much easier if you weren't a baseball player."

And that's easily the sweetest thing she's ever said to me, because of all the people in the world who should want to date a baseball player, it's Mackenzie, but she likes me for all the other reasons *besides* me being a baseball player.

I think I just got complicated.

But my heart's glowing and I can't stop smiling, and this isn't because she was the first woman I've ever gone all the way with.

It's because she throws herself headfirst into everything she does with the kind of passion you don't find every day. It's because she has so much heart her body can barely contain it. It's because I know how easy it would be for a heart like that to hurt, and I will move heaven and earth to make sure that she doesn't hurt.

Ever.

She has more belief in her pinky finger than most people have in themselves and all their relatives combined.

I want her to be my first, last, and only.

Her frowny face is getting frownier. "That wasn't supposed to be funny."

"You're so fucking perfect."

Where I expect her to roll her eyes and tell me she's not, instead, all those frownies disappear behind a soft smile that says it doesn't matter that I didn't get a single hit tonight.

Because I hit a home run with her.

Don't we all want to be perfect to someone? And loved for who we are under the jerseys we wear?

"You're going to hit the ball tomorrow."

Her conviction is contagious, and I smile even bigger. "Yes, ma'am, I most definitely am."

"I should really try harder to resist you."

She slips her hands under my shirt and pushes it up my chest, then follows her hands with her tongue.

Thank fucking god.

She still wants me.

And she's not resisting wanting me.

Mackenzie Montana is seducing me.

One kiss, one touch, one little happy noise at a time.

She doesn't stop me as I tug her shirt off and treat her to the same pampering she's giving me.

Nope.

She reaches between us and strokes my rock-hard dick through my shorts, and *fuck*, this isn't enough.

Not nearly enough.

"Ms. Montana, are you trying to ruin me?"

"Absolutely."

Her playful smile makes my dick strain harder than he's ever strained before, and instinct takes over my body as I swoop her over my shoulder and carry her into her bedroom while she shrieks with laughter.

Coco Puff dances behind us, barking for playtime.

"You're the best! You can do it!" his collar cheers, and Mackenzie and I both crack up.

"Can we get one in Fireball sayings?" I ask as I toss her onto her bed.

"I love when you talk dirty to me."

I love shucking my pants and crawling onto the bed with her. Having her tackle me with a kiss and roll so she's on top.

Her kisses.

Her moans.

Her heart.

She's seen me at my worst. She's brought me back from my worst.

She's getting my best now, and it doesn't matter how little experience I have.

She *fits*. I fit.

Nothing in my life has ever felt this right.

Pretty sure I love everything about this woman.

She pulls out of the kiss and pushes up, stroking my chest. "If baseball didn't exist, what would you be doing right now?"

"You."

"I wouldn't know you if it wasn't for baseball." Gentle fingers thread through my hair, and that smile—*god*, that smile. It puts my dick on edge and ready to explode.

Good thing she's willing to give me a lot more practice.

"I would still want *you*."

She rewards me with the kiss to end all kisses. The one that's not lips and tongues and teeth, but hopes and dreams and dancing souls.

The home run of kisses.

The grand slam of kisses.

The kiss that says *this is my gift to you*.

The kiss that says *I'd want you too even if baseball didn't exist*.

Yeah.

I'm done for.

She's my one.

Forever.

And I'm gonna fucking win the whole damn season for her to prove it.

Mackenzie

BROOKS HASN'T GOTTEN a hit in three games.

I'm pretending like I'm not freaking out about this, but the truth is, I am freaking out about this.

Sarah hands me a plate of loaded bacon cheese fries in Beck's penthouse Friday night while the pre-game talking heads debate what's wrong with Brooks's bat as he returns to the stadium he called home for so many years, but how nice it is that the Fireballs still took their home series with San Francisco early this week.

"But the sex is good, right?" Sarah says.

"The man is still a god, which is ridiculously impressive, but *he can't hit a*—oh my god. *Oh my god.*" I drop a big ol' handful of cheesy bacon fries on the ground and dive for her left hand. "*Oh my god.*"

I'm suddenly crying.

I'm laughing and crying and hugging my best friend in the entire universe while she does the same, because she's wearing the most gorgeous engagement ring I've ever seen, and it's so *Sarah*, and so perfect, and she's glowing.

She's glowing so bright I can feel it.

I pull back and wipe at my eyes, and even though part of my heart is still terrified that I broke Brooks, right now, I can't stop smiling. "When? How? *Why didn't you call me?* I want to know everything."

Beck walks in, takes one look at both of us, grins like he was appointed Best Man Ever To Exist In The Universe, and casually strolls to his kitchen like it's no big deal.

"This morning," she whispers quickly. "It was *so* sweet. And so Beck. And—"

The elevator dings, and Coco Puff flips out.

Like, flips out barking so hard I can't hear his collar translating anything.

"And my parents flew in," she finishes as I lunge for the puppy, who's lunging for the entrance, where Sarah's parents are rushing in with their pet pig, who's also being rushed by Sarah's cat, whom Coco Puff usually gets along with very well, except, apparently, when there's a teacup pig in the house.

"Cupcake!" Sarah's mom shrieks.

"Back, foul beasts of hell," her dad growls while he leaps between the animals.

Beck shrugs, leans over and snags Coco Puff in one hand, the cat in the other, and nods to Sarah's parents. "'Sup?"

Sarah's mom bursts into tears.

Happy tears, I mean.

"It's about time," she sobs.

And then the rest of us burst into tears again.

Which is how my dads find us. All laughing and crying and hugging and making bigger and bigger plans around Sarah and Beck for how their wedding will be, while I know full well that by the end of the night, they'll be on a plane to some amazing location where they'll have a simple ceremony on a beach or in the mountains, and then they'll let Sarah's parents throw the reception to end all receptions later.

Beck's family shows up too—his sister, brother-in-law-slash-best-friend, his parents, and lots of his friends from the neighborhood where he grew up.

They're not my family, but they've adopted Sarah as one of their own, and by extension, I feel like I belong too.

"Oh, Mackenzie, your boyfriend's up to bat," Dad says.

And then I remember the moments I don't want to belong, because now, eighty million eyeballs are all on me.

Or, you know, twenty or thirty sets. It just feels like eighty million eyeballs waiting for me to explain that yes, I, Mackenzie Montana, the woman who couldn't talk to baseball players the last time most of these people saw me, is now dating a baseball player.

"I'll go to the bathroom!" Sarah cries. "Mom, keep Cupcake out of the fries. Beck—get the pumpkin spice candles!"

Beck's sister twists her head and frowns at the screen. "Wait. Isn't that the guy whose sister told us all—"

Beck reaches around and muffles her mouth. "Nope. Not that guy. Nuh-uh. Couldn't be."

"Not him," someone else who was there when Parker and Knox spilled the beans at a cookout last fall agrees.

Agreement rolls through the room, and I hold my breath while I watch the screen.

Brooks is choking up on the bat too high, and his shoulders are too tight. There's also a deep frown marring his normal placid concentration.

He looks exactly the same way I would if the Fireballs moved across the country, and I accidentally got tickets to see the new version of them play while I was traveling to Chicago or New York for work or something.

"Breathe, Mac." Tripp's brother, Levi, pats my shoulder. "He's got this."

I nod. I even lunge for my phone and type out a quick text message, knowing that even though he won't see it until after the game, I need to put the positive vibes out into the universe.

But a *You can do it!* isn't enough, so I snap a picture of Coco Puff and send that too.

And three seconds later, Brooks makes contact with the ball.

It's a ground ball headed up the middle.

"*Yes!*" I pump my fist. "Run, baby, run run *ru*—dammit!"

How the hell did that second baseman both snag that ball *and* make that throw? I mean, Cooper could make that throw, but I dislike the other team doing it.

"He hit the ball, Mackenzie." Sarah jogs back into the living room. "If it was a slump, he wouldn't be able to connect at all."

"Preach, girl." Papa holds up a hand, and she high-fives him.

Right.

So all I have to do is text him before every at-bat, and send him a picture of Coco Puff, and life will be absolutely perfect.

"Mackenzie," Papa sighs.

"Leave her alone, Lou. If she wants to text him every time he's at bat, let her text him every time he's at bat. She's *clearly* good for his chi. Love never hurts anyone."

The screen flashes, and I gasp in recognition.

Brooks's whole family is there.

At least, I assume that's his parents and two other brothers sitting with Parker, Knox, Rhett, and Eloise.

They're all in Fireballs jerseys.

And I think I just fell in love with his family too.

"Sarah," I whisper.

She squeezes my hand. "What?"

"I'd rather have Brooks than see the Fireballs win a championship. Does that make me a bad fan?"

"No. It means you're putting the man before the baseball player, and that's the best thing you can do to support the people you love, and, by extension, the team. And you *know* that."

"But why would he love *me*?"

She clears her throat and points to the screen, where Parker's spilled a giant soda all over herself on national television.

I start giggling.

"Mackenzie Renee." Papa glares at me.

I suck my lips in, but I can't stop laughing. Sarah's snickering beside me too.

Beck shakes his head at my dads, both of whom are glaring at me now. "Dudes. Let the ladies bask in their solidarity however they need to. It's like me laughing when someone gets tasered. They've been there, you know? Cheesecake?"

I hug Sarah. "I'm so glad you two are getting married."

Her smile overtakes the entire city. "Me too. Now, let's go cheer on some Fireballs."

3 8

Brooks

I AM the biggest loser in the history of losers.

It's been five days since Mackenzie rocked my world in the back of my truck, and five days since I've gotten a base hit.

"It's over," I tell my beer.

"Yeah, you're a loser," my beer agrees.

My beer sounds a lot like Rhett.

I squint at the foam at the edges of the amber liquid, then up at the three Rhetts across the two tables from me.

Dude is *good*. Like, he might be retired from being a dolphin, or a sea otter, or a—a SEAL, that's what he was—but he can still make himself be three people and two tables at once.

I hiccup.

"Nice, dude," the beer says.

We fist-bump, and it spills itself all over my pants.

Fuck.

Am I wearing pants?

I squint at my legs.

Shorts.

Right.

I'm wearing shorts. And my broken Fireball Man thong.

That's what's weird about my junk.

Feels different without the cup on. And when my junk is rolling over and playing dead.

Like Coco Puff. The playing part, I mean. Coco Puff isn't dead, because the universe isn't that cruel.

Though I'm probably dead to Coco Puff for how awful I've played this week.

"Wipe yourself up, doofus." Parker shoves napkins at me, and when I don't take them right away, Rhett, Jack, and Gavin—all eleven of them—tackle my legs and tickle the ever-loving fuck out of me.

The beer tells me I'm on my own, so I do the second-best thing I can do to fighting back.

I praise the baseball gods that I'm not as ticklish as Rhett is, and I start singing.

I don't even know what this song is, I just know I need to sing it right now while I'm flopping around on the ground avoiding the tickles.

"Beeeeer, beer beer beer *WHISSSSSSSSSSKEY*. Whiskey and *PIIISSSSSSSSSSSKEY*. They rhyme on a *MIIIIIIIIIIME*."

Jack breaks first, crowing and clapping his hands over his ears as he leaps back.

I sing awesome.

Great self-defense.

"I got your back, Jack," Eloise yells, and she leaps on me too, going for that spot under my arms like I actually showered after the game, which I might not've.

I'm in a piss-poor mood.

A weirdly happy piss-poor mood.

I like it, but I don't want to.

Definitely need more singing. "Rum in a blaaaaaaaanket, shooooooooooes in the *moooooooooorning*."

"*Dammit*, asshole, I hate that song." Gavin shoves a tortilla in my mouth, because there are always tacos when Parker's around.

I love tacos.

I don't deserve tacos.

Rhett and Eloise are still trying to tickle me, but Rhett suddenly yelps, and then Eloise leaps to her feet.

She's fast for a pregnant chipmunk. Might lose the babies out her pouch if she's not careful.

Are we at the zoo?

When did chipmunks get tattoos?

I don't ask why Mackenzie's ghost is threatening to rip the ultrasound picture that Rhett and Eloise brought here to—*Parker's apartment*.

Dude.

I'm in my sister's apartment. That's why there are zebra stripes and leopard prints all over.

And unicorns.

What's a leopard unicorn? A leopracorn? A unipard?

"Apologize," Mackenzie's ghost orders.

Fuck it. "I'm sooooooorry I can't hiiiiiiiiiit a ballllllllllll," I sing.

If you can call it that.

I'm losing the tune I never had in the first place.

Knox falls off his chair laughing.

I forgot he was here.

Huh. He lives here.

He lives here, with my sister, because they're married, and they're in love, and they're normal—for Parker being an Elliott by birth—and they don't have to worry about how having sex ruins their careers.

Fuck, sometimes they have sex *at Parker's office*.

I reach for the closest thing I can find and throw it at him.

And because I'm a loser, it goes right through him and bounces off Mackenzie's ghost.

Rhett punches me in the arm. "Bro, don't throw unicorn sex toys at your girlfriend."

If he's gonna be an idiot, I'mma keep on singing. "Knooooox ain't my giiiiiiiiiirlfrriiieeeend."

"Is he drunk?" the angel ghost asks.

I stare at her, because *fuck*, I miss her, and I really, really want to touch her, but since I can't, and she hates me—even if she says she doesn't when Coco Puff calls—I'm gonna sit here, in a puddle of beer, and watch her until she fades away.

"I think he got into the special brownies Nana brought over yesterday," Knox whispers.

"Oh my god."

Wow.

Hologram Mackenzie sounds exactly like regular Mackenzie would. There's no static or anything.

"Brooks, how many brownies did you eat?"

"Seventy-four."

Parker contradicts me with some number that makes it sound like I'm on a diet, so I flip her off.

I think.

With my toes, maybe? My fingers aren't moving right.

Dude.

I can make the *Star Trek* sign. What is that saying that goes with it? Drink long and stop her?

No, that's not it.

Drink—live—prosper—froghopper.

I giggle.

"Brooks."

Ghost-hologram Mackenzie touches my arm, and *poof!*

That part of my body sobers up.

"You have fingers."

She briefly pinches her eyes shut, but she's also pinching her smiling lips shut like ghost-hologram-angel Mackenzie doesn't want to mock me.

She's so sweet.

An angel.

I said that already.

"You're damn lucky weed's legal in baseball now."

"I'm dry."

"You're drunk and high, crazy-ass," Parker says.

I grin. "I know. Drunk-high. Dry. Heh." They need to be serenaded. "*I'm soooooooo awesoooooooome.*"

The ceiling has glitter on it. And it's moving.

Knox leans into my field of view, frowning. "I think Nana needs to tweak her recipe, and I need to throw those brownies out."

"Fucking pregnancy," Eloise mutters. "I want a brownie."

I grab ghost-angel-with-a-body Mackenzie. "Don't tell real Mackenzie I suck."

"Real Mackenzie?"

"The real Mackenzie. The one I love. The one back home, that I'm disappointing because I broke her team."

Shit. I'm making angel Mackenzie cry.

I'm going to hell. Baseball hell. Where I'll never hit a ball again, and my team will always lose because I'm a loser.

"You love me?" she whispers.

"Shh. Don't tell real Mackenzie. I have to win for her first."

"No, you don't."

"Glow said so."

"I'm going to punch Glow in that big-ass glowing butt." She swipes at her eyes, then bends over and kisses me, and huh.

I can touch her. And smell Cracker Jacks. And taste heaven.

"You're real Mackenzie." Shit. Did I say something stupid about duck porn? Or did I just think that?

Doesn't matter.

She's laughing and kissing my face and straddling my stomach, and one of my brothers tells us to get a broom.

And he thinks I'm the drunk one?

"I don't need a broom," I tell Mackenzie.

She buries her face in my neck and shakes with laughter, and maybe it's the beer, or maybe it's the weed, or maybe it's my dick, but something tells me that I still have a shot at scoring tonight.

Either miracles really do happen, or I'm gonna need a lot more of those brownies before this season's over.

39

Mackenzie

I WATCH the sun come up over New York City and the ballpark that Brooks called home for so many years from the balcony of his condo. He's still sleeping—poor guy was a mess last night, and yes, I enjoyed every last minute of sloppy, drunk-high Brooks being a complete and total goofball until the minute he looked at his bed, said *hi, old bed, are you real too?* and collapsed fast asleep without even taking off his clothes.

He's so damn perfect.

And he's been through so much.

The least I can do is to be here for him today.

I confess, I'm not *only* watching the sun come up.

I'm also texting with his family.

ELOISE: Okay, Meatball Thief. You need to spill all the details on knowing ALL OF THE BRO CODE GUYS immediately, or I'm calling a guy I know who knows a guy who can slip penis-shrinker into Bazookarooka's Gatorade, and I don't think you can afford for his weewee to shrink any more.

PARKER: Cabana pubic hair nightmare.

. . .

JACK: Dammit, Parker, you just ruined the beach for all of us.

ELOISE: Dude, if you're afraid of pubic hair, you have more problems than I thought. Also, thanks for the Christmas present idea.

KNOX: Bro Code. Mackenzie. Please, for the love of I LIKE LICKING PICKLES, tell us about Bro Code.

KNOX: I LIKE LICKING PICKLES.

GAVIN: Shit. Our Parker translator broke.

RHETT: Bugs are contagious. Especially during phone sex. Wash your hands. Private Montana, if you don't tell my wife what she wants to know, I'll come over there and torture it out of you.

MACKENZIE: I'll tell you everything I know about the Bro Code guys if you send me pictures of Brooks as a baby.

ELOISE: Lame. What if I send you his sex tape?

PARKER: *knife emoji* *Eloise emoji*

RHETT: 1. Don't threaten my wife. 2. Where'd you get that tatted up awesomeness? I NEED THAT EMOJI NOW.

JACK: We need to go back to Brooks's sex tape. I thought he was a virgin.

. . .

Gavin: NO SEX TAPE.

Knox: Hot Crazy Pants did it in the back door.

Parker: *gif of woman covering her eyes and ears*

Gavin: *laughing crying emoji*

Jack: I never thought I'd say this, but I think Knox is my new hero.

Rhett: Babe...I think you screwed up in programming Knox's phone. Or you screwed up in downloading porn at the library. Not sure which.

Parker: *picture of a note reading "Eloise downloaded porn at the library and then did a bad paste job of Brooks's face into the video. It's awful. But also really amazing."*

Mackenzie: I legit think I'm in love with all of you.

Brooks: Not the wake-up I expected. Come back to bed?

I DROP my phone and look into the bedroom.

Brooks is sitting up in his bed, shirtless—he pulled it off in the middle of the night before rolling over and cuddling me—with the covers pooled around his waist.

He gives me a hesitant, lopsided smile, and my heart swells at the uncertainty in his eyes.

This poor man.

I made him think he's nothing more than a baseball-hitting machine, when I know he's so much more.

"Morning." I slide onto the bed next to him, practically in his lap, and wrap my arms around him while I kiss his cheek. "Feeling okay?"

"You're here."

"I left Coco Puff with my dads. He wanted to come, but I could get here faster without him."

"You didn't have to come. I was going to be home tonight."

I heave an exaggerated sigh and shift to straddle him, then cup his cheeks. "Brooks Elliott, I am *not* letting you sit here, alone, when you need me."

He winces.

But I don't let him look away. "The Fireballs won. Two games in a row. They've *won*. And do you know why?"

"Because everyone else on the team is awesome?"

"*Because you're a team*. So you didn't get a hit. So what? Are you in the dugout telling people it's hopeless, or are you in there daring them to look better in their footy pajamas than you do? Are you telling Robinson his glove has a hole in it, or are you smacking him on the butt and telling him he'll get the next fly ball?"

"Kenz—"

"*I'm a damn good baseball player, and I'm a damn good teammate.* Say it."

He mumbles it under his breath.

"Say it louder, or I'm going to take my shirt off and seduce you with my breasts."

His gaze snaps back to mine.

"Okay, yes, I'm also going to seduce you when you say it." I can steal a meatball costume, but I can't lie to him.

"You…you're not mad?"

"I'm only mad at me for everything I've done to make you think that I'd be mad."

"The Fireballs are your team."

"And you're the man I love."

It slips out, but I don't want to take it back, because I love him.

I do.

My eyes go damp as he studies me like he's not so sure he's not still hallucinating, and the memory of him telling "not-real-Mackenzie" that he loves her makes me smile as I say it again. "Brooks Elliott, I am hopelessly, irresistibly in love with you. And it's not because you can hit a baseball. And it's not because you wear my favorite team's uniform. And it's not because you let me take your virginity in the back of your car. It's because this heart—" I brush a hand over his chest "—this heart right here speaks to the gigantic mess of a superstitious dork who lives in my heart and who knows how it feels to want to be loved for the weirdo that she is under all the makeup and Fireballs clothing."

His arms slip around me while he blinks away the shine in his eyes. "Do you have any idea how amazing you are?"

"Maybe a little."

"Good." He laughs, and suddenly I'm pinned beneath him on his mattress in this very comfortable, very modern bedroom that he used to call home.

"I'm going to kiss you," he informs me.

"I'm going to kiss you back."

"I'm not doing it for luck."

"I left all my luck behind in Copper Valley, so I couldn't give you any even if I wanted to."

"Did you bring your belief?"

"Brooks." I comb my fingers through his messy bedhead, smiling because I can't help myself. "I will *always* bring my belief, and it's not about what happens in a ballpark. It's about what happens in here."

I touch his heart again, and he lowers his lips to mine.

A relieved shudder passes through my whole body as our mouths connect, because honestly?

It was a little terrifying to find him drunk and high and talking about how he broke my favorite team.

I was afraid I broke *him*.

"I'm never putting baseball ahead of you ever again," I whisper against his lips.

"I love you," he whispers back.

Those words soak into my soul, and all the chaotic parts inside me still.

This is what I've wanted.

It's not about winning and losing. It's about being accepted for who I am.

It's what I've offered my favorite team my entire life, and with three little words, this man who doesn't have to love me, who could've—and probably should've—walked away from me and never looked back two months ago, it's what he's offering me in my *whole* life.

He kisses the tears wetting my cheeks, and then he kisses my jaw.

My neck.

My breasts.

He pauses and looks up at me. "I wasn't born to win baseball games, Kenz. I was born to win *you*."

"Maybe you can do both?"

His eyes flare wide, and I break into laughter.

"So that's how this is going to be," he says as his own smile comes back. "You giving me trouble for the rest of my life."

I push his shoulder, and he obliges and rolls over so I can straddle him. "Brooks Elliott, I'm going to give you *everything* for the rest of your life."

A wicked grin lights his features. "Bring it, Montana."

I do.

And then I do again.

And once more, for good luck.

EPILOGUE

Mackenzie

I NEVER EXPECTED I'd be a Fireballs girlfriend, but here I am, at a meeting for the Lady Fireballs, discussing the auctions we're starting up again during home series to raise money for the new children's outreach foundation Tripp and Lila are starting to bring more outdoor opportunities to kids across the metro area.

We're going to fund everything from upgraded playground equipment to baseball and softball teams.

And I know exactly how to do it.

"We need to auction off the mascots," I announce.

Lila's eyes cross.

Tanesha Greene cracks up and accidentally pulls her boob out of the baby's mouth, and he erupts in the cutest wail you've ever heard.

Sarah, who's an honorary Lady Fireball because she's awesome, ducks her head under the table because while Tanesha can laugh openly, Sarah's still trying to maintain an air of neutrality in the ongoing debate over the mascots.

We're almost at the All-Star break, and they *still* haven't canceled the mascot voting.

It's getting ridiculous.

"Fine, fine." I wave a hand magnanimously, which was a good word from Cooper's word-of-the-day calendar. "We can wait to auction them off until *after* they all lose to write-in votes for Fiery this fall."

The door swings open, and Tripp sticks his head in before Lila can beat me with a foam finger. "Mackenzie. Got a minute?"

"For the sake of my ability to keep breathing, yes."

Sarah laughs openly at that.

Tripp takes one look at Lila, grins, and then quickly sobers back to Mr. Serious Team Co-Owner. "Ah, carry on without Ms. Montana here," he tells the room.

"*Fiery forever,*" I whisper with a side eye at Lila.

They love me.

They really do, even if they pretend they don't.

Out in the concrete hallway beneath the stands at Duggan Field, I smile brightly at Tripp. "What's up, boss?"

"For the last time, stop calling me that."

"I thought you liked to pretend that I work for the Fireballs."

He suppresses a smile, and you can't tell me that's not what his contorting facial muscles are doing. I refuse to believe anything other than a smile is going on there.

It helps that he mutters, "You and Elliott really are made for each other."

Highest. Compliment. Ever.

I turn so he can see my jersey. Brooks brought it home last night, and it has his number, along with *Brooks Elliott's Girlfriend, #1 Fireballs Fan* stitched on the back.

It's a little hard to read, because that's a lot of letters on the back of a jersey, but Brooks made it work.

Tripp really does smile now. "C'mon. We need you on the field."

"We—wait. What?"

The Lady Fireballs meeting was on the verge of wrapping up, because the game starts in like seven minutes, so I'm certain I misunderstood him.

But he guides me to the tunnel heading out onto the field, and huh.

So this is what it looks like.

It's been four months since Brooks and I started dating. He's brought me out to the field many, *many* times, but never when the stands were full and both teams were out getting ready, and *oooh*, there's that stupid umpire who doesn't know where Brooks's strike zone is.

I glance at the Fireballs dugout, find Brooks, and frown.

He ducks his head, but I saw the grin, and I know he knows why I'm frowning.

I'm possibly still ridiculously fanatical about expressing my anger with wrong calls.

"Do *not* talk to the umpire, Mackenzie," Tripp murmurs.

"Like I'd be the first person to offer to have my boyfriend pay for his glasses."

"I had no idea I'd prefer the days when you couldn't talk to the players at all, yet here we are…"

I grin at him.

He shakes his head, then grins back, because he adores me, and I'm the best luck the Fireballs have ever had.

Or so Brooks tells me every night after he hits a home run.

Which he does regularly, both on *and* off the field, because it turns out, he really did just need the right woman in his life.

Or so we surmise.

In any case, he tells me I'm definitely better luck than all those things he and the guys supposedly did in the name of luck at some "secret club" in spring training.

Also?

The Fireballs are only three games back from being in a position to make the play-offs.

"Here." Tripp hands me a baseball. "Try to aim this time."

I look at the ball. Then up at him. "I don't play baseball."

He's grinning. "The entire metropolitan area saw the highlights from that game. We know."

"So what—"

"Ladies and gentlemen, please turn your attention to the field." The announcer's voice booms through the ballpark, and all the boys in Fireballs red pop out of the dugout.

I gasp as realization sinks in.

"No," I whisper.

"Half these people are here because of you, Mackenzie." Tripp gestures to the stands, which are nearly full. "Your *Fiery Forever* campaign has done almost as much good as everything else we've been doing."

"Almost?"

"That's what I said too." Brooks joins us, glove on, and would it be wrong to sniff his glove here?

It would, wouldn't it?

The announcer's voice booms again. "The Fireballs would like to welcome Ms. Mackenzie Montana, who'll be throwing the first pitch today."

Brooks slips his arm around my shoulder, and *oh my god*, I'm going to jump him right here, because he smells like grass and baseball and leather and sweat and it is *such* a turn-on. "I'm catching for you. Throw it hard like I showed you last weekend."

"You *knew*."

He grins, and I fall in love with him all over again.

"Out to the mound, Mackenzie." Tripp shoos me, and my home team erupts in cheers as I step over the third base line and head to the pitcher's mound.

It's not only the players either.

Sarah and my dads are up in the owners' suite, which is really easy to see since there's a camera trained on them and broadcasting their cheers on the video screen over center field.

And a huge, gigantic crowd-roar is circling all around me.

There are whistles. Clapping. Shouting.

Even cameramen following me like I'm some kind of celebrity.

My eyes sting, and while I'll never understand exactly how it feels to be a world-class baseball player like my boyfriend, I now totally get the thrill of being cheered on by forty thousand screaming fans.

I step up onto the mound where so many of my heroes have played, turn, and look at the man I love, who squats down and snaps his glove at me, his warm grin lighting me up from the inside.

"C'mon, Kenz," he calls. "Let 'er rip."

Well.

He asked for it.

I grip the ball.

Pull my arm back.

And then I fling it forward with all my might, letting go at the exact right moment...

To send it flying off toward the visitor's dugout, where Spike the Echidna drops to the ground as my baseball bounces off his spikey head.

"He's out!" the announcer crows.

The crowd goes wild.

I'm talking yelling, screaming, we just won the game of the century, hog-wild, won't have-anything-left-to-cheer-with-during-the-game, full-body celebrating.

Tripp's on the sidelines, shaking his head. Lopez and Rossi and Stafford are all rolling.

Brooks leaps to his feet, jogs over to retrieve the ball and help Spike to his feet while I take a curtsey.

I know what I'm supposed to do, because I've seen this play out a million times before. I'm supposed to head to home plate, and meet the player who caught my ball. We'll take pictures, he'll sign the ball—like he didn't bring me that home run ball he hit in New York the morning that I told him that I loved him—and then I'll disappear into the crowd and someone new will throw out the pitch tomorrow.

I glance at Brooks, and yep, here he comes.

And there's the camera crew.

He's grinning broadly. "That's my girl," he says as he sweeps me up in a hug.

"I threw it exactly like you showed me."

"That you did."

He sets me back on the ground, and when he's supposed to turn for my souvenir photo, instead, he drops to one knee.

Right there.

On the baseball diamond.

In front of forty thousand screaming fans, who are now whooping and hollering even louder.

My eyeballs fall out of my face.

I swallow my tongue.

But my heart—my heart is leaping for joy as he pulls a small box from his back pocket.

"Mackenzie, my love, my joy, the match to my crazy, and the light of my entire world, will you marry me?"

He pops the ring box, and *he did not*.

Except he did.

He got me a baseball diamond ring.

I can't talk.

Can't think.

Can't breathe.

But oh my god, I can love this man.

I'm nodding so hard my vision wobbles. "Yes. *Yes!*"

The whole team swarms the infield.

Brooks slips the ring onto my finger, rises to his feet, and I tackle him with a kiss that's probably not fit to be shown on that big video screen over center field while a mass of big, sweaty baseball players converge on us, making one big happy family.

"I love you," I tell Brooks through the happy tears streaming down my cheeks. "Baseball or no baseball, winning or losing, I love you."

He hugs me tight, kisses me hard, and then lets me go, because he has a job to do.

And when he hits a grand slam in the bottom of the eighth, I don't care that everyone in the entire ballpark knows he hit it for me.

I only care that he's happy.

And that smile as he rounds third and points to me in my seat four rows up down the third-base line—yeah.

That man's happy.

And the two of us are going to be happy forever.

We'll have our losses. And we might steal a few mascots together along the way.

But whatever the universe throws at us, we'll handle it. Together.

BONUS EPILOGUE

Mackenzie

JUST WHEN I thought my life couldn't get any more perfect, it did.

Again.

And now, I'm standing in the hallway beneath the center field bleachers, knowing my entire family, all my friends, and the entire Fireballs organization is out the field, waiting for me to walk out of here in my white dress, with my bouquet of Fireballs-red roses, to say *I do* to the man of my dreams on the field of my favorite place on earth.

No, second-favorite.

Wherever Brooks is has completely surpassed Duggan Field as my favorite place, though luckily, we both spend a lot of time here.

"I can't believe my baby's getting married." Dad's already sobbing in his handkerchief, and Papa's not doing much better.

Neither is Sarah, who has the special kind of glow that's making me highly suspicious about what she and Beck did on their third honeymoon last month.

Yes, third.

After eloping, they were subjected to the wedding reception to end all wedding receptions, and they needed multiple honeymoons to recover.

Me?

I'm getting an entire off-season of honeymoon.

"Who knew we'd be *here* now," Sarah says as she hugs me tight.

She, Parker, Dame Delilah, and Evianna are my attendants today. Brooks has his three brothers and his dad standing up beside him today, and I'm so ready to get this show on the road.

I'm more than ready to be Mrs. Brooks Elliott. "Is everyone here? Can we start?"

Lila bustles down the hallway in heels and a loose Fireball-red dress. "You're ready?"

"*So* ready."

"Good." She sticks her fingers in her mouth and whistles.

There's a scurry of feet, a very familiar scurry, and a moment later, Spike the Echidna steps into view.

I gasp. "You are *not*."

We're two days past the regular season, one day before the Fireballs leave for the first round of post-season play, and all of Copper Valley is waiting with bated breath to find out who won the mascot contest.

I might still be wearing a *Fiery Forever* button on my dress.

My dads might be appalled.

But I refuse to give up hope.

"No, we're not announcing the winner today. It's not after the season yet." She makes a *come on* gesture, and Glow pokes his head around the corner too. "But we *are* adding a few attendants to your wedding. It was in the fine print."

Firequacker dashes in and offers me his arm.

Lila gives him a look, and he hangs his head, then steps up to escort Glow.

Meaty lumbers around the corner, and he and Spike size each other up, then also link arms.

Lila throws open the doors to the outfield, and a cool breeze wafts in from the pleasant fall afternoon.

The speaker system blasts Elton John's "I'm Still Standing," and I start laughing, since my dads have made the song the Fireballs' new theme song this season.

"This is wedding goals," Dad declares.

The two mascot pairs traipse down the makeshift aisle, and I know I should be hiding out of sight, but I can't help peering out to watch Brooks do a double-take at the unexpected wedding guests.

His teammates all laugh and high-five each other. His family all turn their phones to snap pictures.

Except the babies, naturally.

And Brooks grins.

Of course he does.

Turns out all those grumpies he had were a result of being a little lost in his career and personal life.

It's been my utter joy to help turn his frown upside down, and I can't remember ever feeling more proud than I did the day the Fireballs clinched their division, and all of his teammates poured Gatorade on him first.

After getting Santiago, I mean.

The Skipper always goes first.

Parker squeezes me in a quick hug. "I'm so glad I'm getting another sister today. And thank you for ignoring what my phone said to you last night."

I squeeze her back, and she departs to walk down the aisle with Jack.

Dame Delilah strolls down the red runner with Rhett.

Evianna follows with Brooks's dad.

And Sarah gets in one last hug before pairing up with Gavin.

Butterflies swirl in my stomach, but not the nervous kind.

They're the excited kind.

"You ready for this, baby girl?" Dad asks.

He and Papa are both devastatingly handsome in suits today, which they chose so as to not outshine the bride.

I don't care how fancy they get in drag, they wouldn't outshine me today, but if this makes them happy, then it makes me happy too.

I nod to him.

He kisses my cheek. "Then we'll see you on the other side."

"Wait, what?"

He and Papa link elbows, and they take off down the aisle. *Without me.*

I turn to give Lila a *what the hell?* look, and then I freeze.

Lila's not there.

Fiery is.

Fiery the Dragon.

287

All seven feet of him.

Standing there with a new white beard, and white ear hairs sticking out, in a tuxedo, leaning on a cane.

He offers me his free arm.

"You…you want to walk me down the aisle? And give me away?"

I almost can't get the words out, and I'm using every trick my dads ever taught me to not cry as he nods gravely.

I touch his beard. "They're not going to let you come back, are they?"

He shakes his head.

Then he wraps his arms around me and hugs me tight.

I hug him back, hard, knowing full well there's a grown person inside this suit who has to think I'm a nutcase for sobbing all over him on my wedding day, but I don't care.

This is both the best and worst wedding present I could've ever gotten.

He pats my back, and I realize we're not alone.

"Okay, Kenz?" Brooks asks softly.

I nod. Shake my head. Nod again.

He chuckles softly. "I figured."

People are stirring out in the outfield, probably wondering if I'm going to bolt.

As if.

I sniffle and straighten, then look at my soon-to-be-husband. "Thank you."

His easy grin comes back, and there go my panties, melting themselves off.

Or, I should say, my Fiery thong.

Wow.

This just got awkward.

"How about we share the privilege, Fiery?" Brooks says to the dragon.

Fiery nods.

He offers an elbow. Brooks does too.

And for his last act ever as the Fireballs mascot, Fiery escorts us to our happily ever after.

ABOUT THE AUTHOR

Pippa Grant is a USA Today Bestselling author who writes romantic comedies that will make tears run down your leg. When she's not reading, writing or sleeping, she's being crowned employee of the month as a stay-at-home mom and housewife trying to prepare her adorable demon spawn to be productive members of society, all the while fantasizing about long walks on the beach with hot chocolate chip cookies.

Find Pippa at…
www.pippagrant.com
pippa@pippagrant.com

PIPPA GRANT BOOK LIST

The Girl Band Series
Mister McHottie
Stud in the Stacks
Rockaway Bride
The Hero and the Hacktivist

The Thrusters Hockey Series
The Pilot and the Puck-Up
Royally Pucked
Beauty and the Beefcake
Charming as Puck
I Pucking Love You

The Bro Code Series
Flirting with the Frenemy
America's Geekheart
Liar, Liar, Hearts on Fire

Standalones
Master Baker *(Bro Code Spin-Off)*
Jock Blocked (Copper Valley Fireballs #1)
Hot Heir *(Royally Pucked Spin-Off)*
Exes and Ho Ho Hos

The Bluewater Billionaires Series

The Price of Scandal by Lucy Score
The Mogul and the Muscle by Claire Kingsley
Wild Open Hearts by Kathryn Nolan
Crazy for Loving You by Pippa Grant

Co-Written with Lili Valente
Hosed
Hammered
Hitched
Humbugged

For a complete, up -to-date book list, visit www.pippagrant.com

---

Pippa Grant writing as Jamie Farrell:

The Misfit Brides Series
Blissed
Matched
Smittened
Sugared
Married
Spiced
Unhitched

The Officers' Ex-Wives Club Series
Her Rebel Heart
Southern Fried Blues